Table of Contents

I0517314

Front & Back Covers by Laura Givens

Entering the Chrysalis

In the autumn of 2004, I approached the ten-year anniversary editing *Hadrosaur Tales* Magazine. I'd just signed a contract for my novel *Vampires of the Scarlet Order* with LBF Books and I wanted to focus more time on writing. Around that time, I attended the West Virginia Festival of the Book, where LBF had a presence. It was a chance to meet the publisher, Jackie Druga, and some of her staff. She edited a magazine called *The Writer's Post Journal* and expressed an interest in running a genre fiction magazine with me as editor and Nick Johns as art director. We brainstormed the name *Tales of the Talisman* to highlight our interest in horror and the darker ends of the fantasy and science fiction spectra. In effect, *Hadrosaur Tales* became *Tales of the Talisman* without the anticipated break and I kept going for another ten years.

Although Nick left the project early, Laura Givens stepped in and has done a remarkable job over the years finding illustrations for every story in the magazine. What's more, she's illustrated all but two of our covers for the entire ten-year run. Laura is currently finding success placing her artwork in galleries and I'm cheering her on for even greater success in the years to come. I'm also quite proud of the authors we've run in *Tales of the Talisman*. As I write this, three of our alumni—Jennifer Brozek, Bryan Thomas Schmidt, and Lou Antonelli—are up for Hugo awards. What's more, Lyn C. A. Gardner's poem "In Translation" won third place in the 2012 Rhysling Awards for the best science fiction poem.

As we enter summer 2015, I have just turned in my third steampunk novel, *The Brazen Shark*, to Sky Warrior Publishing and signed a contract for a horror novel, *The Astronomer's Crypt*, with Lachesis Publishing, who bought LBF Books. When I started *Tales of the Talisman*, I never expected to return to professional astronomy as I did in 2008. On top of that, the publishing world is evolving at a rapid rate. I am looking at the best ways to present short fiction and poetry to a wide audience and am committed to doing so. With this issue, *Tales of the Talisman* enters a chrysalis. To see the butterfly that emerges, follow us at facebook.com/TalesOfTheTalisman, TalesOfTheTalisman.com, and hadrosaur.com. We have exciting plans in discussion for soaring into the next decade and hope you'll be there to soar along with us.

— David Lee Summers

Tales of the
Talisman

Volume 10   Issue 4

ISBN: 1-885093-79-9

William Grother
Publisher

David Lee Summers
Editor

Laura Givens
Art Director

Kumie Wise
Assistant Editor

Tales of the Talisman
(ISSN 1558-0377)
is published quarterly by
Hadrosaur Productions
P.O. Box 2194
Mesilla Park, NM 88047-2194
www.hadrosaur.com

Subscriptions: $24.00 per year
$48.00 per two years
Subscriptions available at:
www.talesofthetalisman.com

Tales of the Talisman assumes no responsibility for unsolicited manuscripts, photographs or artwork. Unsolicited material must be accompanied by a self-addressed stamped envelope to ensure its return.

© 2015 Hadrosaur Productions
All rights reserved. No unauthorized use of any of this material without express permission granted by the individual authors and artists.

"Delightfully Oddball"
-Dave Truesdale, SFSite

"Hilariously intelligent"
-Luke Reviews

From behind
the bar
To Across
The **STARS**

From The Murphy's Lore Universe of
PATRICK THOMAS
www.patthomas.net
www.padwolf.com

scan here for e-book

Find us on
Facebook!

Final Journey

Story by Stephen C. Ormsby
Illustration by Morland Gonsoulin

I am a part of this train, and the train is a part of me; I am the nGeneer. This steel behemoth is not just connected to me, it is now part of my DNA.

My forefathers were engineers and ran the trains, but then scientists decoded the human genome and built the technology to embed sufficient code into people to create unfathomable cross bred machinery. I was tested at an early age, and, showing the same aptitude as my father and grandfather, my body was used to create this joined beast of metal and skin. I am an nClass 21 diesel locomotive transporter unit.

It nourishes me and I guide it, and together we travel across this Australian landscape supplying fuels and foodstuffs to the major cities. Merged, we separate only out of courtesy for the workers who have not grown accustomed to this level of interbreeding.

My smooth metallic panelling warms in the early morning sun, as I experience the passengers boarding and shuffling for seats. Energy builds as my diesel engine heats, and I now have the strength of a dozen machines. The hills before me will challenge my wheels and my axle yet again, but I know this will be the last time.

My final journey will begin in a matter of mere minutes.

It will be a short journey. The comptrollers and mKanics think I have become unstable. I know I am still as strong as the metal that supports my frame. I know that I can go on for many years. My retirement should not be so early in my life. My wet body is only in its forties, though my metal body is closer to sixty. Even still, an angst resides in me that I am not ready to stop doing this. My life, and body, has been devoted to this job ever since I was young; ever since they changed me. Ever since the metal in my veins made me feel every component of the train that I was connected to. Its metallic skin is as well known to me as my own, for I have spent as much time in it as my own.

But today it ends. Today they de-commission my engine from my brain. I am scared.

The blast of a fanfare starts the proceedings, and I perceive something else; the thrill of the trip begs me to join it, to surrender to the hills and valleys, rivers and streams, the hot breath of my engine. I surrender to my programming, and the pre-trip algorithms flow through my mind.

The driver's seat absorbs my wetware, and my bodyplugs accept the tentacle-like cabling that spiral out. Each connection stings, but the ache is so familiar that I smile in recollection.

The final checks indicate trip readiness. I lose the sensation of my soft skin to the rigidity of my hulking one thousand tonne frame. The perception of arms and legs give away to carriages and passengers. Feet transform into wheels, so many wheels, each finding purchase on the track. I shut my tiny eyes to visualise through windscreen-sized windows.

A whistle blows. The station master waves his flag.

I strain my body to make the first small movements. If I had skin, it would be sweating. As it is, my funnels blow thick, black smoke from the effort. But, slowly, my wheels stop spinning and start gripping, until I pick up speed. The cheers envelope me, and I feel the love these people have. My diesel engine sings in return.

* * *

It is all over. I have arrived and the passengers have long departed. Now I am in the mKanic's repair workshop, waiting for the doctors. My engine has gone cold, and my metal panels have also cooled. The chair has released me, but I still feel the clickety-clack of the tracks upon my toes. The roar of the engine ripping from my throat.

I already feel the loss.

The thumping of boots on the floor. My time is here, and they will clean my DNA of all train residuals, leaving me ... just me. I barely remember that sensation.

The door opens, and in walks a team of smiling men and women. I try to smile back, but it fails to materialise. They are too polite to notice, as a second team brings in banks of surgical machinery. A nurse walks up, and gently guides me to a gurney I had not noticed before.

I lay down, and I close my eyes. The sting of a needle penetrates into my soft skin.

* * *

Air blows through my stacks.
The solid metal tracks
That thud beneath my wheels.
I blow my horn,
And hear it echo,
Far out across the valley.

Over 100 kilometres per hour,
And Freedom is mine.
The children cheer,
And yell for more,
I oblige them,
with a longer blare.

The air blows through my stacks.
Nothing but the open tracks.
My metal skin warm from work and sun.
My engine hums.
I close my eyes,
and let the breeze blow through me…

* * *

Vibrating. Is it the track under my wheels? Am I on a bridge? Are passengers disembarking? No.

The shaking is a physical thing upon my shoulder. In slow movements, I open my eyes to see the same nurse that had been so kind to me earlier. I wonder how long ago that was.

"Three days, Mr. Smith. It has taken almost three days for the procedure to complete. For some reason, it was more difficult than usual, but the doctors have assured me that it was very successful.

"I have run scans this morning to verify the results, and you have absolutely no trace of locomotive DNA in your system. You are clean, and now allowed to go home. Congratulations, and thank you for your many, many years of service. Your retirement comes with many benefits and bonuses. We hope you enjoy them."

I open my mouth, but no words issue.

"Don't worry, Mr Smith. That is a by-product of the operation. Some of the tubing necessary for the operation went down your esophagus, leaving your throat somewhat raw. It will return to you over the next week. In that time, we recommend bed rest."

This time I nod, and notice how different I feel. There is a loss of movement, but also an increase. I feel individual components of this wetware body, and remember that this carcass comes with arms and legs, instead of wheels and carriages. No longer nGeneer, I am empty.

It takes time to coordinate them. In slow motion, I move away from the bed and the nurse. In a tangle, I manage to pull on sufficient clothing to be able to leave.

So, this is freedom? I suppose so, as I don't feel anything else, but me.

Me. A strange concept after so many years of being joined. I walk towards my apartment, and in the distance I hear a train whistle—probably a buddy of mine.

Loss rips through me. I yearn to feel that strength again, but am now drained of it. As a consequence, I feel drained of all emotion. The smell of diesel upon my skin, the churn of metal on metal, the smell of smoke, the relief of a water station; none of these things are a part of me anymore.

It is not freedom.

Again, the train whistle blows, and this time it is closer. I know the route it is on and the track on which it travels. I am not that far away, and I decide to watch it pass.

In a quick shuffle, I move through the city, realizing how much longer it takes to do without dozens of wheels. But I stumble through and around the wet bodies looking for my hard-shelled friend. I bump and knock into walls, feeling the injuries on my soft skin. It surprises me just how delicate this frame is.

With my head in the air, listening for the next whistle, I run into something soft. It stops me.

"Idiot. Watch where you are going."

All I can do is nod, as I fall towards the hard concrete footpath. Thrusting my hand out, I feel something snap when they connect. Pain.

"Serves you right, arsehole."

There, the whistle. I am close, so close.

I run, my hand now dangling loose upon my arm. The pain is intense, but that can be fixed later. I run fast, but have already learnt to avoid 'people'. The fourth whistle; the last whistle, which means they have reached the underpass.

Only another minute now, and I will be there too. Will there be enough time? I climb onto the train tracks, and can see the road traffic on the bridge. The tracks below my feet do not feel right. I do not feel right.

But I stumble over rocks and sleepers, and fall. I get up and run again, only to fall again. Now though I see the light in the darkness. My quarry is just ahead, and I can hear the engine. I hear it in my heart and in my head. I feel it, and I don't feel it enough.

I need to be it.

I stand at the mouth of the tunnel, as I hear the 5:15 approach.

I smile.

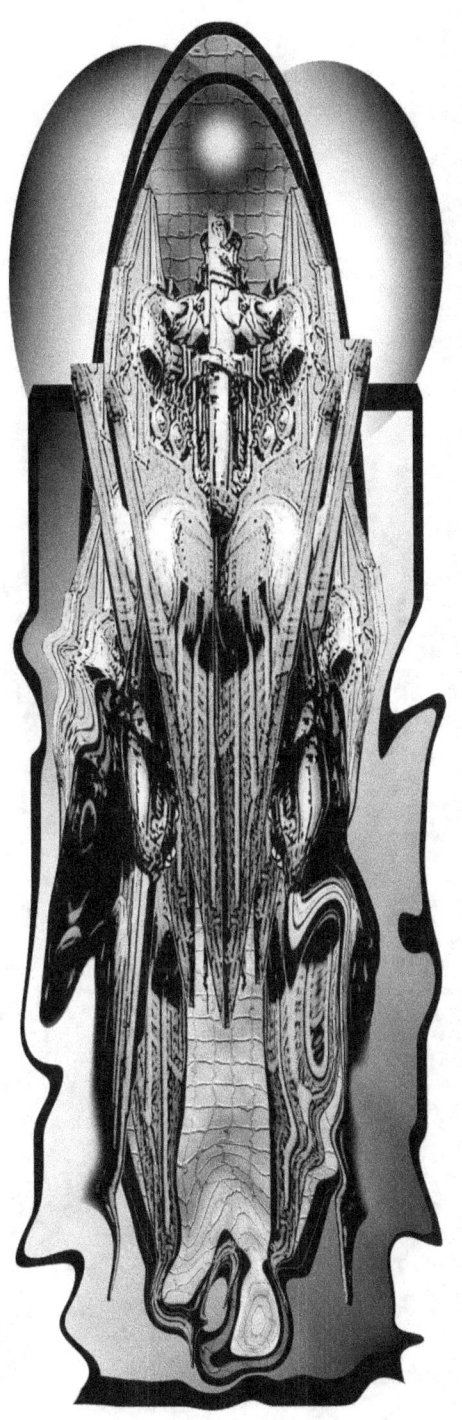

The Last Gypsies

"Before the last gypsies are
enshrined in glass along
the pillared skyway,
I want to visit the dark
glens of incantation."

"Before the stars are
fixed inviolate
in the static heavens,
I want to know the planets
circling Alpha Centauri."

"Before the dream dies
dormant in its tracks,
never to be dreamt again,
I want to discover a world
where I could belong."

In the coffeehouse
I frequent most often,
odd marginalia scribbled
by a variety of hands
in the tattered books
left there to read.

— Bruce Boston

Shady Moons
Story by William R. D. Wood
Illustration by Teresa Tunaley

Maddie sighted down the length of the plasbine rifle, her finger tight on the trigger. A hundred meters away evening sunlight glinted on the flopper's fur as it hopped onto the grassy rise. She took a breath and held it. The creature paused as if getting its bearings and leapt into the air. Maddie squeezed the trigger and bloody tufts of orange fur rained down on the hilltop.

She cackled and rocked back in her chair, the wooden floorboards of the porch creaking as she craned her neck to the left, peering in the screen door. "Did you see that, Errorstotle? That there is a record if ever there was one."

"Yes, mum," answered the brass and chrome bot from her right side.

Maddie jumped, her grip tightening on the plasbine. "Don't you creep up on me, you sneaky old bucket. Get your danged fool head blown off is what you'll do." Maddie quickly surveyed the homestead, taking in the house and the outbuildings, all of which rested on a half-square-klick of stone fused into the native landscape. No floppers in sight. She returned her gaze westward. This time of year, the critters always came from the west.

"Yes, mum. Sorry, mum."

"Danged tootin' you're sorry. I wonder why I even keep you around some times."

"Perhaps one of few remaining mysteries of our time, mum."

The bunched wrinkles in her face relaxed. "You saw that shot, though? Not bad for an old woman, eh?"

"Yes, mum. You've still *got* it."

Maddie's smile widened. "Danged straight. Back when I was a girl, my daddy—"

"Mum?"

"What is it? I was about to reminisce."

The bot pointed.

Maddie rocked forward in her chair and leaned into her squint.

Two klicks away, maybe three, across the rolling hills and purple grasses to the south, a shining object in the sky slowed as it descended. Shimmering exhaust spilled from the drive end of the cigar-shaped clipper ship, swirling as it dissipated.

"I ain't got time for visitors," Maddie grumbled. "Probably that dog-faced Rigellon wanting to convert me to the church of the holy flipsmacker again. I done told him—"

"No, mum."

"No? Nobody else has the unmitigated gall to land on our planet—on *my* planet--unannounced."

"Yes, mum," said Errorstotle. "Of course, no one comes *at all*. You and the mister were never *neighborly*."

"Hush up and leave the mister out of this, bless his soul," snapped Maddie, her voice catching. "If it ain't that no-good data thumper, who is it?"

Optics clicked softly amidst the whir of Errorstotle's uplink to the house's subspace modem. The bot accessed thousands of databases. Retrieving, sorting, comparing. He was good at that sort of thing. Maddie cleared her throat.

"A common model used throughout Contracted Space," said Errorstotle. "The hull is registered to the Sector Central branch providing transports to administrative functionaries."

Maddie grunted and grabbed the pair of hunting spectacles linked to her plasbine. She didn't use them for actual shooting but the gun required them to be close by or it wouldn't shoot. She hated the innumerable safety features built into new gadgets. The old days when she and the mister had first staked their claim were gone. Back then they'd had the whole planet to themselves and done as they pleased. Then the danged bureauticians arrived with a cargo hold full of red tape, forms and grants.

She zoomed the spectacles and squinted through lenses. The ship settled onto three sweeping tail fins. Dust and bits of scorched grass still billowed from the ground as an airlock irised open near the nose. Whoever was aboard was in a hurry.

Stairs unfolded and assembled down the side of the fuselage.

A man in bright orange excursion wear stepped out of the airlock onto the landing field, flipping through several pages on a clipboard before descending.

"Only danged house on the whole planet, but he needs to check his paperwork to make sure he's in the right place."

His eyes were small, set close together over a zit-sized nose and thin mouth, like his features had been pinched together in the middle of a pale, flat face. Small ears stuck out high on the side of his head and his close-cropped hair was a sparse blue-white smear.

"A dang Margmali," Maddie grumbled.

"Indeed," agreed the bot. "They do hold prime jurisdiction to this wedge of Contracted Space, mum. If memory remains uncorrupted, they reserve the right—"

"I know all their nitpicky rights and easements.

Ain't good manners to come dropping in unannounced is all."

Movement played in her peripheral vision from the edge of the lot. Maddie swung the plasbine around and squeezed off a shot. A *screep* pierced the evening air.

"Excitement's got me all flustered, Errorstotle—throwing off my accuracy. Must've missed the flopper's head completely. Dang thing actually had time to squeal."

"I fear the excitement might not be over, mum."

"Why? Who is that fellow?" She lifted the goggles back to her face and fiddled with the controls. "Can you make out his patches?"

"Yes, Mum. He's just paused at the base of the egress mechanism. His lapel insignia reads—oh…" The bot let the sentence hang for uncomfortable seconds.

"Crunch it out, bucket boy."

"Shady Moons Retirement Domes."

"Dang."

* * *

She heard the Margmali step up onto the porch but didn't turn to face him. Instead, Maddie took careful aim at three floppers a klick out to the west. They bunched as they crested a hill.

The round from the plasbine, set for a tenth-degree dispersal, toasted the tightest of the two, the third dropping to the grass several hops later.

The gasp from the Margmali garnered a grin from the old woman. Her shooting skills wouldn't stop a true bureautician from speaking his piece, but maybe this one would stick to the abridged version.

"Welcome," said Errorstotle to the man. "How may we help you today?"

Their visitor gave the bot a nod, consulted his clipboard and addressed Maddie. "You are Madeline Adelaide Finnsawyer?"

"Maybe I am." Maddie shrugged and spread her blanket evenly over her knees, placing the plasbine across her legs. "What's it to you?"

Her visitor's gaze lingered on the weapon as if he expected her to suddenly swing it to bear on *him*. Hell, maybe she would, if he acted up any. She knew it was a gross generalization, but the Margmali, as a race, tended to fluster easy-like. Flipping through the pages on his clipboard, he stopped near the bottom, tapping a particular point of data. "According to the last census drone, this world held only two high-order organic residents. Mister Zekiel No Additional Names Finnsawyer—whose passing was noted one cycle ago—and his wife Madeleine—"

"Yeah, yeah, yeah." Maddie, already bored with the visitor, scanned the horizon with the targeting goggles. "She's me. What do you want?"

"Ms. Finnsawyer," said the Margmali, "before we begin formally, I'd appreciate your restraint from further slaughter of the indiginies."

"You mean the floppers?"

"Yes." He shuddered, looking to one side a moment as if his composure were at stake. "I find such wanton disregard for life … disturbing."

"Are you serious, sonny?"

"I should say so," said the Margmali. "*Floppers* lack protection under current animal cruelty laws since they've only recently become available in Contracted Space, but—really—you should be ashamed. Their adorability quotient—"

"You've taken a shine to 'em, have you?"

"Personally, no, but my kithren are somewhat enamored and I've promised them—"

"You haven't touched one since you landed?"

The Margmali's jaw worked soundlessly.

"Why, of course you did," said Maddie with a shake of her head. "Well you best be getting on with it so you can get back to your pretty ship. We ain't got all day."

"Yes, well. I am Field Minister Trannon bu'Rowesnouser—"

Maddie laughed. "That's a mouthful, ain't it Errorstotle? How about I just call you Clem?"

The Margmali choked in midsentence, beginning again. "I am Field Minister Trannon bu'Rowesnouser, public health representative from the Contraction Department of Social Mandates. Recent upgrades to department policy, specifically those dealing with special interspersion, indicates diminished suitability for your continued homesteading grants and permits since your husband's passing. My spot-assessment, on arrival, concurs. I am here to offer—"

"Look, Clem, I am a tolerant woman, ain't I, Errorstotle?"

"Mum is the epitome of manners and patience."

"Oh, shut up, you old bucket."

"You asked me, mum," countered the bot.

The Margmali cleared his throat. "If I may continue?"

"You look like a nice young man," said Maddie. "Cut to the end of the chase, would you?"

"I believe I have. I am here to assist you with shutting down your homestead and transporting you to a highly desirable facility." The field minister pulled a narrow booklet from his clipboard and held it on his open palm, allowing the holo-gami images to unfold in the air before Maddie's eyes. "Shady Moons Retirement offers wonderful Dysons, each with programmable quantum arc sunthetic tertiaries, eliminating all those higher energy UVs you humani-descended are always citing—"

"You're here to kick me off my land?" Maddie's hand tightened on the plasbine.

"No, no, no," stammered the Margmali. "I am only concerned about your continued well-being, Ms. Finnsawyer. The Department of Social Mandates has simply determined for your species, at your age and under the stressor of having recently lost your mate to the rigors of the harsh life endured as sole proprietors of this world, you should be relocated to a facility where you are free to live out your remaining days in comfort and peace. These are *your* rights, Ms. Finnsawyer. I am but a servant of the public health."

"Sounds like a hold full of jumblejangle if you ask me, Clem." Maddie relaxed her grip on the weapon and leaned forward enough to give the Margmali a pat on his forearm. "I'm going to pass. But thanks for stopping by."

"I'm sorry?" said the Margmali.

"Sakes alive, Clem. Don't you people understand plain Omnish? That all sounds real nice, it truly does, but I'm just gonna stay here."

"This is awkward, Ms. Finnsawyer, but I'm not sure I've made myself clear. You are to be evacuated and transported with respectful grace and decorum, but without further delay." He collapsed the brochure and held out the clipboard for her to inspect the document beneath.

"Whatever that Margmali butterslug scratch says is all well and good but I made up my mind to stick this out a year ago when the mister went on to his reward." Her voice quavered, but she pushed through, volume rising just enough. "And I aim to do just that."

"Ms. Finnsawyer, your relocation is not open for discussion. You may lodge all the appropriate complaints, but that will have to be done after your new resident indoctrination. Your health and happiness are my only—"

"Clem, you must be out of your mind," she said. "The mister and I received our homesteading grant over one hundred fifty cycles ago and I'll be ding-danged if I'm gonna just pull up roots and leave just because a bunch of bureauticians have decided I'm better off elsewhere, just because he's not with

us anymore. Errorstotle, tell this fine flat-faced gentleman to get the *health and happiness* off my planet."

"...Mum?"

"What!" Tears welled in her eyes but her voice was iron.

"This is Margmali space," said the bot. "You and the mister agreed and—"

"—done told you to leave the mister outa this—"

"—knew when your homesteading grant was signed—"

"—I ain't reneged on my end—"

"—that the Margmali maintained the right to reoccupy in the event of death—"

"—dead? Do I look dead to you—"

"—environmental catastrophe—"

"—only environ*mental* hoopla is those dang floppers—"

"—or incapacitation, either mental or physical—"

"—why, I'm fit as a saxstring." Maddie pushed up from the chair, the blanket dropping to the porch as she deftly caught the plasbine in a two-hand hold across her thighs. "Are you questioning my mental acumen, Clem?"

"Ms. Finnsawyer, I assure you this is not personal."

"Maybe not to you, but it's damned personal to me." Placing the butt of the plasbine against Errorstotle's torso, she gave the bot a shove, causing him to take a step back to maintain his balance. "And just whose side are *you* on, anyway?"

"Always the mum's, mum."

Maddie raised an accusing finger at the bot. "Then start acting like it, you danged bucket."

Screep!

Maddie spun on the Margmali, eyes narrow. Barely in the audible range, a trill hung in the air. With the side of the plasbine's muzzle Maddie prodded the minister's pocket.

Screep!

The Margmali sputtered, "Ms. Finnsawyer, please—I—"

"Mum, I recommend you lower the weapon and allow the good field minister a bit of space."

"What? Like he's giving me *my* little piece of space?" Her words were slow and deliberate. "What's in your pocket, Clem?"

Slowly, the field minister pushed a hand into the broad side pocket of his trousers. The trill became a coo and Maddie's face twisted in disgust as he pulled out long, orange-furred ears followed by a small frog-like body. Tiny, dumb eyes stared up at the three of them.

"Ms. Finnsawyer, it's j-just a harmless f-flopper," stammered the evaluator, holding the creature in folded arms, half turned from the woman to keep it from her pitiless gaze. "It was hopping along as I walked from my clipper and—and—"

"Put it down, Clem. You don't want it. Trust me. Nothing but a dang vermin."

Jaw set, the Margmali took a step toward her, moving the flopper to a one hand hold in order to push the plasbine muzzle toward the planks at their feet. "See here, Ms. Finnsawyer. I acknowledge you clearly have strong feeling regarding these creatures, but they seem to be quite plentiful here—"

"Oughta be. I think they come from here."

"Indeed? Well, I apologize for circumventing the normal Contraction vetting process for pet ownership. Be that as it may, my desire to take a single flopper from this world is not the matter at hand."

"Oh, I think that is exactly the matter at hand."

Transparent goo dripped from between the floppers butt and the field minister's palm. The creature squeaked as he switched hands and attempted to wipe the substance on his trouser leg.

"Good luck with that," said Maddie with a chuckle. "Best toss the thing aside and let me deal with it."

"Wholly unnecessary, I assure you, Ms. Finnsawyer. With a little training—"

"It didn't just sprat on you, Clem. That there is a pheremonal ejaculate. She's done marked you as food. If we don't get you cleaned up, the whole migrating squarm of 'em will be here by morning."

The Margmali shook his head. "They're not dangerous, Ms. Finnsawyer. Next to cats and butterslugs, flopper ownership is the newest and biggest trend in all of Contracted Space. I hardly think the quarantineers would allow—"

"Not dangerous unless you get too many of them together."

The Margmali looked to the bot who nodded. "But—"

"But nothing. Sure they're all sweet and *coo-ey*, until the population reaches critical mass. If there's no other food, Clem, they'll eat their own when squarming season hits. Shoot fire, that's what keeps the ones out front of the squarm moving." Maddie took a piece of jerky from her housecoat pocket and tossed it off the porch. "They don't want to get ate."

The flopper leaped from the field minister's protective embrace, landing on top of the jerky where it stood on its haunches and began to nibble at the meat. The electric crack of the plasbine ended its meal in a flash of carbonized vapor.

* * *

"…and your memory, Ms. Finnsawyer. Suppose you forget—even once—something vitally important about survival in this vast lonely wasteland? What then? These are the concerns of your fellow citizens."

"Well, that's what Errorstotle is for. The mister's done programmed him just fine to look out for me, ain't that right, Errorstotle?"

"Yes, mum."

"And besides, Clem, this ain't no *wasteland*. This is my *home*. Has been most of my life."

"Ms. Finnsawyer, if it eases your mind, please understand, I graduated third in a class of over two thousand and currently hold the highest office in the field minister corps. I've conducted, or participated in hundreds of such visits. My credentials alone would take an hour to expound and the flowcharts and checklists I have poured over concerning your case are exhaustive. In my expert opinion you will be happier and healthier at Shady Moons than you could possibly hope to be here."

"And all that hooey makes you better qualified than me to decide my own life?"

"Yes."

"Well, Clem, I got news for you. I *ain't* convinced. You might want to consider checking *yourself* into Shady Moons."

"Myself?" asked the Margmali. "I don't understand."

"Poor thing." Maddie gave his forearm another pat. "All I'm saying is that if you're the expert and I'm still not convinced, you must have forgotten something important about how to do this. Else you must be wrong. Which do you think it is? Might be time to wander out into the pasture yourself."

"Ms. Finnsawyer, I implore you. Allow the Department to look after your health."

"My health? I'm in perfect health for my age, Clem. I'm in perfect health for someone *your* age. Besides Errorstotle here has a full first aid and triage package. And for anything he can't handle, I've got a Doc In The Box in the shed." She pointed the muzzle of the plasbine toward the closest of the outbuildings.

"I sympathize with you, Ms. Finnsawyer. Sincerely, but the Mandates are for the betterment of all. My position remains wholly unchanged. What belongings do you wish to bring? If my holds are too small, a cargo drone will be sent for the rest."

"With the mister gone, this here is my planet, Clem." Maddie's words were quiet, hardly audible over the stiffening breeze. "That makes you a trespasser. Onto my world and into my life. And that ain't right."

Maddie looked toward the small plot on the homestead where the mister's grave marker rose. The setting sun cast its shadow long enough the tip touched the porch. Shoulders slumped, she sighed. "You're not going to let this go, are you?"

"I am charged with your safety and health and, despite your assurances, I cannot in good conscience leave you to your own devices."

"Then I ain't got a choice."

"No, Ms. Finnsawyer, you do not. But rest assured—"

"Fine. Errorstotle, take care of this rube."

The field minster's eyes widened as he clutched his clipboard to his chest.

Errorstotle looked from Maddie to the Margmali, then back to Maddie. "Mum, surely you realize I cannot *take care* of Field Minister bu'Rowesnouser."

"Just so," said the Margmali giving the bot a look of relief.

The butt of the plasbine struck the man in the temple with a *thunk*, freezing his face in mid-expression before he dropped heavily to the porch.

"Of course, I realize that, you dang bucket. I just needed him to look at you long enough to whack him good. I may be fine to live out my days here where I'm happy, but I ain't as young and quick as I used to be either. Now you take Clem back to his ship and set the autopilot for the next poor soul on his list. I just hope they got the gumption to give him what's for too."

"Very well, mum."

She stood over the field minister, lips pursed into a crooked smile. "Least he wasn't that dang Rigellon."

* * *

Errorstotle brought the ground transport to a stop just as the Margmali stirred in his seat, one hand rubbing at the lump on his temple as he groaned.

"My apologies," said the bot.

"Think nothing of it. A few minutes in the trauma bay and I'll be better than new."

Once they stepped off of the transport it loaded itself into a service slot which promptly sealed in preparation for departure.

"Thank you for coming, field minister. And my thanks to your superiors."

"The trouble is minimal," said the Margmali. "This world is on a frequently traveled route."

"Still, your department's support, stopping in every few months, is critical to Ms. Maddie's continued independence."

"And she truly does not remember our previous visits?"

"No, sir, she does not. Nor that Mr. Finnsawyer's passing was eight cycles ago—not one. Your department's visits, though, are instrumental in provoking her to assert her independence to the degree necessary and thereby regain an optimum level of cogency."

"As long as she continues to respond, this arrangement is acceptable. Suppose she realizes what you are doing?"

"Then I will call that day my greatest success, field minister."

The Margmali nodded and turned to ascend the stairs.

"And, field minister," Errorstotle added, passing a small vented container to the man. "Ms. Maddie is correct about the floppers. Critical mass is more than a billion within a standard planetary diameter, but finite just the same. The worlds of Contracted Space should be informed."

Giving the container a gentle shake and receiving a *screep* as reward, the Margmali agreed. "Fare well."

Errorstotle's optics zoomed on the homestead. Shawl pulled tight over her shoulders, Maddie rocked back and forth scanning the horizon to the west through the plasbine's targeting goggles.

"We shall."

A Brief History of Human Evolution
Or
How I became a Bloodthirsty Pyromaniac Fornicating Naked Ape

First let's start with the facts
that the existence of human beings
is not evidence of some long progressive chain
which culminates in sentient consciousness.
The existence of human beings is more or less an accident,
a random coincidence of happenstance.
If an asteroid had not slammed into the Yucatan,
dinosaurs might never have gone extinct
and apes never would have learned to stand and think.
Mammals cowered beneath the fearful shadows
of their terrible reptilian overlords
for entire geological epochs.
Our tiny ancient ancestors were egg thieves and insectivores.
We are descended from a long line of egg thieves,
something to ponder the next morning you eat breakfast.

The Apples of Eden allow me to write this poem.
Once upon a time our ape ancestors
stopped living in the nighttime
and began thriving in the daylight,
using their improved diurnal eyesight
to tell which fruit was the most ripe.
This learning to discern different subtle shades of color
is the root of all language.
In the African homeland the drying of the savannahs
created vast expanses of grasslands
giving Australopithecus incentive to stand
and survey the terrain for predators like leopards.
As they walked and wandered their diet changed
from mostly vegetarian to carnivorous omnivore.
We were forced to get faster to capture more meat
and this allowed us to wander farther and farther
until we had covered the entire planet like an outbreak of infection.
Chasing our dinner changed our body types,
we became taller and thinner and lost most of our hair.
This allowed our bodies to sweat as we ran chasing game
and added considerably to our sexual response.
This improved sexual response gave us
reasons to cooperate, form families, bands and tribes.
That's right, being a bunch of feverish frenzied fornicators
greatly aided our evolutionary process.
We invented blades on projectile points
about the same time we learned to paint
and we think language jumped forward at the same time
but things really took off once we discovered fire.
The first mischievous men set entire valleys ablaze,
fires that burned for days and days.

While harvesting the dead animals someone must have discovered
that cooked meat stayed preserved longer
and once we began to eat charred flesh
our stomachs shrank and our brains grew larger.

So there you have it and here we are,
builders of a magnificent civilization
but if you think the whole purpose of the universe is to evolve
a species of bloodthirsty pyromaniac perverted naked apes
you are a sadly mistaken victim of your own egocentric expectations.
We still make weapons, more for war than hunting
and we still build fires
but we have language too, an art which leaves no fossil record.
Which means we can write poetry,
to romance a woman, remember the departed, or inspire a child.
We can write poetry to discover and reveal the magical mysteries of the universe.
Grab a pen and write something, remember you are the result
of billions of years of genetic engineering
to put you right here, right now, today
and you already know exactly the right words to say.

— Gary Every

The Day the Electricals Ended

Story by
K.S. Hardy

Illustration by
Tom Kelly

TKELLY2015

To begin, the light was strange that day. Too much light, a rich golden, almost daffodil light. I thought nothing of it, as the night before over tea, in an extra edition I had purchased in the city from the corner newsboy, I had read that the astronomers at Greenwich were noting unusual sun flare activity.

Little did I suspect, that this glow that suggested joy and all is well with the world, did portend something more ominous was on its way.

My morning journey into Londontown on the Tesla locomotive was as normal except my eyes were often drawn away from my copy of the most recent scientific romance by Herbert Wells by the passing landscape outside the compartment's window, all bright and crisp like a new autochrome photograph of exceptional quality. Even when the train coasted through the outskirts of Londontown with its soot- and smoke-stained buildings I noted how everything and all seemed to reflect an unnatural glow.

This was all quickly forgotten at my work place where as usual I was symbolically chained to my desk, adding up the column upon column of figures generated by the financial institution I was indentured to as Quality Control Inspector for the Accounting Department. It was my task to randomly double check the work of the twenty clerks that were under my supervision. And of course, the room that housed our office had no windows, to limit distractions that might slow our mathematics. So for several hours I was isolated from the sun and the almost magical gleam that infused that day. I did notice however that occasionally the Edison bulbs would flicker in their ceiling fixtures.

It was at lunch that it happened.

I was taking lunch with Nesbit, a colleague who oversaw the Loan Remittance Department, who oddly enough, was a little mouse of a man whereas his work may have implied a much more intimidating hulk but as he had so often assured me, his size and demeanor inspired feelings of pity in the delinquents and they paid up because they felt sorry for him.

As usual we had walked around the corner from our building to the tiny Earl of Sandwich franchise we had come to enjoy for its privacy from work as well as its tasty assemblages. On our short journey I made a remark about the quality of the daylight, which had not diminished, it may have even increased.

"Yes, it makes one consider investing in the shares of a manufacturer of smoked glass spectacles," Nesbit replied.

After ordering from the menu we sat at the table

for two about half way back in the shop, discussing the previous day's rugby matches broadcast on the wireless the night before.

The waiter approached to refresh our tea. Without any apology for the interruption he bent to pour.

Then a sudden brightening occurred, like the flash powder of a thousand photographers being touched off at once. I blinked. Nesbit's eyes squinted shut. When I reopened mine the day had returned to its normal English gloom. A murmur rose in the shop.

"Oh, dear," said Nesbit.

I at first thought that Nesbit was commenting on the strange event that had just transpired, but no, it referred to the fact that the waiter was still pouring and that my cup runneth over.

I wrestled the china pot from his white gloved fingers with some difficulty. It was as if he had a death grip upon it.

"Sir?" Nesbit asked with concern and reached out to touch the waiter's arm.

He did not react to word or touch. The glass eyes did not even twitch in the sockets of the waiter's wax face. He was frozen in place.

I looked around the shop as did Nesbit. All the other automatons on the staff were likewise frozen.

"What the bloody..." Nesbit began before he realized that ladies were present and curtailed his exclamation.

I pointed to the Edison bulbs in the chandeliers which were lightless.

"The electicals must be out," I commented.

"Oh, well then, they will be back on shortly," said Nesbit picking up his sandwich to attack it again.

But it didn't. So we settled our chits as the owner profusely apologized for the inconvenience and went back to work where we could still crunch numbers because the frugal company we slaved for had yet to upgrade to the new electric adding machines and somehow managed to still have oil lamps shelved away in some back storeroom.

At quitting time for that day the electricals had not been restored. I was faced with a new dilemma. How was I to get home to my wife and our little cottage in our village outside the metropolis? The Tesla locomotives would not be running, could not run without power in their magneto.

And nothing else either I discovered when I stepped out onto Marlowe street. Lorries and autos were stalled everywhere in their journeys. Not a hansom to be found of course for our good King in his royal wisdom had banned working horses from the

British Isle, it was rumored he was heavily invested in both Tesla Inc. and Edison stock. So I set out on foot for I knew my wife Franny would be worried not only at the state of things due to the electricals being off but at my not coming home at the expected time. I thought about sending her a telegram but then realized that that also required electricity.

* * *

By my pocket watch I had been almost three hours on the road. The outskirts of Londontown were behind me and I was in one of the rural stretches between hamlets. My home was still ahead of me. Fortunately, it was the season when sunset came late. I had an hour or more of daylight to go.

I trudged on, jacket over my shoulder, thirst at my throat.

Then a miracle before my eyes. An old stagecoach inn of the previous century often located at crossroads had now been converted into a pub. I made my way directly inside.

"Pint," I requested.

"What's your desire?" asked the pub keeper.

"Anything will do as long as it is wet."

I gulped down a third of it straight away. I paused to look around. An old man I took to be a farmer was the only other patron.

"Any word on what might have happened to all the electricals?"

"No. My Marconi is out also," said the proprietor.

"Witchcraft!"

We both looked at the farmer.

"They are still around, I tell you, and to be reckoned with," he continued.

"Actually, it was the sun," said the pub man wiping dry a pint. "We have a retired professor nearby. Was an Oxford don. Was an astronomer. Taken up bird watching and water colors now. Comes in every noon. Was here when it happened. Said it was a solar flare, whatever that is? Cooked the wiring, he said, magnetized it or demagnetized it, I forget which. He was quite excited. Ran out of here saying he was going to write an article to the Royal Geographic about it.

"From the city?" he asked once he finished his tale.

"Aye."

"Walking?"

"Trying to get home to the wife," my hand strayed to the locket she had given to me that I used for a watch fob.

"Where to?"

"Abbotsgate."

"Got a ways then. Will not get there before dark."

"I can get you there," interjected the farmer. "Cost you a pound."

"How?"

"Got a wagon around the side."

The pub keeper shrugged. I was curious.

"Show me."

* * *

He did have a wagon that appeared older than he was, wooden and just as cracked and creaky.

"You will have to help me with my horse," he said.

Puzzled, I walked with him around to the front.

He did have a horse. Its coat a brown weathered leather. A large brass key protruded from its left flank.

I helped him wind it up, feeling the tension in the massive clock spring tighten, and then we were off.

* * *

An hour or more later we were at my gate. I gladly paid the old man his requested pound note and rushed inside.

"Franny!" I called. "Franny?"

I found her in the bedroom sitting on the bed edge. A welcoming smile on her lips.

I unbuttoned her blouse. Located the spot on her breast. Opened the locket that had come with her and extracted the key.

Thank the Lord, I still had an old fashioned wife.

I wound her up.

Willicicle

Little Willie in the snow
doesn't have so far to go.

Pluto's just a tiny rock,
soon he'll find a door to knock.

Willie's tired and soon he's dozin'.
Oops, too late—now he's frozen.

— Neal Wilgus

Chained Pearls

fugues adorn her glittering *If only*
draped iridium pearls

worm-holed, strung together
across her nape and through the night

a necklace of multiverses, of *Maybe*
points of divergence

from her capacity for destruction
and (convulsive) rebirth along other lines

hands webbed gossamer with age
cradle the misbegotten past, uncertainty

for its shroud a Brownian solution
that rips into every proof against the dark

energies and *What's the matter?*
existential bulwark

— W. C. Roberts

Good Samaritans
Story by Mark Silcox
Illustration by Teresa Tunaley

The Benefactor lay face-down in a ditch by the side of the road. His upper orifice quivered and flexed, slick with the faintly glowing, yellowish liquid that oozes out of his kind whenever they're tripping on potassium-40. Scattered in the grass around him were at least a dozen greasy black banana peels.

A lot of traffic was passing on the highway, and it wasn't like he was inconspicuous with his limbs all spread out down there in the dry mud. I could sort of understand why folks had been reluctant to stop and help out, though. The pungent, swampy smell he was giving off was so thick you could taste it in your mouth. His kind always stink—it's probably one of the main reasons we don't get along better with them, even after everything they've done for us. But when you come across one who's been on a bender, it's bad enough to make you consider getting your nose amputated.

I pulled onto the gravel shoulder and climbed off my floater. "Excuse me," I managed to choke out though the noxious fumes. "Um, sorry, but you look pretty bad. Is there anything I can do?"

He didn't notice me at first, so I walked up closer to get his attention. His flabby limbs were shivering slightly, so I knew he wasn't dead. I was about to pull out my tachphone and call 911 when he turned his head-thing toward me, and his green eyespot flickered. There was a soft, squashing sound from somewhere inside of him, and he let loose a new wave of aroma that made me hold both hands up to my face and whimper. I knew I was being rude, but the human body has its limits.

He'd somehow managed to lose his chatterbox, so he had to struggle to shape those airy exhalations his species produce into something that sounded like human language. I thought I could tell what he was saying after the fourth or fifth barely audible gasp. He seemed to be repeating just one word, over and over again: *"Hospital. Hospital. Hospital!"*

This was obviously a pretty sensible suggestion. "I can call for a medical drone," I said. "I dunno, though—they're not really built to transport you guys."

He flicked the moist tip of one of his ropey upper limbs. I looked back over my shoulder to see what he was pointing at, and drew a long sigh. The sidecar of my floater. It was empty, and just about the right size to carry him. I'd been riding out that morning to participate in a race at the Etobicoke Kinetic Arena. I'd only attached the car to my machine because I had planned to pick up some groceries on the way home.

My GPS told me that the Osler Medical Center was a couple of miles away. "Okay, I think I can help you," I said. "Just give me a second."

I reached into my pocket and pulled out a thick bandana, which I tied hard around my face. It blocked out enough of the smell to stop me from feeling dizzy. Then I slid down into the ditch and helped the sick alien pull himself upright. He wasn't especially heavy, but his limbs flailed around a lot. A couple of times I slipped on banana peels, a sight that must have looked pretty comical to all of the drivers speeding right past us.

This was not the type of day I'd planned for myself at all.

* * *

When we rolled up outside of the emergency room, an orderly came running out with a clipboard. "Nice floater!" he said, and waved us over toward the entry doors in a friendly way. Then when he got to within about five yards, he reeled backward and clawed at the air.

"Oh, dude!" he moaned. "That thing smells totally P-40ed out. Where'd you find it?"

"Him, not *it,"* I said. It always makes me uncomfortable when people refer to the Benefactors as though they're dumb animals or pieces of furniture. "At least, I *think* he's a him. He was lying by the road."

"So, I'm guessing bananas?"

"Sure, what else would it be?"

"Usually it's bananas. But Brazil nuts and lima beans are radioactive too. Plus, I've heard stories that some of them will actually break into chemistry labs, looking for the hard stuff."

That sounded to me like a hokey urban legend. "There were a bunch of old banana peels on the ground next to him."

The orderly took out a pen and scribbled something. "First Benefactor we've had here in quite a while. I'm not so sure what the protocols are. But we need to get it ... sorry, sorry, get *him* inside. Give me a hand, will you?"

The two of us hauled the alien out of my sidecar and slid his two sturdiest-looking appendages over our shoulders. For a second, I thought I'd pass out. The poor critter couldn't have been more than about eighty kilos, but the potent stench made it harder to breathe while we carried him.

"So with a vehicle like that, I'm guess you must be headed to the track out in Etobicoke," the orderly said. "I tried floating once, but it made me nauseous."

"That used to happen to a lot of people. They've

given us meds for it, now."

"No kidding?" The orderly glanced furtively at the wheezing Benefactor, trying like so many others have since their arrival to reconcile his gratitude with his revulsion.

"You should try it out," I said. "You'll love floating, it's the best feeling in the world. And the pills don't even taste funky like those cancer-immunity drugs they gave us last year."

"Awesome!"

There were about half a dozen people in the ER. Most of them were waiting in line to use the Therapy Cabinet. One tall guy with tattoos and two fingers missing scowled at us. "Hey," he shouted, "Get that stinky fuckin' thing out of here! This hospital's for *people*."

The orderly tried to ignore him. I got ready for a testy exchange, but before the injured guy could get all worked up it was his turn to use the cabinet. I figured that when he stepped out a few minutes later with a brand new hand, he would probably be feeling a lot more peaceable.

The girl behind the check-in desk crinkled her nose at us. "Ew. Bananas, I bet. Room 17-E is open." She pointed down a corridor.

"Thanks, Greta," said the orderly. "If there's a spare chatterbox lying around anywhere, have it sent over—this guy's lost his. And I think we might actually need a doctor."

"Oh, wow—like, a *real* doctor?" said the girl. "That's exciting! I'll check and see if there's one around."

We started walking in the direction she'd indicated. As we stepped into the empty hospital room the alien started exhaling frantically again. "*Sick. Sick. Sick!*" he moaned. The he sort of folded over in the middle and puked (or whatever you'd choose to call it) all over the shiny linoleum. The stuff that came out of him was a radiant yellowish-gold, about the consistency of thick oatmeal.

"Oh, mother." The orderly staggered backward and leaned against the doorframe. "I'm out of here. You can stay here with your, ah, *friend* till we scare up a real doctor for him, all right?"

The Benefactor drew slowly upright, then crashed headfirst onto the creaky cot at the back of the room. As he lay on his side wheezing and quivering, I sat down on the room's sole chair beside him, hoping I wasn't getting irradiated by the pool of shimmering barf.

A nurse came into the room and turned him over onto his back. She used some oily adhesive from a plastic tube to attach a brand new, chrome-plated chatterbox to the alien's skin about halfway up his midsection. "I'll call down for somebody to bring over a mop and bucket," she said, looking at me like I'd just stepped out of a spaceship myself.

"Thank you," said the Benefactor a few moments after she'd left. The tinny, uninflected voice coming out of the chatterbox gave me a little chill. You'd think they'd have designed a version of the device that would make them sound more human.

"No problem," I said. "You were pretty messed up. Feeling better now?"

"The convulsions will begin shortly. I should probably be restrained." He managed to get his head-thing propped up onto one of the slender pillows, then turned his twitching eyespot in my direction. "Your name?"

"Ken. Ken Hinton."

"I have heard of you. The floater champion. You came second in last year's Greater Metro time trials."

"Yeah, that's me." I was surprised. There were always a few Benefactors sitting in the bleachers at big races, watching the amazing vehicles they'd given to us back in the '20s swooping around the rubberized track. The other spectators found their presence disturbing, so they were usually asked to sit in a group by themselves. Apparently, this one was a fan.

It occurred to me that this was the first chance I'd ever really had to conduct a genuine conversation with a Benefactor, something that went beyond just a "pardon me" on the monorail or a "those look good" in the produce aisle.

"You know, I guess really, I should be the one who's thanking you," I said. "You and all your people, I mean. When your guys first landed here, our cities were all covered in smog, and food was still really expensive all over the world. And just that very week, some doctor had told my dad he had six months left to live. Now he's doing fifty pushups every morning!"

I could tell I was blathering, but the alien still had his face turned toward me, and his eyespot was trembling and dilating in that way that's supposed to mean they're paying attention.

"Nobody ever really talks much these days about what things might have been like if your mission hadn't stopped off in this part of the galaxy. But I still remember all the fighting in the Middle East. Plus that big flu epidemic that was just getting started in Pakistan, the nukes in South Africa..."

"We estimate that your species would have

self-terminated within less than a hundred of your years."

"Wow, no kidding?" Was it my imagination, or did he sound just a little petulant through that squeaky metal box on his chest?

Then suddenly, the Benefactor fell over onto his back and all of his appendages started thrashing wildly. I jumped up and ran out of the room, frantic. "Nurse! Anybody!" I shouted. "Need a little help here!"

A short guy with wispy grey hair dressed in cream-colored scrubs was running toward me from the far end of the corridor. "Stay cool," he shouted. "I'm the doctor!" As he got closer I was able to read his plastic nametag. "Dr. Klimke," it said. His face was mottled red and he was flailing his arms to keep his balance on the slick flooring. He was definitely the least mellow-looking old person I'd seen in a long time.

"Is there really one of *them* in there?" he asked me, puffing and panting as he slid to a halt on the polished tiles.

"Uh huh. All wired up on bananas. He's having some kind of a seizure."

"It's okay! It's okay! I have one of these." The doctor pulled a fist-sized injection gun out of the pocket of his smock, took a deep breath, and walked into the room through the sticky mess drying on the floor.

The Benefactor's midsection twisted to and fro and his limbs beat at the empty air. A horrible sound was coming out of his new chatterbox— "...agah... agah...agah...agah..." like a scratchy antique CD. Dr. Klimke darted back and forth, looking for a place to administer the drug. His glasses got knocked off his face and he started cursing as the cot began to jitter across the floor on its squeaky casters.

Finally, he found a spot and fired the drugs into the alien's system. The gun went off with a pop and the seizures stopped almost immediately. The poor creature's chatterbox screamed out a burst of ugly static as his limbs flopped down over both sides of the mattress.

"Will he be better now?" I asked the doc.

"Damned if I know," said Dr. Klimke, retrieving his glasses. "We're in luck, though—one of their ships is in orbit right now somewhere over the Niagara Escarpment. We shouldn't have much trouble getting him off our hands. You're his friend?"

"Well, not really, but I guess if you..."

"Okay then, come with me." The doc swept out of the room and headed off down the corridor. "We need to make a call."

* * *

We walked through the quiet hallways until we passed into a whole different wing of the med center. This part of the building had lush carpets and brightly colored walls. Schmaltzy piano music was playing over the P.A. system. "Is this some kind of luxury ward?" I asked.

Klimke shook his head. "Recreation center. We'd just built a brand new wing of the hospital when the Benefactors showed up, and everybody suddenly started getting healthier. We had to do something with all the extra space."

He strode past several big abstract oil paintings and a long window that looked down into a squash court. I followed along dutifully. "So what's the normal treatment for one of the aliens when they get into that kind of state?"

"You're asking me?" he said. "How the hell would I have any idea? I'm a people doctor! I didn't get my degree in radioactive potassium removal."

This pulled me up short. "You mean, you don't get taught how to care for them?"

"What're you so surprised about? Those critters scrubbed the Earth clean, replaced our fossil fuels, then gave us all enough food to eat and a bunch of toys to play with. Surely you'd think they'd be able to look after themselves!"

"But they obviously don't! Almost half of the Benefactors who came down with their mission turned into addicts! *Everybody* knows that. There must be hundreds of them in every city on the planet, getting high on cheap fruits and vegetables!"

The doctor turned to face me, frowning. "There's no need to raise your voice, young man. Look, I think it's great that you have a place in your heart for our stinky friends from beyond the stars. You're a real good Samaritan."

I often have a hard time telling when somebody's being sarcastic, but this guy didn't leave much up to the imagination. "So because they smell bad, we're not supposed to help them?"

"Well, now, I didn't say that. But listen, that alien's just an administrative hassle for as long as it's here. We obviously can't kick it back out onto the street, but nobody for five hundred miles around here can do a blasted thing to help it, including me. So instead of standing around making speeches, why don't you just help me get your buddy safely sent away?"

We had reached a swinging door that led into a dark, mostly bare storage room. Against the back wall a computer monitor was sitting on top of a shoulder-high piece of convoluted machinery made out of greenish-gold-colored metal, and covered with twisted plastic tubes, little trap-doors, and patches of grease.

"Wow," I said. "That's Benefactor technology, isn't it?"

"Uh huh." The doc walked cautiously toward the machine. "It's a ... well, we call it the space phone. It's for contacting their ships in orbit, in case of a crisis."

"The 'space phone' huh? So how does it work?"

"Curious soul, aren't you? You see that big orange button on the side?" He spoke to me like I was some kind of feebleminded adolescent.

"Let me guess—you just press the button and wait."

"Yep—you got it." He took a deep breath, then slapped the button hard with the palm of his hand. "And that's about the limit of my expertise."

The screen slowly crackled to life. It was broadcasting a picture of a plain, corrugated metal wall. Nothing else happened for a few minutes.

"That's the inside of their orbital ship?" I asked.

The doctor just shrugged.

A broad, pulsating alien eyespot suddenly slid into view. Both of us jumped backwards, startled. The patch of green flesh receded a little, leaving the screen about half filled-up by the image of a Benefactor's wrinkled, fleshy head-thing. This alien seemed a bit more spry than the one we had left back on the hospital bed.

"Please state the reason for this (buzz) *summons,"* said the machine in a loud, mellifluously masculine voice.

"There's a voice synthesizer inside the phone,'" Klimke explained. "It's a classier model than the chatterboxes. I think the guy on the screen is one of their mission leaders."

"That is (buzz) *correct,"* said the machine. The big eyespot throbbed slightly.

"Please excuse the disturbance, sir," said the Doc. "It's a very great honor and a privilege to be speaking to a leader from amongst your race."

You would occasionally hear people talk to the Benefactors in this servile way, as though the aliens were some sort of conquering army. Even though they'd never done anything violent, or demanded any payback whatsoever for their assistance to us. It always creeped me out.

"Please dispense with the (buzz) *formalities, Dr.*

(buzz) *Klimke. Kindly state your business."*

"H-how does it know my *name?"* the Doc whispered to me.

I pointed at the plastic nametag on his chest. He exhaled, obviously very relieved.

"I picked up one of your guys on the roadside," I explained to the strange face looking out at us. "Pretty sure he's overdosed on P-40."

The loose skin surrounding the eyespot crinkled. This was what their species usually did when they were irritated. *"How* (buzz) *regrettable. It is the fifth such case in your region this month."*

"I administered 600 milligrams of propofol and restrained the patient," Klimke offered.

There was a short silence. A few of the Benefactor's appendages rose and quivered near the bottom of the screen. *"That is an oddly* (buzz) *generous dosage, Dr. Klimke!"* it eventually said. *"Was there some pressing need to* (buzz) *sedate this* (buzz) *unfortunate for close to an hour? As you know, Doctor, my species are subject to the risk of prolonged* (buzz) *apnea if they are left unconscious while* (buzz) *under the influence."*

The doctor glanced over at me, a little red in the face, then turned back toward the screen and shrugged. "I just wanted to be sure he wouldn't come around too quick. He was thrashing around pretty badly, like he was gonna tear the place up or something..."

"There are no records whatsoever of P-40-induced seizures causing significant (buzz) *injury or* (buzz) *property damage!"* The skin at the top of the Benefactor's head-thing was twitching feverishly as the synthesized voice rose in pitch.

"Yeah, well, there's a first time for everything," said Klimke. "Things would sure be a lot simpler all around if you'd just tell your boys down here to lay off the damn bananas!"

The machine emitted a slow, wordless exhalation. It was strange how much trouble it seemed to be having translating the alien's speech into English—there was a long pause and an angry buzzing sound just before every halfway esoteric word. In spite all of the amazing technology they'd managed to develop, the Benefactors had never been much good at communicating with us. For some reason, it seems to be their one big blind spot—aside from the freaky fruit fetish, of course.

After another minute there was a clunk from deep inside of the machine and a small door on the front swung open. *"Please take this* (buzz) *device,"* said the alien, *"and attach it to the patient's body, just below his (buzz) verbal emulation mechanism, then stand well back. Please try to perform this small task with (buzz) competence, or serious injury could result."*

The Doc reached in cautiously and pulled out a slender, circular disk of shining metal, with a plastic suction cup on one side. "You guys sure are a pain to deal with," he grumbled. "How come every one of you seems to be either a junkie or a petty tyrant?"

"Perceptions are (buzz) relative," the Benefactor replied. *"My species cheerfully anticipates the end of our (buzz) obligations on your (buzz) benighted planet."* Its eyespot contracted once more, then the screen went dead.

"What do you think he meant when he said 'the end of their obligations?'" I asked Klimke on the way back to the hospital room.

"Dunno." The Doc was obviously still in a sulk after being chastised by the alien. "They talk about being on a *mission* to Earth, though, right? I guess their mission must have some sort of timetable."

"So, they're just going to up and leave one day?" It was a possibility I'd heard people talk about, but one that I'd never really reflected on before. "Are they going to take all of their stuff with them?"

I thought about how my life would change if I couldn't race my floater any more. That sleek, inscrutable machine sitting out in the health center's parking lot was the most beautiful thing I'd ever encountered. Silent, swift, and delicate, but seemingly indestructible. Sometimes when I was riding it, it made me feel a little that way too, in spite of all my natural insecurities and gracelessness.

"Well, I'm sure they wouldn't do that," said Klimke. "If they tried to take some of the stuff, we'd fight them for it—the therapy cabinets, for example, or the fusion reactors. Hardly seems like it'd be worth the trouble for them."

I guess I could see his point, more or less. "But even if they leave their gifts behind, I guess we won't be getting any more help from them. That's pretty scary."

"Why?" said the Doc. "The human race was doing okay before they got here. I'm sure we'll be just fine."

I laughed out loud when he said that. The sound of it echoed down the corridor, causing a couple of nurses and one hobbling patient with a mobile I.V. to turn their heads. "My gosh," I said. "Come on … you don't really think that, do you?"

I guess I just assumed that he must have been joking. But when I turned to look at Klimke he was staring grimly ahead. He was holding the smooth metal disk out a little in front of him between two fingers like it was something filthy he'd picked up off a bathroom floor.

When we got back to his room, the sick Benefactor was still unconscious, but his lower extremities were shuddering under the hospital sheet somebody had pulled over them. The patch of vomit was gone, but the air still smelled foul, and there was a yellowish-brown stain left behind on the floor.

"Holy hell," said Klimke, flinching back from the doorway. "I think it's starting to come around!"

"So do your thing, already." I pointed to the disc in Klimke's hand. "He'll be off your conscience soon enough."

The alien's chest expanded sharply, and his chatterbox let out an eerie electronic howl.

"Tell you what," the doctor said. "How about *you* do it?" He shoved the cool disc into my hand. "He's *your* friend, after all." Before I could argue, he was making his way toward a nearby stairwell, with pretty impressive speed for an old guy.

I took a few cautious steps into the room. The Benefactor's head-thing lolled to one side. He was awake and looking straight at me.

"W-what?" he said with a crackle, and one of his appendages pointed to the thing in my hand.

"Easy, now. It's something from your own people, up in orbit."

His lower limbs started shaking more violently.

I inched closer. "They don't know how to make you better, here," I explained. "But this thing is supposed to help, somehow. I'm supposed to…," I held it out just above his chatterbox, to show him.

His voice came through very slowly. "It will … transport me … back to the ship … for rehabilitation."

"Really? Straight from here? This little thing?"

"It is … a teleportation … device."

I whistled, astonished in spite of it all. Teleportation! You occasionally heard vague stories that the benefactors had their own private stash of technologies that they never shared, stuff that was way beyond anything they'd ever let us see. But I guess I'd always found these fables difficult to square with my image of them a species that got drunk on bananas.

"Well, being teleported will help you out, right? I'm sure they have something up in that big orbital ship over Niagara that'll fix you up in no time."

"But I … do not want … to leave the Earth," said the alien. "I am … happy here!"

His eyespot was swirling with unfamiliar

pigments. I looked into it for a long time, but couldn't think of anything to say to console him. I wanted to ask: *What's the attraction? What is it that makes you want to cling for dear life to our wretched world?* But I guess I also didn't really want to hear his answer. It would have been hard to live with the knowledge that the very best thing our planet has to offer is faintly radioactive produce.

I clapped the disk against his upper torso then staggered backwards. There was a flash of white light as he disappeared, and a brief whoosh as air filled up the space where he had just been. In less than a second, nothing was left of him there but a stained floor and the slightest trace of his sickly aroma.

* * *

I missed the first floater race that afternoon, but ended up winning the tournament after the double elimination round. When I climbed up onto the podium and held up my trophy I said that I wanted to dedicate my victory to a new friend I'd just made. Everybody looked confused, so I took a few minutes to tell them all about my strange adventure earlier that day. Then I turned to face the Benefactors who were there and thanked them for everything they'd given us, including the wonderful machines that we'd just finished racing. I don't know what I'd hoped would happen. But when I stepped away from the microphone, nobody applauded.

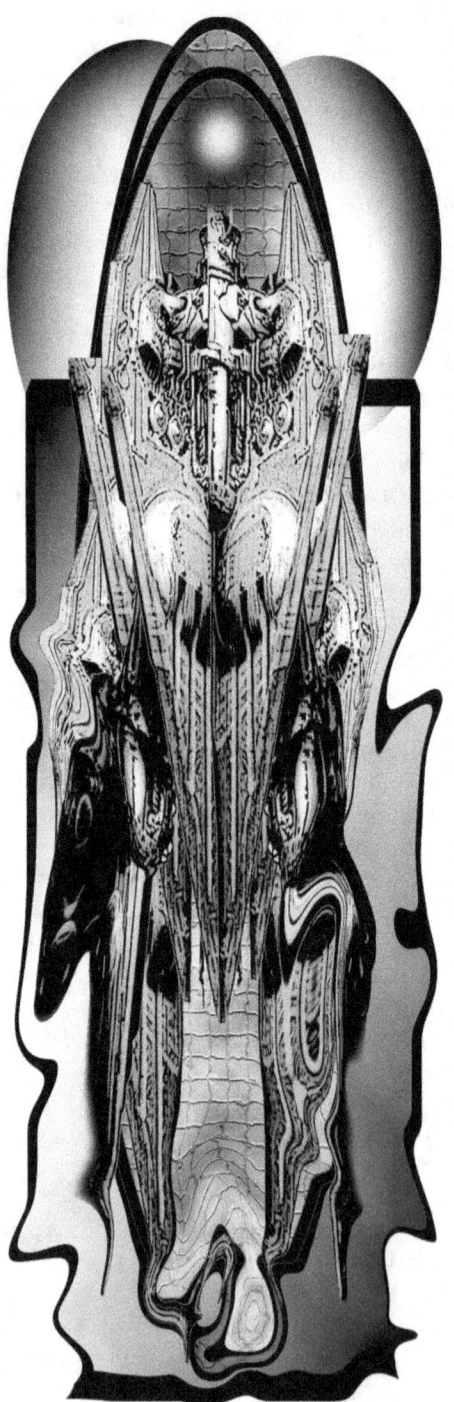

Aggression: Deleted Genome Project

The other scientists
call me hot-head;
I prefer passionate,
personally committed
to the Aggression: Deleted
genome project.

Success finally!
Within the cellular soup
we isolated alleles,
receptors, neurotransmitters
with any link to aggression.

Developed genes for
enzymatic inhibitors
and modifiers—
tried to avoid
competitive, impulsive,
and assertive traits
to preserve
a sense of self.

Fortunately no stab, no jab—
a quick sniff
and the complex cocktail,
complete with starter enzymes,
vectors by nanobot
along olfactory nerve cells
straight to the brain.

I grow impatient waiting
for proper clinical trials
or violent criminal volunteers—
the reason for this research:
a means of rehabilitation
for release back into society
from overcrowded prisons.

Imagine less crime!
Peaceful streets,
World Peace with wide use—
a Nobel Prize!

Will test on self;
make notes of any effects
large or small, fast or slow
make notes to learn,
to learn
should have learned
from Kirk, Miranda …

Make notes why?
why bother to type
why bother to try
to try to help
to try
to take
even one
more
breath
one
more
br

— Lauren McBride

Author's Note: "should have learned/ from Kirk, Miranda . . ." refers first to Captain Kirk from "The Enemy Within" episode of the original *Star Trek* television series, and second to the planet Miranda from the *Serenity* movie following the unfortunate cancellation of the *Firefly* television series.

Thursday's Child
Has Far To Go

Story by
Mark Anthony
Brennan

Illustration by
Tom Kelly

Monday

"Good morning. Is Mr. Johnson there, please?"

"I'm sorry, no," said the woman on the other end. "Who's calling?"

"Am I speaking to *Mrs.* Johnson?" asked Malotte, eyeing the read-out on his screen: 'Irene Johnson (Mrs.) Divorced'

"Yes."

"Well, Mrs. Johnson, this is Jason Malotte of RMS Securities. Your husband asked me to call the minute an opportunity like this came along. Is he around?"

"No. You see he doesn't live here anymore. We're not … together."

"Oh, I see, that's too bad," said Malotte, tapping his desk with his pencil. Irene Johnson sounded friendly, trusting. He had a real shot here. "I had this great investment opportunity that just came up. I was dying to tell him. Perhaps you'd like to hear about it?"

"Well…," said Mrs. Johnson hesitantly. "I don't know much about these things."

"It's nothing complicated. Don't worry. When I was speaking to, um…" Malotte quickly checked the information on his computer screen. "…Bill, he wanted something simple. Now this is—"

"Bill? Did you say 'Bill'?"

"Yes, ma'am, your husband, Bill."

"No, no, he goes by William. No one's ever called him Bill. Bill is our son's name."

"Oh, your *son*." Malotte scoured the page looking for her age. There it was: 63. "Yes, of course, I remember now, Bill is your son. OK, well, when he and I spoke we—"

"Wait," stated Mrs. Johnson. "Just wait, Mr. … er…"

"Malotte, ma'am. Jason Malotte."

"Mr. Malotte." Her voice had turned to ice. "You never spoke to my son. Bill has been dead for 14 years. Really, do you people have no shame?"

The line went dead.

Malotte ripped off his head-set and flung it down on the desk in disgust.

"Jerry!" he yelled.

"He's off shift," came a voice from the other side of the office.

Malotte took a deep breath. That god-damned Jerry. Worst fucking fact-checker in history.

He could have tried tweaking with Mrs. Johnson. But how? Change her husband's name to Bill? Bring her son back to life? No way. Too drastic. Tweaks like that could do him in.

He spotted Hanson, the Shift Supervisor, over top of the cubicles. Hanson raised his hands with the silent question: 'Why aren't you on the phone?' Malotte gave him a sarcastic smile and wave.

Hanson could go fuck himself. Malotte was the best closer on the floor, and everyone knew it.

He pulled his head-set back on and glanced at the time. 9:13, was that all? The thought of another three hours until lunch was unbearable. A simple tweak should do the trick.

He closed his eyes and selected a point in his brain. A pin-point, centre-front. He clenched his fists, willing the point to grow. Ow, ow, ow. Sharp, stinging pain. As the point grew the pain grew. Don't forget the time. The time, yes, nudge it just a bit. And … let it go…

He let his body go limp, his fists relaxing. The pain in his head became diffused and weak. It was ebbing away. He opened his eyes. 12:01. Perfect.

He rubbed his forehead with three fingers, but there was less than a dull throb now. More of a memory of pain. His stomach suddenly lurched, then slowly, slowly subsided. He sighed. He was fine. As usual, he was fine.

But he never got used to it. Even after all these years the pain was still nasty. Migraines. At least, that's what people called them. Flashes of real unpleasantness. But, so long as *he* brought them on, so long as *he* controlled them, they were tolerable. Not like those involuntary ones he used to get when he was a kid. Those were killers. He hadn't had those kind in years. Not until last night, that is.

It had struck him in the middle of the night like a bolt of pure pain. A lightning strike out of nowhere. Searing white-hot agony. He had no idea how long it lasted. During the white torment there is no time.

"Shaky start," said Hanson as Malotte walked by him, "but a good morning for you after all."

"Yeah," sneered Malotte, "well some of us have to actually earn money around here, you know what I mean?" He turned back before opening the door to the elevator. "Hey, what's with the smell in here today anyway?"

Hanson shrugged. "What smell?"

"I dunno," Malotte called back as he passed through the door. "Like someone lighting matches or something. Friends of yours?"

A good morning? Just 'good'? It was supposed to be better than that. He had to work on that tweak.

* * *

In the coffee shop they were playing Dire Straits

—their first song, his favorite.

'...*and the vultures, yes, the vultures wait eons*...'

Wait, wasn't that where they sing, '...and the Sultans play creole...'? He'd never noticed anything about vultures before.

'...*they are the vultures, they are the vultures of Spring*...'

Malotte gave a short laugh. The young guy behind the counter looked at him, puzzled.

"It's just the song," explained Malotte, pointing upwards. "It's funny how they do remixes. You know, alternate versions."

The barista cocked his head. "I dunno, man. Pretty sure it's the original."

Malotte smiled. The song was even before *his* time. But this kid? No, he clearly had no idea. "This song is called '*Sultans of Swing*', not '*Vultures of Spring*'."

"No, you're wrong, dude. My dad is like the biggest Mark Knopfler fan there is. This is 'Vultures of Spring'. I should know."

"Huh," said Malotte, holding his hand out for his change.

Okay. Well, that was weird.

Tuesday

"Aaaah!"

Malotte sat bolt upright in his seat. He hated falling asleep on the train. It was even worse when you woke up screaming in pain.

Several people in the compartment were looking over at him. One or two seemed genuinely concerned, but most of them were just annoyed.

"Holy shit," muttered Malotte to himself. He'd had many a bad headaches, but this was something else. Like someone had split his head open with an axe. The scorching hot blade was still in there. There was even a metallic taste at the back of his throat.

His head throbbed, but the pain was billowing, getting lighter. His stomach heaved. He felt nauseous enough to vomit but he didn't. It was getting better. Almost back to normal.

He rolled his head to the side and looked at the fields sliding by. They were close to the city center, but the commuter train was passing through one of the green belts. Most of the fields were brown, with rows of vegetables, but there was the odd green patch. These grassed areas were dotted with stacks of hay, cows, and...

What was that? Malotte twisted his head around, trying in vain to look back at what he'd just seen. It had been an animal, taller than cow. It was pink, and he could have sworn it had the head of a pig. He straightened back up in his seat. It was probably just the after-effects of that horrible migraine.

By the time he reached his stop downtown he felt much better. Physically, anyway. He was still out of sorts. The station looked the same as ever but it was unfamiliar somehow.

It was no better when he reached the street. Same storefronts, same buildings, same everything, but it just wasn't *right*. When you are driving through somewhere headed in one direction it seems different from when you drive through it in the other direction. Same place, just different. That's how Malotte felt as he walked to work—he was heading outward but he had the inbound view.

And it reeked. Like burning garbage. He had thought it was just a funky smell on the train, but it was everywhere. What could make that smell?

When he reached his office, or at least where his office was supposed to be, he dropped his briefcase in astonishment. His building was gone. The entire block was gone. In its place was an old apartment building. Old, not new. He recognized it. This building was here when he was a kid. It had been torn down decades ago.

He looked around nervously. New cars, new stores, new signs. No, he hadn't travelled back in time. But, what the hell...?

His stomach churned. He wasn't sure that he could keep it down. He had to sit before his legs gave out under him.

Plunking himself down on a city bench he fumbled in his pocket before pulling out his cell phone. With trembling fingers he dialed a number.

"Hello."

"Marcie? Marcie, don't hang up. It's me, Jason."

"Jay?" Marcie snorted. "I'll give you one minute, that's it."

"Don't be like that. Please. I'm having a real bad day."

"Okay. What is it? What's wrong?"

"It's the tweaking, it's out of control. It's out of *my* control. Things are happening that—"

"Jay!" Marcie snapped. "Are you still talking about that stuff? You still think you can change the future?"

"I never said I could change the future," said Malotte defensively. "I just ... change the option. Time is on a ... a track. But there are others, other tracks. Like in parallel. I just ... you know, switch."

"Are you off your meds?" Marcie sounded disappointed.

"I don't need medication."

"Oh god, Jay, you're off your medication?"

"They don't *do* anything. They don't change anything. Those doctors are wrong."

"This is so like you, isn't it? Everyone else is wrong, and you are right. You know what Dr. Chang said."

"I know what he said, Marcie, but Dr. Chang doesn't understand. The migraines aren't having an effect on *me*, it's the other way around. *I* bring them on. *I* tweak them. I use the migraines to shift things."

"Your minute is up."

"No, wait, please. Can we meet? I need to talk."

"Don't do this, okay? It's not fair. I can't deal with it. You know I can't. Get help, Jay, please. I gotta go."

Malotte stared at his phone in disbelief. 'Call ended'. She'd hung up. How could she hang up on him?

He looked around despondently. What was he going to do now?

Wednesday

Suddenly the guy in front of him turned around and faced Malotte, placing his arm on the back of his seat. "This is the one."

Malotte groaned inwardly. What now? He was in no mood for some clown talking to him on the commuter train.

He hadn't slept well the night before. He kept imagining there was a dark, sinister figure approaching his bed and he was paralyzed. Then he would jerk himself awake. It was one of those disturbing, but really annoying, 'waking' dreams. He'd lay back and there he was again, but this time, no, he really *was* unable to move and the figure drew near. Then he'd wake up again. It went on and on. Finally he gave up and got out of bed.

Now he was exhausted. He shook his head to keep himself from drifting off. He didn't want a repeat of yesterday.

"What?" he said irritably.

"This is the one, Jason," said the guy. He was obviously heading for the business district—his suit was expensive. A power suit, similar to the ones Malotte normally wore. "This is the one where a man on the train turns around and talks to you."

"What ... what do you mean 'the one'?"

"The reality, Jason." The 'suit' had a stupid smile hung on his face. It was out of place—there was nothing funny or pleasant going on. It was aggravating. "This is the reality. One of an infinite number, right?"

"Look, I don't know you. Why don't you just—"

The 'suit' held up a finger. "Wait, just wait. Let me finish. You know what I'm talking about, don't you? Of course you do. But you've got it wrong, you know that?"

"Wrong?" Malotte wasn't sure why he was talking to this guy. He should just change seats, but he was too tired to bother.

"You think too linear, Jay my friend. It's not like a bunch of tracks. This reality, the one we're in, it's like a sheet of fabric. Okay? Every point on that sheet represents a place in time and in space. With me so far, buddy? Now that is just *one* sheet. This old universe has no bounds, has it? How could it? Everything that exists, everything that has existed, everything that could possibly ever exist, the universe has it all. That's right, Jay, there is an infinite number of sheets. But you knew that already, didn't you?"

Yes, he did. Malotte had never thought of it in those terms, but the 'suit' was right. Undeniably.

"Now, here comes the kicker, my friend. Those sheets are discrete—they exist unto themselves. No touching, no interconnecting. They remain intact, and never the twain shall meet. At least, that's the way it's supposed to be. But sometimes there's holes."

Malotte's heart sank. He didn't want to hear this. "Holes?"

"Yeah, like perforations in the fabric. Then things trickle through. They slip from one sheet to the other. You've been a bad boy, Jay Jay. You shouldn't have done it. You *knew* you shouldn't have. But you couldn't help it, could you? Over and over again, you couldn't help yourself."

Malotte blinked. This was getting scary. "Look, whoever you are, this is bullshit. I mean—"

"Bullshit?" said the 'suit'. "Really? Really, Jay, you think so? You know what happens when you put too many holes in a fabric? It gets weak. It begins to rip. It's torn, you moron. It's torn because of you."

"Okay, enough," said Malotte. "Just who the hell are you?"

"You know, Jason. You know who I am. Asshole."

Still wearing his silly smile, the 'suit' turn away from Jason and faced the front of the train.

"Hey," said Malotte, lunging forward. He grabbed the guy by the shoulder. "Who are you? Tell me."

The guy turned to Malotte with a look of surprise. It was as if he'd never seen Malotte in his life.

"What *is* this?" said the 'suit'. "What do you want?"

"Those things you just said, how did you know all that?"

The 'suit' grabbed Malotte's hand and wrenched it off his shoulder. He frowned. "Buddy, I've never talked to you, ever. You've got the wrong man."

Malotte searched the guy's face for a second. He finally slunk back into his seat.

Yeah, I know. I know who you are. Asshole.

* * *

It wasn't until he reached to the station that he realized he had nowhere to go. He was acting out of habit. It was lack of sleep—he wasn't thinking straight. What was the point of being downtown? He had no job to go to. None that he was aware of anyway.

It rarely rained, even in winter. This was summer, so it was always sunny. Not today, however. As Malotte left the station he looked up at the heavy clouds that filled the sky. They looked about ready to burst at any second.

He wandered aimlessly down 33rd Avenue, hoping that something, anything would provide some guidance. He didn't know where to turn—he was at a loss.

Finally he stopped at a street corner. He had to call his dad. His dad always knew what to do. Of course, that was when Malotte was a kid. So what? There was no one else he could talk to.

"Hello?"

"Hi, Mom."

"Jason! How are you?"

"Yeah, well ... you know, been better. How about you, Mom?"

"Oh, the hips are still acting up. The left one especially. Dr. MacDonald, he says I should get braces. I don't know. He's awfully young. I don't think he really knows what he's talking about, you know?"

"Mom, you should listen to the doctor, okay? Um, I really wanted to talk to Dad. Is he there?"

"Jason, don't do that."

"Don't do what?"

"It's not funny, that's what. It's bad enough I have to live here on my own. You don't have to be cruel. You know, since your father died I haven't had—"

Malotte dropped the phone in shock. Dad? His father was dead? When? *How?*

"Ah, Christ!"

A searing hot sword pierced his skull, his brain exploding in excruciating pain. His very being became the pain. There was nothing else, just the burning flame of agony.

The white torment. White. White...

* * *

Malotte was confused. He wasn't sure of anything. All he knew was the pounding in his head.

Oh yes, a migraine. He'd had a migraine, and it was fading. Where was he? On the ground?

The side of his face was wet. Puke. He was lying in a pool of vomit. His chest heaved and he coughed up a few more chunks.

"Haka, moof, add kee noo?"

Malotte didn't want to get up. He wanted to relax and enjoy the bliss of having the pain seep away. What was this guy saying anyway? He sat up, wiping away the vomit from his face.

"What did you say?" asked Malotte, blinking. Why was the sky so bright?

"Add kee," said the man standing over him. He looked more scared than concerned. He pointed at the top of Malotte's head, agitated.

Malotte felt the top of his head. Hair? The guy was pointing at his hair?

The man was much shorter than Malotte. He wore an odd, one-piece outfit with a rope for a belt. He was completely bald.

Malotte rose shakily to his feet, rubbing his eyes. He glanced around as he dusted himself off. Where the fuck was he? It looked like downtown, but it was no street that he recognized.

The other people on the street were dressed in the same, one-piece outfit. And they were all bald. Some stared over at him nervously, but they kept moving.

"Talla kwag, moof," said the man next to Malotte, shaking his head. With that he turned on his heel and scurried off.

Malotte tried to wipe the puke off his shoulder with his hand. It was then that he noticed the cars, if you could call them that. Trundling along in silence, the vehicles were boxy and flimsy. Electric-powered, no doubt. They all had the same color scheme—pale green, beige and cream. Those three colours were everywhere—on people's clothes, on storefronts, on signs.

The signs. They weren't in English. In fact, they weren't in any language that Malotte had ever seen.

Just crazy squiggles.

People continue to stare, making Malotte uncomfortable. It was time to go. He ducked into an alley, hoping it would lead him to a street he knew. He batted at the air—it was teeming with insects, so many that he kept breathing them in.

Malotte was dismayed to find that the next street over was no more recognizable than the last. He stood surveying the street for a while, so at first he didn't pay much attention to the chattering behind him. Finally, someone tugged at the back of his jacket. He spun around, surprised to find that a small crowd had gathered. There were about seven or eight of them. Happy and excited they pointed at him and then pointed at themselves. In horror, Malotte realized why.

They all had his face. He stared out at eight miniature, bald clones of himself. The vision of them swam before him and started to recede. He almost fainted, but he caught himself.

Malotte staggered off, bewildered. He was going insane, he had to be. He needed rest, that was it. He had to go home and get some sleep.

He just hoped that 'home' was where he left it.

Thursday

Malotte moaned as he woke up. He really felt like shit. As a young man he'd often woken up after a beery night with serious jungle mouth. That was nothing. Right now the inside of his mouth was as rough and dry as sandpaper, and it tasted vile.

He'd had an episode during the night. Another white flash of blinding pain. He was so tired, though, that he just fell back asleep.

His nostrils twitched. There was an acrid tang in the air. It was hard to breathe.

He threw off his blanket with a crackling noise. Static. Lots of it. So much that he'd felt the discharges on his skin like thousands of tiny pinpricks.

The curtains were drawn, so the room was still quite dark. In the gloom he peered down at his hand. Minute points of light danced all over the surface of his skin. He was alive with electricity. In despair he brought his hand up to his brow. The air hummed. It got louder as his hand approached his face. He pulled his hand away. Sure enough, the sound went away.

Malotte rose up out of bed, emitting twinkling ripples in the air. He gulped hard, and then headed for the window, sparks snapping at his feet with every step.

The diffused light around the edge of the curtains was unsettling. Surely that was the wrong color.

Miniscule bolts of lightning shot from his fingertips as he reached for the drapery. He paused, taking a deep breath. Finally, he drew back the curtain.

"Oh, holy Jesus Christ! No!"

Dear Cthulhu

by
Patrick Thomas

Dear Cthulhu,

I am a writer who has spent at least thirty to forty minutes every month for the last year dedicated to my craft. I have started over fifty novels and one day hope to finish at least one of them. In the meantime, I've tried my hand at poetry and short story writing.

Sadly the world has yet to recognize my brilliance. I feel a very large part of my lack of success as a writer stems from that failure. That lack of recognition of my genius is to be blamed for my not completing anything. Because—and let's be honest here—the moment the masses bow down in the praise I deserve, I'd have the encouragement and motivation I need to finish one of my epic works. Maybe even two. I mean, it's not easy to write and still have a job and a social life.

The latest in the long line of those not recognizing my literary mastery is David Lee Summers, the editor of that rag *Tales of the Talisman*. I liked what I read in his magazine and figured this guy might have something on the ball so I sent him one of my unfinished novels about how Christopher Columbus really used nanotechnology in a ghost bus built from chocolate pudding and sunbeams to discover the hidden city of Newark and covered it all up by saying he discovered America in order to prevent an invasion of alien cyborg llamas that were harvesting humans for their uvulas. As soon as I got Summers's reply, I lost all respect for the man. First off, he told me he expected me to read his writer submission guidelines, obviously not understanding that someone as special as I am is exempt—nay—beyond any artificial construction such as man-made restrictions on brilliance. Then he goes on to tell me that the magazine doesn't publish novels, particularly unfinished ones. Then he complains that he thought it was difficult to read because I "accidentally" assembled the chapters in a random order without any numbering. Let me tell you, that was no accident. That was *brilliance*. A true reader or editor would realize that and simply read the whole book at least once, then go back and try and assemble

the chapters in the right order just to be a part of my greatness. Didn't he see Pulp Fiction? That didn't go in order. And this is even more brilliant because even though that movie didn't go in order, it was at least put in a sequence where it could be understood by the viewer. My novel wasn't challenged by any such limitation. I figured Summers could publish it before it was finished and then I would arbitrarily place the final chapters on different Internet sites and stapled to telephone poles on random street corners for my hordes of fans to find on their own.

I wrote this so-called editor back and explained to him in no uncertain terms about how wrong he was, about how shortsighted his thinking is and that he wouldn't know art if it bit him in the butt. Not that I would do such a thing—my real name is actually Art, short for Arturo although I hadn't decided for sure if I would write under that name. It seemed too plebeian. I'm thinking Fluffy McBoomroom IXX.

However, I'm not an unreasonable man so I gave Summers another chance and sent him three more of my novels. This time he complained that my submission made even less sense because I had randomly mixed the chapters from not just one but three different unfinished works. Summers again failed to see the *genius* of what I did. Can you imagine the reaction when people realize they got not just one, but three novels that would allow them the joy of searching and figuring out not just what order the chapters went in, but to what novel? People would be thrilled by the novelty and they'd be excited because they got three for the price of one. Summers wrote back again, once more going on about these writer's guidelines and the importance of following them if I wanted to be published in his little rag.

Truth be told, I am partially to blame. One time shame on you, two times shame on me. I shouldn't have given him a second chance. Still I'm having trouble letting it go. Then I noticed that you appeared in nineteen of the last twenty issues. I figured the reason you didn't appear in the one was you probably had some sort of beef with this editor as well, so you'd understand where I was coming from. Would you speak to this David Lee Summers and point out what an imbecile he's being? Then tell him that he needs to publish my work. And let him know I won't take less than a half million dollars as an advance, but he can pay half on acceptance and half on publication.

— Artful Author in Albuquerque (aka Fluffy McBoomroom IXX)

Dear Artful,

Cthulhu is continually amazed at the ability of so many humans to refuse to accept responsibility for their own actions or to blame their failures on others. Cthulhu is not going to lie to you and tell you that this David Lee Summers is the greatest editor who ever lived. He is not. However he is better than most, if for no other reason than his good sense to carry the *Dear Cthulhu* column. The man is only human—which is not meant as a compliment by any means—and only has so much time to devote to his literary endeavors. In fact Cthulhu was saddened to learn that this very issue will be the last *Tales of the Talisman*. Summers has decided that he wishes to spend more of his limited lifespan on his own writing, which Cthulhu understands goes in the more traditional chronological order. Mostly books about the Order of the Scarlet Steampunk Space Pirate Vampire Owls or some such thing. Tolerable if you enjoy that sort of thing. Most of what you spouted at me is dreck and nonsense. You think because you came up with an offbeat concept that the entire world should think it is as wonderful as you do and bow down and worship your brilliance. This is a fool's dream. Even as great, wonderful and insightful as the *Dear Cthulhu* columns are, not everyone enjoys them. People have different tastes. Those who like and enjoy *Dear Cthulhu* have the good kind. The others have the wretched and bad variety.

Writer's guidelines exist for a reason. Humans prefer for today to be similar to yesterday. When they watch or read something, most find it preferable to have some idea of what they are about to take in. For Summers or any other magazine editor to abruptly change what he or she has used to build an audience would likely spell the end of their publication, although admittedly in the case of *Tales of the Talisman* it really would not have made much difference as this is the last issue.

Perhaps you should take a look at your imagined and perceived literary talents and give them an honest assessment. Hand off your work to others you trust and have high regard for. See what they think of your work. Join a writers group to get input from peers. Of course another way is to simply keep sending out what you have written in hopes of finding an editor who feels the same way as you and is willing to publish and pay you for your work—good luck getting your requested advance without a scandal or popular reality show. Cthulhu has also heard the argument that people should just simply put their work up for sale and let the readers decide. This is an equally valid concept and easily done with the online venues available today. If after putting your work up for sale, you find that tens of thousands are paying money for your writing, your belief in your work's quality will be validated by the voting by way of currency exchange. If instead you sell five copies and four are returned, then the opposite will be proved.

Or you can simply start your own magazine, one without guidelines, but make sure you have open submissions. I guarantee you will change your views on guidelines before your first issue comes out.

Dear Cthulhu,

I read with interest the letter in your column from the woman who was in love with and physically intimate with a duck and was troubled by the unusual nature of his member. I find myself in a similar predicament, albeit with a different animal.

My husband and I bought a petting zoo and animal sanctuary years ago. I love animals and it's worked out pretty good overall. There have been a few bumps in the road like the time I found my husband offering to sell alpaca meat on the internet or when he decided it would be cheaper to feed the occasional pot-bellied pig to our mountain lion. The straw that broke the camel's back (not literally—thankfully our camels' spines are fine) was when my husband offered to send me off to a spa for three days and take care of all the animals while I was gone. Normally I do the mountain lion's share of the work. The zoo makes just enough money to pay our bills and keep going, so I hadn't been on a real vacation in years. I was a bit suspicious since he hadn't done anything that nice for me since we were courting, but really wanted the massage and seaweed wrap treatment, so I went. It took me hours and when I got there I was told nothing was paid for. I hadn't brought my credit cards so I turned around and went home. By the time I pulled in the driveway, it was dark and I was furious. The parking lot had cars I didn't recognize and there were lights on in the habitats. I snuck in and found out my husband was making some dirty deals. He had a couple of mobsters with a dead body they were trying to get rid of over by the pig pens and a bunch of guys in camouflage with guns who had paid him a grand each to hunt exotic animals. A flamingo may be exotic, but it's not exactly hard to shoot in a fenced in area.

Hubby was shocked to see me and even more surprised when I started throwing the hunters out.

They wanted their money back and didn't want to leave until I pointed to our security cameras and asked to see their flamingo hunting licenses. I told them my husband and I were separated—as far as I was concerned it was only a matter of minutes until it happened—and to take it up with him.

Next I turned toward the guys in suits who I thought were more hunters until I saw the corpse. Turns out Hubby owed ten grand for betting on cock fights, something he knows I hate for the unnecessary cruelty. He made a deal to help them get rid of dead bodies by feeding them to our pigs.

As soon as I saw the body, I hit the panic button on the alarm keychain I carried. It sent a signal to the zoo's security system.

I ran away and the mobsters chased me. I ducked into the nearest habitat which housed our kangaroo. Kenny had been declawed and mistreated by his previous owners and we had taken him in as a rescue. The mobsters followed me in and pointed guns at me. I've never been so scared in my life. I thought I was going to die. Then Kenny hopped out and boxed one man in the face and kicked the other man in the groin. Both hit the ground in pain.

By the time they got up, the cops had arrived. Luckily they hadn't been far. The cops had a speed trap where they hid behind one of our billboards about a mile down the road.

The cops captured the bad guys and with the dead body, had enough to put them away. Hubby got convicted as an accessary after the fact and I got a quickie divorce. In exchange for me not testifying against him, he signed his half of the zoo over to me. Idiot didn't realize I'd already turned the security footage over, so the DA didn't need me to do anything to get a conviction. Especially since it showed him holding the gates open as the killers carried the body in for disposal.

I was happy to be rid of the deadbeat. I was even happier when I found out one of the crooks had a two hundred grand reward for his capture and because I'd summoned the cops, I got it.

You'd think my life would have been great, but it wasn't. I was lonely. My ex was a loser, but he was good for one thing and it wasn't conversation.

Taking care of the animals was satisfying, but didn't take care of my womanly needs. I started having a glass of wine with dinner, then a bottle. One night I was drunk and wandering the paths and I came to Kenny's cage. I went inside and drunkenly told him thank you, then how lonely I was. He came

up to me and I hugged him. Then I noticed the kangaroo was dry humping me. He was almost as tall as my short ex and only a little less hairy. I closed my eyes and it almost felt like I was holding a man who was thrusting against me. Maybe it was the loneliness or the white zinfandel, but some part of me decided it was a good idea to drop my trousers and let Kenny have his way with me. Part of it may have also been guilt that he was one of the few animals we hadn't been able to find a mate for and I knew that even a kangaroo guy had needs too.

I was so happy I did. OMG, it was amazing. The speed at which he took me was incredible, using those powerful legs to hump me like a freight train piston. And he felt bigger than my ex.

I had more organisms than I ever had with a man.

It was only after the afterglow faded that I freaked out because I thought Kenny had two penises. Or is that peni? I looked closer and realized there were two ends.

I'm worried. Do you think Kenny has a conjoined twin that is attached to his penis? I checked but didn't see any teeth or eyeballs or other stuff. Does he need to have it removed? I hope not, because the added width makes our special time together *really* amazing. Still I'd hate for him to get hurt.

— Girl Down Under a Kangaroo

Dear Down Under,

There is nothing wrong with Kenny. Marsupials have a bifurcated penis. All kangaroos except the largest two species have this procreative feature. It helps them match up to the females which have two lateral vaginas. They can even store a fertilized embryo in the second of the corresponding wombs while another develops in the first and bring it to term later.

Your kangaroo is fine. However, you might want to check and make sure your procreative activities have not been caught by the cameras of your security system. While persecution for bestiality may not be a priority of your local District Attorney, it would not take long for video of your trans-species trysts to end up on the internet if it fell into the wrong hands. And I cannot imagine that kind of publicity being good for what I assume would be considered a family friendly business. Use your reward money to build a private area in the kangaroo's habitat where you can enjoy each other away from prying eyes and cameras.

Have A Dark Day.

Dear Cthulhu welcomes letters and questions at DearCthulhu@dearcthulhu.com. All letters become the property of *Dear Cthulhu* and may be used in future columns. *Dear Cthulhu* is a work of fiction and satire and is © and ™ Patrick Thomas. All rights reserved. Any one foolish enough to follow the advice does so at their own peril. For more *Dear Cthulhu* get the collections *Cthulhu Knows Best; Dear Cthulhu: Have A Dark Day;* and *Dear Cthulhu: Good Advice For Bad People* from Dark Quest Books.

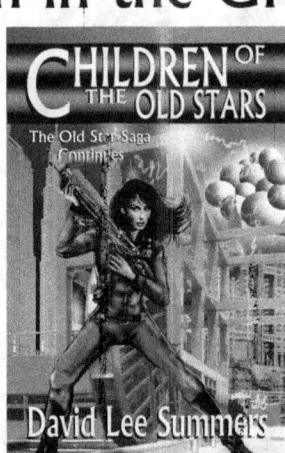

Science Fiction in the Grand Tradition!

"*The Pirates of Sufiro* offers extraordinary storytelling..." Nicole Kurtz, author of the Sybil Lewis Detective Series

"*Children of the Old Stars* presents an engrossing vision of the future..." S. Derrickson Moore, The Las Cruces Sun-News

"[*Heirs of the New Earth* is] a well-crafted and thoughtful piece of science fiction. Highly recommended" Mark Anthony Brennan, Author, Editor, and Publisher

Trilogy available at Amazon.com, LachesisPublishing.com, BN.com and more!

Crows

Story by
Melinda Moore

Illustration by
Laura Givens

Summer

I used to be indifferent to crows. On occasion, I'd notice their silhouettes changing a Jane Austen spring to an Edgar Allen Poe fall, but that was just the pithy observations of youth. Once, a dense murder installed themselves in my neighbor's yard and adorned his roof the month before he died. Sometimes their caws and clacks struck me as conversation, but mostly I wished he'd stop filling his bird feeders. I didn't even think anything of it when they vanished after his death.

Then, they visited my mother.

The heat broke records the first day I saw one talking to her. After a quick trip to the drugstore, I took my children to the local library and read to them in tax-payer provided air conditioned comfort. I was avoiding not only a huge electric bill but also the little box I had bought at the drugstore.

When we left the library to go to my mom's house, the plastic bag crinkled every time I turned a corner as the box slid around inside it. To drown it out, I shouted at my kids to stop decorating each other with a marker they had found in the back seat.

"Not on the face!" I yelled after glancing in the rearview mirror. And not another child, I thought to myself as I cast a sidelong glance at the bag in the passenger seat. It wasn't that I hated my children. I loved them as much as any mother and even felt lucky my husband made enough money that I could stay home with them. But babies were slave drivers with their little wails and stinky messes. When would I have time to play and read with the older two?

I turned the last corner and tried to decide if I should sneak the bag into my mom's house like a nervous teenager. No, it would just remind the kids to ask me what was in the bag again. I pulled up to the white, pitched roof house with the Pepto-Bismol pink shutters: "The house with character," my mother had said when friends had teased me about it. I stopped in the driveway, and my two children tumbled out of the back door. They ran up the stairs like a chaos storm and were all arms and fingers over who got to ring the bell. It must've been rung a dozen times before I got there, looked down at their marker-decorated bodies, sighed and said, "I told you not on the face."

"But I want tattoos all over my body when I'm a grown-up!" proclaimed my bohemian four-year-old. She had brown hair bobbed around the ears with bangs over the eyes. Always the epitome of preschool fashion, she wore a pink tutu over green shorts and a yellow top.

"Where's grandma?" asked my impatient six-year-old who had opened the screened door and pressed his face against the glass of the front door. Tall and skinny, most people thought he was eight instead of six. Too bad his maturity was closer to four.

The sun was already baking me despite the clinging chill of the car air conditioner. Mom had to be here. She knew I was coming, and it was Thursday—laundry day since before my time began. She must be hanging clothes on the line in the backyard. I turned the knob, and the kids pushed the door open, shouting "Popsicles!" as they ran through the living room and into the kitchen. I expected to hear a washing machine chugging through a load or a dryer churning through towels, but only silence greeted me. A clump of DVDs stood next to the TV, and books were piled haphazardly on the lamp table looking as if they would fall off any minute. I guessed she hadn't started the house cleaning that normally accompanied laundry day. I told my son to get the Popsicles as I walked through the book and media library to the backyard.

Perhaps if I hadn't opened the back door to see the empty clothesline, my life would've continued along its predictable route. But really, it wasn't the empty clothes line that forked my road and sent me down an unwelcome path; it was turning my head to see my mom under the apple tree, looking up into the branches, and talking to a crow.

The crow was large, and even its beak was black. My mom's hair was as black as the crow's feathers except for a few grey streaks here and there. It clacked its beak when it saw me and swooped away with a caw that could rip the planar fabric.

"Everything okay, Mom?" I called.

She jumped and turned around. "How long have you been here?" Her eyes widened, and her hands flew to her flushed cheeks.

"We just got here. I've never known you to talk to birds. Were you trying to shoo it away?"

"Shoo it away? Oh, yes … yes. I was shooing it away. Where are my grandchildren?" "Grandchildren" was the magic word that snapped her eyes back into focus.

I said, "Inside. They're artists today."

The kids had managed to stay in the kitchen while they ate their Popsicles but had not managed to keep the Popsicle juice inside their mouths. The marker and syrup mixed into a psychedelic whirl around their faces, and I sighed in relief when my mom decided to wash it off them immediately.

During their protests, I noticed the kitchen phone had a red light blinking. "Looks like you have a message."

Mom glanced up from the soapy paper towel swishing over my son's face and frowned. "Yes, I know what it is, and I don't want to listen to it."

"Who is it?"

"Test results."

My mind raced, wondering what I had missed. She had had an annual check-up recently but never mentioned anything unusual. Surely, being cancer free for fifteen years meant it wouldn't come back now. I wondered at the undone laundry, the house cleaning not in progress. "If it's test results, don't you think you should listen?"

"I don't really want to." She was now scrubbing Bohemia and tickling her at the same time. I decided not to argue with her. I'd leave that for Dad.

"Well, I guess I'll head out then. Happy hour is at Chelsea's this week if you need me, but I have my cell phone. Mark will be by in an hour or so for the kids. Love you guys!" I started towards the door for my monthly get together with moms I had known since my son was one. But as I opened the door to leave, Mom called out, "Better stick to Coke tonight." I whirled around and stared at her. Her back was towards me as she bent down to give my daughter a hug, now that she was clean. Without saying anything, I left the house and headed home to take the pregnancy test I had picked up earlier that day.

* * *

The crow flew in every dream that summer. I was always watching my mother pushing a baby in a stroller with the bird maneuvering like a jet pilot around them. In the dreams where my mother pushed the stroller to me, the crow would fly straight through her heart, shattering her. In the dreams where I rescued my mom, the crow would dive bomb the stroller and I'd wake up with a baby wail ringing in my ears.

I never mentioned the dreams to Mom who was now under the vigilant watch of doctors and family. We made her stock her refrigerator with all the blueberries and broccoli it would hold and eat chicken every night in preparation for the onslaught of treatments that were coming her way. Thursday became laundry day once again and not a single book or DVD was out of place.

The day she called to say her doctor thought she could beat the cancer again, I had to answer the phone from my doctor's waiting room. "That's great,

Mom," I said. I bit my lip with indecision and then told her about the possible miscarriage, "Nothing for sure yet. But he wants to check to see what's going on."

"Oh, honey, no," was all she said as the sunlight of summer dimmed to let the fall in.

Fall

I caught the lid to the pot when it tried to slide off as I turned the last corner to my mom's house. The gentle smell of potato soup escaped, and I wondered if my unborn baby would love it as much as her grandma did. I hoped Mom wouldn't balk too much at the chicken I sneaked in. The recipe had been passed from my grandma to my mom and then to me, but we each put in our own additions, our own individuality. My mom had cooked this soup hundreds of times for sick friends and family. Now it was her turn to be cooked for. The baby kicked as I snapped the lid on, and I automatically pulled my hand back to rub my growing belly. The miscarriage scare had melted like spring snow and left behind a rosy pregnancy glow. The huge maple tree in the middle of my parents yard was almost bare, its branches reaching to the sky like gnarled hands. Leaves crunched below the car as I turned into the driveway, and they tried to push their way into my shoes and socks as I walked up the steps. I sneezed as the dust settled in my nose. I would have to remember to bring my son by to rake them up. Dad had his hands full taking care of Mom, keeping up the housework and still going to his job.

Silence answered the doorbell ring.

I thought I heard what might have been a crow cawing somewhere.

This was our big ladies' day out while the kids were at school: a morning of shopping for strollers and wigs followed by lunch with Dad. She should be ready to go. I set the soup down to open the door and called in to her, but no greeting answered me. I picked up the soup, carried it to the kitchen and deposited it safely in the refrigerator. When I turned to look out the window, I caught my breath. The backyard was a night time of crows, whirling counterclockwise around my mom. She was waving a broom in the air, but the crows never seemed to get hit, despite how thick they were. I ran out to the back as fast as I could and entered the eye of the storm.

The cawing of the crows seemed to fill the world, more insistent than the nurses telling my mom she needed to get back to eating protein. But shouting above the cacophony was my mom repeating, "I don't want to make your decision!" over and over as she swung wildly with the broom. I froze in the mayhem, remembering the nightmares of the summer. She nearly hit me with the broom, but I ducked just in time. I grabbed her by the shoulders and moved her toward the door. Surprisingly, the crows parted to let us through; I closed the door quickly, in case they decided to follow us. The broom clattered to the floor. Mom's bald head rested on my shoulder, and her tears soaked my shirt as if I was the mother and she the child. She had switched to baby soap because it was easy on her skin; its scent mingled with the moment to add to the role confusion. I tried to comfort her by patting her back, but my questions were frantic, "What the hell were those birds doing? What decision? Why are they out there?" Mom just kept crying and didn't quiet down until several minutes after I had shut up. Then she suddenly stood straight, went to get a tissue and asked if I would like a Coke. The only answer seemed to be yes.

The living room was filled with the sound of fizzing as the bubbles in the soda finished popping, but I could still hear the crows calling to us in the backyard. My mom seemed to want to ignore them, so I played along, not sure I really wanted to hear about them anyway. I let the acid in the Coke sting the inside of my mouth as I looked at the lamp table with the counted cross stitch she had started a month ago. It only had a few rows done. Normally, she would've been finished with it by now. Beside it was a pile of books, closed with no bookmarks protruding, so I asked, "Is reading easier than cross stitch right now?"

My mom gave the pile a withering look as if it was the bane of her existence and stated, "They won't cooperate."

"What?"

"The cross stitch loses count, and I have to rip out dozens of rows. The words in the books mix themselves up so I can't make sense out of them. I've given up and just watch movies."

"Have you mentioned this to Dad or the doctors?" I felt blood rising to my face.

"It doesn't matter anyway."

"Have you given up?" I said more loudly than I intended. In fact, I hadn't even intended for those words to leave my mouth. "I know they found it in your liver and lungs too, but I thought it was all receding?"

Mom stared at my face, at my belly, and then rubbed her eyes with her hand. "No, of course I'm not giving up. It's just different this time around." Her eyes moved down to the floor as she took a sip of Coke. "I was younger when I had the first diagnosis. I had energy back then. Now, I just have senility. I'm a crazy old woman thinking the books aren't sharing their secrets and the crows are, are—. I'm sure once I'm done with the treatment everything will go back to normal. And the crows will fly away." She stood up as quickly as my son does when a friend knocks on the door to play. "Let's get that stroller and wig. We'll really paint the town red."

I could still hear the cawing of the crows and wanted to ask about them, but clearly my mom was done with the discussion. I opened the front door, expecting to hear a loud chorus of crows, but the sound was gone.

It was a good afternoon with Mom using her mother's magic to erase all concerns. We laughed at our attempts to lift the huge stroller box into the car and wondered why two people in our conditions hadn't asked the clerk for help. We laughed when Mom tried on the hot pink wig at the store and asked me what Dad would think. And Mom started to laugh when we walked out of the store and a crow swooped down and tried to take her new wig off her head.

I didn't find it funny.

Winter

I spilled Coke down my shirt as I turned the corner to my parents' house. Tears sprang up immediately, but I had spent the last few months mastering the quick blinks that absorbed the tears into the eyelashes so no one ever saw them roll down my cheeks. Christmas had been a bright beacon fueled by the fear of loss. We had sung louder than usual, and our belts should've burst from all the cookies we baked, except no one could ever eat them. I wondered what my mom had thought of the spectacle. The highlight for her seemed to be when she wrapped herself in gift paper and thought someone had bought her a new shawl.

Dad had gone on sabbatical to take care of her when they found the tumors in her brain, but I drove to their house every morning to give him a break. Unfortunately, today I couldn't sit with her. I would have to sit at the hospital instead. My baby had stopped kicking, so they told me to drink a Coke and come down to be monitored. I could've just called and told Dad I wouldn't be there, but it seemed important to tell Mom in person, even though there was a good chance she wouldn't understand me.

Snow was falling in winter's last attempt to blanket the world before spring chased it away. As I pulled onto the street, I saw crows perched all over the yard in the snow, looking like a black and white patchwork quilt. My mom was standing in the middle of the yard, her bald head exposed and bare feet in the snow, feeding the crows bread. I screeched to a halt, not bothering to park in the driveway.

"What on Earth are you doing out here?" I yelled as I ran out and around my car.

Mom looked up with a focus in her eyes that I hadn't seen in months. "Feeding my friends," she said.

I looked down at the black birds, eating the chunks of bread she was scattering. I wanted to kick the feathers off each one. "Do you realize it's snowing?"

She looked up, not as if to confirm it, but as if to enjoy the light sprinkling on her face. "Yes. Maybe there will be enough to make a snowman. Did you bring the children to play with me?"

My mouth hung open. The conversation was so normal and the situation so absurd. "Where's Dad?"

"He's asleep. Poor man. He's really been working hard. He does such a good job taking care of me." The beaks of the crows clacked together as we spoke, but their voices remained silent. They didn't deserve her bread.

"I think we should go inside, Mom."

"Probably."

I grabbed her by the elbow and led her up the front steps. Inside, my dad was snoring on the couch. I wrinkled my nose at the smell of medicine and death that had pervaded the house for a month.

"Put your slippers on, for heaven's sake. Your toes must be frozen." I sounded exactly like my mom had when I was a little girl. When she had her slippers on and a blanket around her shoulders, I said, "I can't stay today, Mom. I just came by to tell you I'm going to the hospital."

"Yes! The baby's arriving today."

"Well, I don't know. They want to monitor me a little. I just wanted to let you know I might not be by again until tomorrow."

My mom placed her hand on my head and pulled back my brown hair like she did when I was small, reminding me that she was still the mother. "Everything is going to be okay now," she said. "You're a good daughter and mother. Thank you." I tried to hug her hard, but my belly was too big, so I squeezed her hands before I left, wondering if the radiation treatments had caused the miracle I had just witnessed.

My husband was already at the hospital and held my hand as they told us the baby wasn't responding as she should. I gripped his hand hard when the first induced contraction came, but had to let it go when they started changing my position every five minutes. Through the haze of pain I could hear, "Baby signs are good. No, now they're gone. Turn this way. That's good."

My husband provided a constant string of encouragement, "You're doing good. Keep it up." But I could hear the strain in his voice as he watched the baby's vital signs go up and down.

I wish I could've thought about the beautiful children I already had, or the amazing conversation I had had with my mother, but all I could think about was the clacking and cawing of the damn crows. Finally, late into the night, I was allowed to push. Then, the baby got stuck between the womb and life. The doctor's calm vanished as he talked to the nurse, and I saw a crow hovering in the lamplight. It was not going to get my baby. With the help of a contraction that raged through my whole body I pushed my baby out and held my breath as they unwrapped the umbilical cord from around her neck. I cried at her first wail and sung to her about her baby blue eyes while she nursed. Still in the delivery room, my husband held up the phone for me to hear that my mom had passed away.

Spring

The absence of crows at the funeral was notable only to me, but I fumed over it. They had started this disaster, so they should pay their respects. Instead, they chose to haunt my dreams, silently drifting through the skies in murders like large, black clouds.

Then, on one of the first days of spring, I took the baby over to cheer up dad. As I pulled into the driveway, I saw a crow sitting on the front steps. We stared at each other through the windshield, me wishing I had learned to shoot a gun. After several minutes, I opened my door and yelled, "Get out of here! You're not touching my baby." It cocked its head at me and flew off beyond the roof.

Satisfied that I had chased it off, I carried the baby in the car seat and set it on the porch. Turning my back on her, I rung the bell and opened the screened door. When I went to pick up the car seat, the crow was sitting right on my baby's stomach. It bowed its head toward her ear, the black feathers and my daughter's mess of black hair mingling as one. There was a whispered caw before it took flight, tickling my baby with its feathers. She woke up and stared at me—the newborn blue eyes gone and replaced by my mother's mahogany eyes. She smiled her first real smile.

The Cursed Land of Dreams

Under the cold stare of the Moon
I wander about the city centre.
The tortuous symmetry of the buildings
Looks down on me from far above.
There is no pulsating heart within
The perfection of steel and glass.

Near the river I stop, breathless,
Feeling the dampness in my boots.
This is the last haven of wilderness
In this soulless city where everything
Must form an orderly, rational pattern.

A mute sillhouette hands me a wooden box,
I grab it and willingly pay my fare to the
Stranger who melts into the darkness.
I rush through streets and avenues, mad
With anticipation to indulge in
The sensuous, taboo purchase.

Lying down in bed, all I want is
To lose myself in this shameful pleasure.
My eager hands plunge into
The void of my magical box.
My eyes immediately close,
And I sigh, taken into the vortex
Of the ominous, the banished,
The cursed land of dreams.

— Livia Finucci

The Stones Next Door

Story by Linda Maye Adams
Illustration by Laura Givens

Every neighborhood has one of those houses. You know the kind. The parents look at it and discuss housing values, and the kids dare each other to sneak into the yard but no one ever does.

I lived next door to it. The house itself is one of those clapboard ones, painted a glossy dark green. A big oleander is trying to take over the right side of the house, and the walkway is tenting up from tree roots. A black wrought iron fence with spikes closes off the house like a prison. Every time I walk by, I catch the faint smell of urine.

My parents told me the house was normal at one time, at least until the day the stones appeared in the front yard.

I remember that day. It was while things were still good between my parents. They went out to stand on the porch, murmuring about the stones. The

stones hadn't been there last night, and this morning they were.

"Maricruz," my mother tells me, "don't go near that house."

Useless words. When school was in session, I walked past it twice a day. Better than walking across the street with that yard with the Rottweilers that try to come over the chain link fence.

This morning, I wake up to the muffled anger coming from my parents' room. I'm not ready to get up, but I can't shut out the voices. Finally I step down to the floor, barefoot to hardwood, trying to find spots that don't groan under my feet. Weariness drags at me as I sneak outside.

It's still early enough out that the moon is stranded in the coming daylight, a white disk hovering above the mountains. The mountains have jagged lines and hard edges, but the Douglas Firs soften that sharpness. I used to think of them as gentle giants, watching over me.

But not any more.

A shiver finds me again, and my gaze lands on the house next door. To the stones in the yard.

There are five, all shaped like giant fingers. It's like someone just stuck them right into the earth. No fresh digging, no holes. They just, simply, are there. The stones are made of granite, and about five or six feet tall. They always remind me of grave stones. But who puts gravestones in a front yard?

I stand outside the iron fence and stare at the yard, wondering what those stones mean. The heat of the day is coming in to stay, though it's not too bad with the breeze blowing. Ninety down here, and the granite mountains in the distance are topped with snow.

A screen door creaks open, and then the hollow metal bangs.

A man comes out of the house and looks at me. He's older than my grandparents, and every time I see him, it seems like he's getting thinner and thinner. Like something's eating away at him inside.

When he sees me, he comes to the fence and studies me with beady blue eyes. His skin is so pasty that I can see green streaks underneath. A sickly smell rises off him that makes my throat contract. I have to remind myself to breathe.

He gives me a sideways glance, and his mouth splits into a brown-stained smile. "Too young," he cackles. "Too young."

It makes me shudder. But fear makes me bold with my words. "What does that mean?"

A door slams at my house, loud enough to make both of us look toward the house. Dad has come out, a storm rolling down the sidewalk.

The old man follows him with those beady eyes, running his tongue along his too red lips. It reminds me too much of a cat thinking about making a meal of a bird.

* * *

Three days later, I come home and find my mother at the table crying. She's got no makeup on, and her face is brown and splotchy.

"Your father is not coming home," she tells me. She has a crumpled piece of paper in her hands.

The world is empty.

* * *

That night, a storm blows in. It's different than other storms. The wind makes the white oaks sway, and the clouds want to rain, but it never comes. Lightning flashes above the mountains, and thunder does a drumbeat.

I can't help it. I look out the window, hoping to see my father coming. He always comes to my room when it storms to make sure I'm okay, and I already miss that.

A flash of lightning snaps a moment like a picture, and I see the stones in the yard.

There are six.

* * *

The next morning the storm has washed the world clean and empty. I go outside to look at the house with the stones. Maybe I dreamed it. Maybe there are still five.

But there is indeed a new stone in the yard. I always look at that yard, every day. It hadn't been out there yesterday. How had it gotten out there?

The door to the house opens and the old man comes out. His body has filled in and looks much healthier. His gnarled hand caresses the newest stone.

I can't help it. I glance up at it, where I think a face should be. For a moment, I see one, blurring on the stone and it's my father's.

Before I can think or breathe, I run. Behind me, the old man cackles, "Just right."

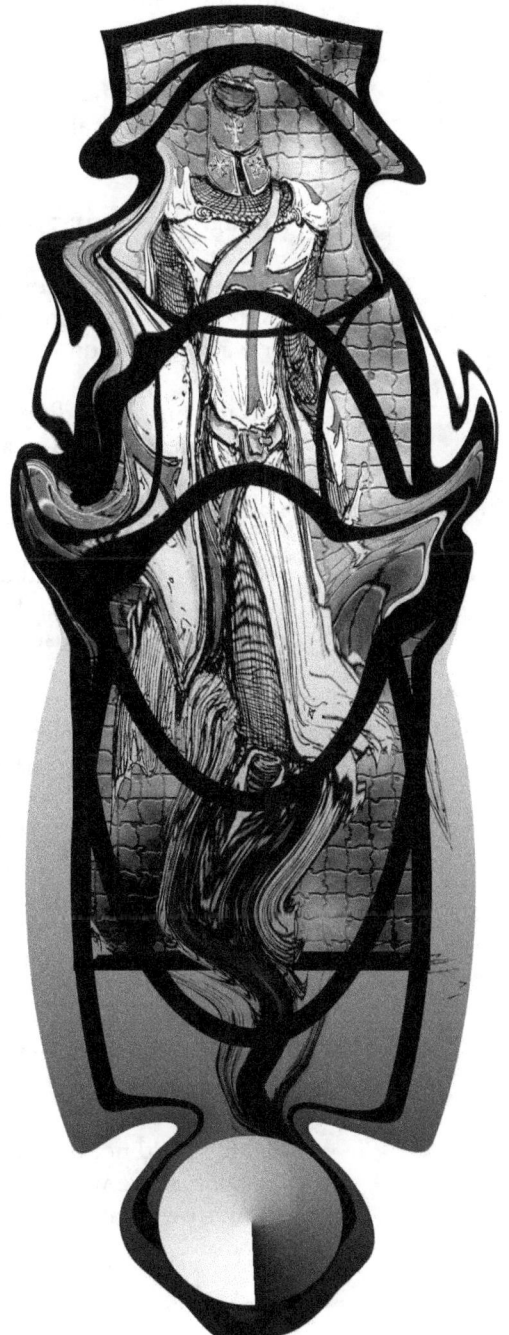

Passage Through a Shifting Past

The surrounding landscape was lit by distant scattered fires,
revealing the twisted forms of dead and dying men,
and the rushing shapes of those who were wounded
and sought for some escape.

Through this landscape of carnage and suffering
the old wizard walked serenely,
as if untouched by horror or fear.

Though distant cries could still be heard on all sides,
as struggling survivors engaged in desperate combat,
Saleiessen passed through all of this unassailed,
as though he were invisible,
or walked as an untouchable ghost among the living.

Around his tall striding form there was a glow,
as though he moved in a protective orb of light,
but none turned or spoke to him,
and his passage seemed to leave no trace,

save that where he walked there was a calm and silence,
which spread through the night like the descent of sleep
upon a wakeful house.

In the distance a burning farmhouse could be made out,
and the sounds of bleating sheep scattered through the night.
Toward this blazing shape he made his steady way,
as though following an unseen path.

When he reached the farmhouse gate,
now hanging on a single hinge,
he stepped quietly through the opening,
scanning the dark ground for a familiar shape.

Eventually he saw it,
the form of a child, huddled behind a small wooden shed,
holding in his arms a small dark shadow.

Neither child nor dragon made a sound,
even when the wizard stooped and gathered them
into his own arms.

Shifting his warm bundle to his left arm
and holding his glowing staff in his right,
he made his way out of the yard,
and back out into the dark night.

Where he walked a peace and quiet descended,
and by the time he stepped out of the dark landscape,
and onto the moonlit top of a stone tower
overlooking the sea,

a quiet had descended over all the tortured land,
like a nightmare that is ended,
and whose suffering is long past.

— Nicolo Santilli

A Trivial Case of Haunting

Story by Jeffery Scott Sims
Illustration by Jag Lall

Vorchek contacted me at my office. Angie, my devoted secretary, took the call, carried in the dubious news, announced with unabashed distaste, "It's that one again, Sterkie, the professor. He told me he's got business for you. Shall I tell him to get lost?" I waved her away, shrugged with a frown, replied, "I'll take it," and once she'd returned to her outer nest I reached across my littered desk and picked up the telephone.

"Sterk Fontaine here. What do you want, Anton?"

"Professor Vorchek to you," he responded with a hint of bemused complacency, his normal tone, spoken in that precise, slightly accented English of his. "Good day to you, Mr. Fontaine, and best wishes to your comely assistant. I have a job for you, sir. I will pay reasonably for an acquisition. Let us get together for a talk."

"Not interested, not now, not ever."

"*Very* reasonably." We made a date at the Bistro for lunch, a halfway point between my downtown Phoenix office and his digs out in the nowhere toward Wickenburg. Angie tried to argue me out of it, noting that my previous dealings with this man had been fraught with peril, fraughtless—if that's a word—with profit. I said, "What the hell, he's got his racket, I've got mine." Professor Anton Vorchek investigates weird mysteries to further the cause of science or satisfy his private curiosity; I locate and acquire strange artifacts for big bucks, regardless of source or current ownership, no questions asked. That's how I make my living, chancy but lucrative, if the object pans out and I don't get caught.

I'd have settled for a hamburger. Vorchek ordered us dainty, fruity sandwiches cut in wedges and stuck with colored toothpicks. They were edible. Tall, trim, dapper as always, dressed to impress, he stroked his clipped beard and eyed me keenly from beneath his broad-brimmed hat, attempting to engage me with Old World pleasantries and witticisms. I said, "Vorchek, you're a bad risk. The last time I made the mistake of dealing with you, I lost everything but my life, and barely held on to that. Make a solid pitch, pal."

So he cut to the chase. "I must have the urn containing the ashes of Chief Karasota, which is buried in an unmarked grave under a slab of volcanic rock at the Casa Malpais ruins near Springerville. Do you know the site?"

"I know the town."

"I possess the geographical particulars. It is government land. The authorities currently consider my presence objectionable, a foolish lingering after-effect of that Montezuma Well contretemps."

"I heard something about that, through the wacko grapevine. Didn't you get somebody killed?"

"Someone died," he said indifferently, "an unforeseen complication logically unrelated to my research. Regardless, my lurking in the vicinity might arouse tiresome comment, even inappropriate actions on the part of officialdom. Therefore, I turn to a professional. Enter there, Mr. Fontaine, win for me the prize, enjoy subsequently the fruits of your labor."

"Why?"

Vorchek squared his shoulders, craned forward. "Perhaps you may understand. A series of surprisingly well-attested legends reference Karasota, prehistoric medicine man to a populous and aggressive tribe of ritualistic cannibals who plagued the region centuries before the white man arrived. Although ultimately extirpated by a coalition of their desperate neighbors, the stories of their appalling behavior, and his amazing magical prowess, linger to this day, whispered among the descendants of their enemies. So absolute was the arcane might of the wizard Karasota that he could be destroyed only in the molten fires of a fresh, blazing cinder cone, the last to erupt in that region, a natural calamity associated in song with his overthrow. Be that as it may, Karasota departed this world, accompanied by all of his people, but as befits his exalted rank the victors entombed his ashes in a clay pot deep in a hole under a massive chunk of cooled lava, with stern warnings against ever exposing him to the living world. His charred remains, they aver, retain elements of his supernatural strength. That claim, sir, I would put to the test."

"Got it," I replied. "Vorchek, you're a kook, in genius' clothing."

He grinned, adjusted his natty tie, flicked a crumb from his tailored jacket. "Bring me that urn, with its contents intact. Not a particle must be lost. For that service, Fontaine, I pay handsomely." He named a figure. We shook on it.

Angie said I was nuts. She said Vorchek was nuts. "One way or the other, you'll lose on this deal." Maybe right on all counts, only this type of "contract" was my stock in trade. In this insane age of ours people accept and believe so much rubbish, the gee-whiz crapola peddled to them through stupid video documentaries on cable TV or garbage paperback books. Rest assured that's all nonsense, meal tickets for charlatans and carnival-style promoters. Yet there is the real, the actual strange stuff, the unearthly and the incomprehensible that truly exists, festering behind the facade of normal life. There are those men who, for good or evil, glimpse fragments of that outer reality, seek to understand or master it. Whatever I might think of Professor Vorchek, I knew he was one of those. They don't advertise, never pop up on late night talk shows. They function quietly, behind the scenes, seldom sharing their discoveries. Often they're wrong, on occasion frightfully correct. Sometimes they call for me.

Two mornings later I spun out of town in my banged-up Jeep, equipped for camping, a suitable cover for the region targeted. I slid through Payson shortly after dawn, spent the next three hours on the good highway that slices a fire-break through the endless forests of the eastern Arizona highlands. I rolled into Springerville, hugging the New Mexico border, in time for a late breakfast. The landscape had changed, become one of grassy plains cut by perennial watercourses and studded with hundreds of dead cinder cones. It had been a lively place once, alive with flame and explosions and spouting magma, in the times of the dinosaurs I guess, even so late as the heyday of Karasota.

Before embarking on my latest mad venture I read—courtesy of Angie's research talents—everything openly available on the long gone big chief. A fearsome fellow indeed, the terror of his enemies, at best a problematic friend. Judging by the oral tales handed down the generations to the earliest anthropological scribes, nobody would put in a good word for the guy. The blackest of sorcerers, Karasota ruled his folk with joyous cruelty, while the dooms he visited upon other tribes can not be nicely described. He turned them into nasty things, or conjured nasty things to pester them, or sent them to hell and brought them back in pieces, alive; oh yes, and he ate them, too. Scientists had collected copious evidence of ancient cannibalistic feasts. Morbid stories and gloomy songs related those blackened, marrow-cracked bones to the ugly myths that fouled the name of Karasota.

Big deal. All I had to do was receive into my hands a dirty clay pot, pass it on to the Professor. After that he could do the worrying, if any be required.

I spent three days scoping the territory, tent-squatting by night on the national forest, by day learning the ways of the locale. Naturally I took the guided tour of the Casa Malpais ruins, the fabled citadel of Karasota, the crumbled wreckage perched atop harsh and forbidding volcanic cliffs overlooking the modern town and, as it always had, the winding, shimmering serpent of the Little Colorado River. Malpais must have been an ominous joint in the olden days, with creepy Karasota glaring down on his darkened domain, his intended victims quailing at the thought of him selecting them for the next fancy dinner.

I toured in disguise, of course. I carried nothing on me to connect Sterk Fontaine of Phoenix to this quiet, unassuming sight-seer and camper. Had anyone dreamed of investigating, they could have questioned the number and variety of tools I brought with me, tucked inside my inordinately large tent until I used them.

Came the night of the main event, as I inched the Jeep into position with lights dimmed to the gate that blocked the end of that dark, lonely road. From personal study I knew the layout of the ruins, and I had Vorchek's map to the secret site of the burial. I appreciated that bit: officially Karasota's grave didn't exist, so if I minded my Ps and Qs, got in and out undetected, left no obvious traces, no one would ever think to come after me. It's not really stealing, if you didn't know you had it to miss it. Hah! My job isn't always that simple.

I got the goods. I identified the crude basalt column, fifteen feet high, the same one noted by my good-natured guide on the tour. He had also drawn my attention to the unusual petroglyph, an old Indian scrawl of a picture, which resembled a kindergartener's stab at a spider, only with too few eyes and too many legs. Vorchek had clued me to that as well. My guide didn't mention the roughly rectangular slab at its base, resembling the million other volcanic stones in that bleak landscape, a place pretty eerie by night. My guarded flashlight beam generated weird shadows from those angular rocks as I maneuvered. The slab looked like it weighed a ton, but though broad enough to cap a full-sized grave, it was very thin. I scraped around its edge with a shovel, cranked it up with a crowbar, heaved it aside.

I'd opened a perfectly square hole, almost a shaft, three feet across by five deep. At the bottom, just like clever Vorchek told me, sat the urn. The burial chamber, if you will, was entirely unadorned, but when I scrambled down to examine the clay pot I found it chased with freaky designs on every inch of its surface. As a relic it wasn't much, a typical rounded, kiln-fired vessel, flat bottomed with a wide, heavy, gum-sealed stopper—a sleazy pot-hunter could get something for it—the designs, however, brought me up short. Seriously, I hesitated, perhaps a few seconds, to drink in the curious artistic craftsmanship of yore. Somebody with a really sick imagination had painted that thing. Those awful, nightmarish monsters, miles beyond the column spider, suggested such unpleasant surmises, seemed to scream in a universal language: KEEP AWAY.

I yanked the urn out of there, careful not to crack the stopper's brittle seal. I slid the slab back into place. I checked the ground, obliterated my footprints. I wrapped the pot in burlap, gingerly transported it to the Jeep, came back for my tools. Then I got the hell out of there, returned to my tent, packed up everything, was hundreds of miles away, approaching home, at first light.

I delivered the package to Vorchek at his retreat, that isolated old converted ranch house (on some historical register) high on a scrubby hill overlooking desert, where he crowed with delight and went into paroxysms of pleasure at first sight of the thing. "Yes, yes, the imagery matches—late Anasazi pictorial writing—this symbol here, the red-eyed one, the classic representation of Karasota. My findings must hold validity."

"My finding," I corrected him. "I've done my bit. Pay me."

"Of course, my boy, of course. I shall commence experimentation immediately. If you wish, Mr. Fontaine, I will keep you abreast of developments."

"Just give me the money." He did, in cash, a satchel full. It puzzled me, how he found access to funds like that, but I knew, vaguely, that he got around. I thanked him politely, reminded him to remember me if his oddball studies demanded such an easy and juicy caper in the future. I let myself out; he'd already run off into his private basement laboratory. That was that, a dramatic score for remarkably little effort.

Then the world turned upside down, and the bottom dropped out of my life, and I plummeted headlong into the pit of horror. Here are the salient facts.

For two days I basked in the glow of unalloyed success. Angie and I celebrated, with abandon, and she was oh so grateful for my largesse. Everything went my way, as I expect it to without fail (a simple

soul, all I ask from this world is that I get everything I want, when I want it), until the night of that abhorrent dream. It roared out of slumber to hit me like a sledgehammer in the face, darkness falling away to reveal a hideous swarthy face daubed in red and yellow shouting in a frenzy of hate and rage, plainly gabbling its unrestrained fury at me. The intensely focused anger struck with the power of a body blow, and then I'd dashed to the floor, awake, perspiring and shaking. It took a stiff belt direct from the bottle to calm me down. I'm not prone to nightmares like that. Usually I rest like a babe, consciousness and conscience drifting happily.

Thus began the day. I'd slept alone that night, but for some reason my apartment seemed unusually small that morning. Corners and shadows disturbed me, as if a sixth sense warned me of uninvited company crouching nearby, just beyond my vision. I'm wary like that, when it's called for, my instincts having served me well at times. They jumped and pinged now, only nothing was there.

I reached the office at nine, helloed Angie, brushed off her lovey-doveys, which didn't suit at the moment. Retreating into my inner sanctum, I attempted to occupy myself with busy work, scrutinizing documents pertaining to pending cases. Little got done, time hung heavy. A senseless annoyance bugged me. Despite having all the lights on, with all of my cubbyhole perfectly visible, I squirmed anxiously, constantly adjusting my position that I might peer to the side or behind. It was worse than in the apartment. I couldn't shake the notion that someone spied on me.

At length Angie entered with a sheaf of papers, stared at the contents of the ashtray, the open bottle on the desk, examined my face. "What's wrong?" she asked.

"Nothing," I snapped, surprised by my own curtness. I do try to keep on her good side. "I'm out of kilter today. I need some air. Excuse me, I'm going for a walk."

My stroll through one of the least scenic portions of Phoenix failed to restore my equilibrium. It's a rotten neighborhood, okay for me because the rent is low and whatever transpires there happens under the radar, a benefit in my line. Certainly the sights and noises and smells weren't conducive to cheer. I'd settle for standard peace.

I didn't get it. Envision the scene. I'm walking down the shabby street, cars whizzing by, a few local hoodlums lounging or meandering. Here came another one, far down the avenue, this character appearing different from the rest even at a distance. Only a black spot at first, framed against concrete and plaster, approaching me steadily with a peculiar rolling gait. It crossed the street to my side, visibility enhancing. I froze, numb and dumb. Forgetting its inordinate size—about that of a Volkswagen—it wasn't precisely a spider. Dozens of skittering legs and a trio of bulbous eyes supplemented the basic form. Suddenly it raced quickly toward me.

I screamed, fled madly from its charge. A couple of pedestrians lunged aside, shying in panic from my crazed flight. It only occurred to me a tad later that they acted to avoid me, not that awful thing. They didn't see it; the beast existed to terrorize only me.

I didn't return to the office, once I'd shaken my pursuer, choosing instead to hole up at home, despite concerns derived from the last night's events. Wisely I worried. A murky incident at the elevator leading to my floor warned me that unpleasantness continued to dog me. I entered the box, pressed the button, waited impatiently for the doors to slide closed. Shadows shifted in the hall, indicative of large, nebulous shapes in hasty motion. I backed into a corner, gritting teeth. The doors inched together. As they joined I heard an impact, as if a flabby mass had rushed up against them and abruptly collided. I almost fainted before the elevator lurched into ascent.

The rest of that day rates poorly in my annals. Minor but insidious tidings periodically assailed. Out of the corner of my eye shadows trembled like live creatures. Lights darkened, as if presences unseen had passed before them. Regular noises at the curtained windows hinted at unwelcome calls from things, never observed, that sounded nothing like birds, bigger and more determined than insects. I sat most of those hours in the living room, in a chair backed against a wall, squeezed between the entertainment center and the sofa, where I could watch all the doors and windows. I thought a lot, put two and two together, tried to come up with three or five, reluctantly accepted four. With evening coming on, dreading the inexorable night, I telephoned Vorchek.

I outlined for him, the summary replete with lurid detail and expletives, an account of my experiences. He recommended I pop by to see him in the morning. No, he was quite busy, could not be disturbed until then. Really, now, I must wait.

Courteous as ever, but when I violently protested the delay he hung up on me.

A description of that night can be reduced to capsule form: a waking nightmare. I hadn't a prayer for sleep. In the morning I noticed a cracked window pane, where some stinky black goo had seeped through. I lit out early for Vorchek's place.

The professor, dressed in a long flannel robe, met me at the door, greeting me with congenial and jocular comments. "Difficulties accrue, Mr. Fontaine? You look as if the vicissitudes of life weigh heavily."

"Spare me the chatter, Professor. I feel like death." I tersely brought him up to date on my problems.

"A trivial case of haunting, eh? Perhaps you theorize an overt connection to our old friend Chief Karasota."

"You know I do. It's the only explanation."

"A plausible one, certainly. Come with me, young man." Entering into his lair, quaintly decorated with old-fashioned furnishings enlivened with bizarre relics of ancient or primitive cultures, he started me off with a drink, insisted I eat something, a bowl of cereal at which I barely poked a spoon. The booze—not my first of the day—steadied me somewhat, or took the edge off my wobbles. Then, at his urging, we descended into his bleak basement, a cavernous chamber carved from bedrock which, he said, had been devised by the original owner as a fruit cellar.

"It admirably serves my purposes," he opined, flicking on a dazzlingly bright lamp. Behold the secret private laboratory of Professor Vorchek, a chaotic, musty jumble of books, papers, strange machinery, weird artifacts. A long table occupied the center of the room, above which dangled a naked bulb. On the table rested that damned pot, and other stuff too.

"May I reacquaint you with Karasota?" Vorchek asked politely, indicating with a wave of his hand a pile of granular brown powder mounded on a sheet of wax paper next to beakers of various fluids. "I have been working non-stop since your delivery. My chemical research alone provide rare insights, tantamount to arcane breakthrough. This ash possesses amazing properties. You may find them difficult to conceive. For instance, young man, this material reacts favorably to specially enhanced organic tests. How about this: Karasota's incinerated substance responds similar to a live organism. Think of it!"

"I don't care to."

"The magical essence survives," continued the professor, his eyes gleaming behind the thick glasses he'd donned, "to an incredible degree. Intellectual power, at a superhuman level, without physical mind; for such discoveries I live and breathe. These notes tell the tale, Mr. Fontaine. Harken to the evidence that Karasota's persona endures beyond the grave—"

"No, I won't," I snapped, louder than intended. I realized Vorchek had been speaking in a whisper. My voice cracked and resounded hollowly from the rough stone walls. More in control, I added, "I don't need to hear your notes. I'm convinced. Karasota lives, he's out to get me."

Vorchek nodded, removed his glasses, smoothly replied, "I concur."

"Why me? Why not you?"

He reacted with astonishment, real or feigned. "Me? It has nothing to do with me. You raised the slab, you purloined the urn. You, sir, defied the curse that protected his remains, by deliberately ignoring the warning petroglyphs and—" he gestured at the pot—"the extremely cruel and vivid threats inscribed thereon. My activities, all in the name of pure science, constitute secondary factors, apparently of no account. Your action is the primary, thus subject to supernatural … discipline. Yes, that is the word I choose."

"What am I going to do?"

"Do? I have not the slightest." Vorchek patted my shoulder, an avuncular touch from which I pulled away sharply. "I shall continue my research, Mr. Fontaine. Perhaps, in time, I may formulate the beginnings of a solution to your predicament. That, surely, must cheer you immensely."

Finally I got angry. "Won't do, Professor, not for a minute. I can't stand it as is, and how do I know it won't get worse?"

"I expect you to keep me abreast," he advised with an encouraging smile. "I relish the opportunity. Make your own notes, leave out nothing. Report to me frequently."

"To hell with that. I want the urn and the ashes. I plan to return them where they belong."

"I reject that," he said, still polite, yet with ice creeping into his tones. "I am a busy man—"

"And I'm desperate. Fork them over, or I'll make life hard for you."

Vorchek patted his robe pocket, which I now noticed visibly bulged. "Try nothing foolish, sir. I

am prepared for the unbecoming hot-headedness of which you have proven yourself capable. You have my answer. Be gone … and good day to you."

So we parted, after I saluted him with a snide comment concerning his ancestry. I didn't really want to beat up Vorchek, not if it could be avoided. I couldn't turn him in, not without involving myself in the risk of years-wasting incarceration. I had to explore other avenues.

That wasn't easy, since my travails didn't let up. Horrors pressed, intensified. I scarcely made it home alive, for in the midst of city traffic a dark, leathery object hurtled against my windshield, flapping frantically. I recall jagged yellow teeth. Only a fierce concentration of will kept my hands steady on the wheel. The incident passed, sure, but more followed, and more doubtless lay in store.

Next morning, after a ghastly night, I dragged myself into the office. Angie squeaked at sight of me, put on her Florence Nightingale act, but I nixed that fast. "This you do for me," I commanded. "Cook up the perfect alibi, with you the perfect witness. If anybody asks during the next forty-eight hours, you've been with me round the clock. Exquisite detail, naughty winks if necessary. Got it?"

"Why not make it real?" she queried, leaning over the desk to offer me a tempting view.

"I got work to do. I'm out of here. Hold the fort, honey, until you hear from me."

I burgled the fortress of Professor Anton Vorchek. With all that valuable or unique stuff on hand he took all kinds of measures, but I'm a past master at evading security tricks. That night, the dead of night, I gained entry, slunk along walls under grotesque wooden masks, by stone idols of repellent aspect, skirted piles of moldy books and yellowed papers, reached the basement stairs, all without a sound, without observable light thanks to a night-scope headlamp. I slipped into the heart of Vorchek's scientific empire, and there, under his slumbering nose, I broke the bank. The goods lay where I'd last seen them, the urn and the ashes. I carefully scooped the latter into the former. That old dead dust felt hot to my fingers, fiery hot, that I must wrap my hands in a handkerchief to finish the operation. Vengeful Karasota bit at me any way he could. I couldn't refuse the gesture, left a scrawled note pinned to the table with one of the professor's antique daggers: "My way, then, sucker."

The remainder of that night I drove like a madman for Springerville. It was a wearing ride through those black tunnels of forest. When I focused on the road before me, I glimpsed catty-corner something hunched in the passenger seat, a revoltingly inhuman shape that gestured dangerously with horrid appendages. When I couldn't stomach it anymore and looked that way, I saw emptiness. I lost my lane three times, the road once, and almost squashed an elk.

I contrived to check in early at a motel on the western outskirts of town. They had free Internet service—not bad for such a cheap dive—so I connected with Angie, reminded her to prop me up from her end. I laughed bitterly when she typed back that Vorchek had called, urged an immediate interview. I signed off, hunkered down for the day. I ate, sparingly, canned pork and beans, washed down with whiskey. I didn't go out, didn't dare show myself under the sun. Also, recurrent fumblings at the door inhibited my penchant for wandering.

As soon as Springerville closed down I hightailed for unlovely Casa Malpais, where I quickly, professionally, performed the same operation that first brought me there, only in reverse. I had one final, really bad moment. Having lowered the hellish pot into the hole, I felt a sudden loony desire to crawl in with it and pull the big slab over me. A voice whispered in my head, cajoling me to self-destruction, then thundering orders in a crazy screech. The individual words came across as gibberish, but I got the gist of what Karasota demanded: he craved my company down there with him, forever, in the blighted darkness of his implacable hatred. Incredibly, that suggestion struck me as momentarily alluring; I lowered a leg over the lip of the cavity before I braced myself mentally, zapped by a thrill of horror that physically rattled me, and I heaved myself aside, pushed the stone into place, rolled and groped away, leapt up and ran.

The haunting stopped then and there. I'd undone my cursed crime. Drained, peculiarly exhausted, I retreated to my motel room, where I crashed hard and slept like a corpse until late morning. The spiteful jangling of the telephone roused me, limp and ravenous. Still groggy I pawed for the phone, took the call. It was Professor Vorchek. The cunning old bastard had tracked me down.

"A despicable act, Fontaine," he declared, the words clipped, in a tone of heated iron. "I will not forget this. You think me powerless, young man. Revel in such dreams while you can. There shall in the end be balance."

I groaned, "Get off my back, Vorchek. I had to do it. Were the tables turned, you'd have done the same, just not as cleverly."

He belched a loud, hostile snort, said, "I dealt in good faith. I paid you well. I have nothing to show for my costs. Unfairness requires compensation." He chuckled, an ostentatiously evil sound. "I must teach you my capabilities."

My throbbing head lolled on the pillow. "You got a bagful of data," I pointed out, "that should keep you jolly for a year. I'll return half the fee, not a penny more, on your guarantee of no comebacks. Bear in mind, Vorchek, that you might need me again."

A long, long pause, not so much as a breath on the line, then: "Agreed. A personal check will suffice." The connection died.

And I would have lain there the rest of the day, only insatiable hunger seized me. I went out, hunted up Springerville's finest, and treated myself to a juicy steak. I considered it a celebration in honor of a job well done ... medium well, anyway.

Ooze Blues

Owl hoot haunts the darkened swamp
Cajun spirits rise
Water drowned trees turn to logs
Alligators' yellowed eyes

Snakes swish through the thickened bog
Poison on their breath
Humid air floats like a ghost
Smothering as death

An old jalopy was pulled out once
Out of that clutching ooze
The passengers were never found
Boot-leg whisky blues

— Louise Webster

A Kepler's Dozen
Thirteen Stories About Distant Worlds
That Really Exist!

A new anthology of action-packed, mysterious, and humorous stories all based on real planets discovered by the NASA Kepler mission. Edited by and contributing stories are David Lee Summers—best selling author of *Owl Dance*, *The Pirates of Sufiro*, and other novels—and Steve B. Howell—project scientist for the Kepler mission. Whether on a prison colony, in a fast escape from the authorities, or encircling a binary star, thirteen exoplanet stories written by authors such as Mike Brotherton, Laura Givens, and J Alan Erwine will amuse, frighten, and intrigue you while you share fantasy adventures among Kepler's real-life planets.

For orders or more information visit:
http://www.hadrosaur.com/kepler.html
Also available at **Amazon.com** and **BN.com**
Search for "A Kepler's Dozen"

Just Another Indian Kid

Story by
David B. Riley

Illustration by
Neil T. Foster

Amouhtak looked over to his brother. His brother shrugged. That dog was really fast. The horses couldn't keep up with him over the rough terrain. "Let's head back, little brother," he said. "The horses are worn out."

Jordan nodded. "Thought we might have some meat tonight."

"It was not meant to be. There is something about that dog, almost like he has Coyote in him," Amouhtak said. "We'll never catch him."

Jordan pointed to the west. The sky was growing very dark.

His brother nodded and pointed to the south. "There will be shelter that way."

The sky continued to darken. It was almost like night. The wind was getting stronger and colder. Amouhtak pointed at an outcropping of rocks just as the sky began to open. "Let's camp up there."

"We can make it home," Jordan argued. "It's just across the river."

"No," Amouhtak warned.

Jordan pulled the reins and ordered his horse into the river. The river was different, swollen from rains upstream. The water was moving fast and it was so deep. His horse reared. Suddenly, he was in the water. The cold water was swirling around him. He wasn't even sure where the bank was. Everything was so dark. He thought he heard his brother yelling for him, then that voice slowly faded away and was replaced by the roaring torrent of water all around him. He couldn't breathe. Then, there was nothing.

It was so quiet. There was nothing but quiet. The water was no longer swirling around. He opened his eyes. A campfire burned right next to the water's edge. He reached down and the water was only a few inches deep. He sat up. This was an odd place. It looked like the outcropping of rocks his brother had wanted to go to, but it also seemed like a cave. Joseph looked around. There was no sign of his horse anywhere.

The warmth of the fire felt good. As he began to dry out, he looked around and wondered how he'd gotten to such a strange place. If the water swept him into an underground cavern, then where was his horse? And who made the campfire?

Joseph sensed a presence. He turned and looked over his shoulder. A pair of green eyes glowed in the darkness. Then they were gone. His heart skipped a beat when he realized an animal was right in front of him, just across the fire. He hadn't heard it approach.

It was a dog. A really big dog. A terra cotta dog. The dog he and his brother had been chasing. A terra cotta colored dog? They each stared at the other for a minute, maybe even longer.

"What is this place?" Joseph asked. He looked around for anything he could use as a weapon. There was nothing, not a single rock. There was not even a stick of firewood.

The strange dog sat quietly across the fire from him. It was not threatening him, but he was terribly confused. How did this fire burn with no wood?

"Why have you come to the Canyon of the Ancients?" the strange dog suddenly asked. "Were you not told this land is sacred?"

"It is the easiest way to get back home," Joseph replied. Only then did his thoughts catch up to him. None of this made any sense. "What are you, talking dog? My brother thought you were Coyote."

"Do I look like Coyote?" the talking dog asked.

"No."

"I am Dahgo. Were you not told to avoid this place?"

"It is too far to go around. Our horses were exhausted," Joseph said.

"Then why not rest them?" Dahgo asked. "Then they would not be tired."

"I do not understand," Joseph said.

"If you rest tired horses, then they are not tired anymore," Dahgo said. "Surely you can understand this."

"No, I mean, I am so confused," Joseph said.

"It is not complicated. Horses, like all creatures get tired. If you let them rest, that tiredness fades away," Dahgo explained yet again.

"I understand that," Joseph said.

"Then why are you confused about it?"

"I am confused about you. I don't understand what this place is. Why am I here?" Joseph asked.

"I am confused as well. Tell me Joseph, why do you have a white man name?" Dahgo asked.

"My mother is white. She liked the name Joseph. My brother, we have the same father but my father's first wife died," Joseph said. He seemed to be babbling. "What are you?"

Dahgo seemed to give just the slightest nod. "I am Dahgo. I live here in the quiet. I have lived here a very long time. I am the god of medicine."

Joseph took a quick look around. There was no obvious exit. Everything away from the fire was black. "You are the trickster god."

"No. I am the god of medicine. No one here is

going to trick you," Dahgo insisted.

"The Ute people have no such god like you," Joseph said. "The great creator, Senawahu did not make this place."

"At least you know something. I was starting to wonder if you knew anything. I have never seen a boy who did not know that tired horses can rest and get restored."

"I didn't say that," Joseph defended. "And you are no god of the Ute people."

Suddenly the fire was gone. There was nothing but blackness—blackness and those glowing green eyes. Then the fire was back. "I am Dahgo. I am the god of medicine."

"We have no such god. If we get sick, our people pray to the god of blood—not to you." Joseph was determined not to show fear, though the sudden darkness scared him. "Our gods do not hide under the ground."

"I know that," Dahgo replied. "I never said I was a god of the Ute people."

"Stop confusing me," Joseph pleaded.

"I never said I was one of your gods. I live here now." There was a certain tone of sadness in Dahgo's voice.

"The elders, they tell of a people from long ago, before the Ute, before the Navajo," Joseph said. "Are you the Anasazi?"

"Yes, Joseph." There was silence for quite a long time. "My people are gone now. They died long ago and I could not help them."

"What do you want of me?" Joseph asked.

"Want? You came here. You fell in the river," Dahgo pointed out. "Even though you were told not to go to the Canyon of the Ancients, here you are."

"I want to go home," Joseph said.

"As you wish," Dahgo said.

The fire went black. The sound of the water returned. The cold waves were suddenly swirling around him. Joseph couldn't breathe. The water was filling his lungs. Then, somehow, he was clinging to the branch of a tree. Someone grabbed him and pulled him away from the water.

"I have been looking for you for hours," Amouhtak said. "You could have died."

"I thought I had." Joseph noticed his horse and his brother's horse both stood next to the bank of the river. "Let's go home."

"You are cold, brother. Let's make camp," Amouhtak said. "We'll build a fire."

"Let's get home. I'm okay," Joseph insisted.

It was well after midnight when they got back to their village. The moon had already set and the sun would soon be returning to the sky. But something was wrong. People were up. People were coughing.

Joseph stabled the horses. Amouhtak came running to him.

"Joseph, father is ill. He feels like he is on fire. Half of the village is this way," his brother informed him.

Joseph raced to his father. His mother was tending to him as best she could. She was trying to use cold water to cool him down.

"Joseph, I think this a disease called smallpox. It is very bad," his mother said. "I saw it once when I was a little girl."

It all made sense. "Has anyone come to the village while we were gone?" he asked.

She nodded. "Just the Indian agents from De-lores. They gave us blankets. The *Farmer's Almanac* says we face a rough winter."

"I must go into the forest. I'll be back soon. Burn all of the blankets and have everyone who touched them wash their hands in hot water," Joseph said. There was no reason why they should listen to him, though he spoke with such authority the people started bringing out the blankets.

Joseph soon found the trees he wanted. He took his knife and peeled off the bark. He brought back as much as could carry. He placed the bark on a stone and ground it up as best he could. He then took the bark, ground it into a paste along with some water. He then took it around to those who were ill, starting with his father. "This will not cure the disease, but it will lower the fever and give the sick ones a fighting chance. It is the best I can do."

His father struggled to speak. "How do you know this?"

"I just know," Joseph said.

By late afternoon it was obvious the fevers were down. The feeling was the people were going to recover, although a baby and one of the elderly women did not make it.

Joseph found himself sitting on the bank of the creek that ran past the village. He looked to the other side. The strange terra cotta dog was watching him. Joseph gave a very slight nod. The strange dog god did as well. Then, it was gone.

Three vampyrs. Three lives. Three intertwining stories.

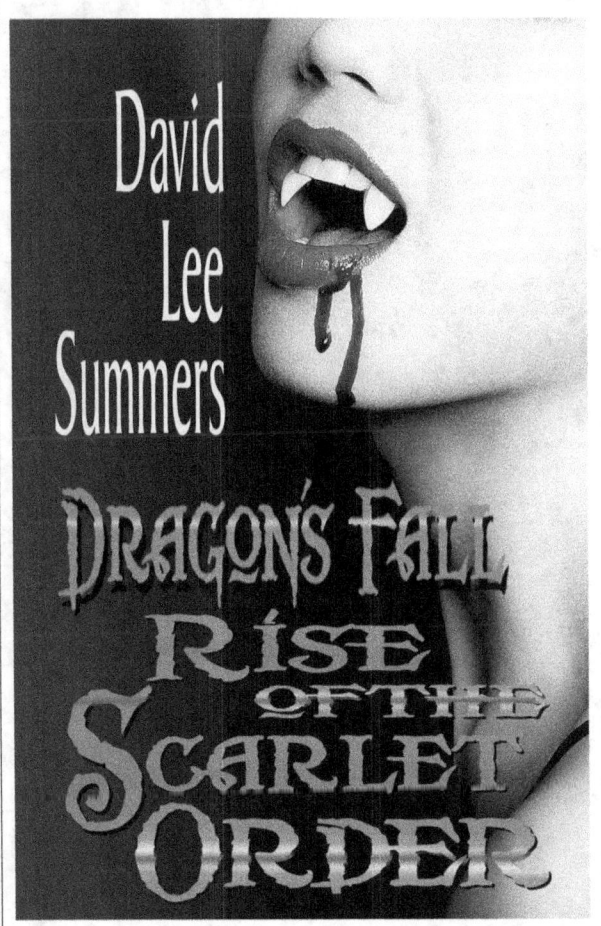

Bearing the guilt of destroying the holiest of books after becoming a vampyr, the Dragon, Lord Desmond searches the world for lost knowledge, but instead discovers truth in love.

Born a slave in Ancient Greece, Alexandra craves freedom above all else, until a vampyr sets her free, and then she must pay the highest price of all—her human soul.

An assassin who lives in the shadows, Roquelaure is cloaked even from himself, until he discovers the power of friendship and loyalty.

Three vampyrs traveling the world by moonlight—one woman and two men who forge a bond made in love and blood. Together they form a band of mercenaries called the Scarlet Order, and recruit others who are like them. Their mission is to protect kings and emperors against marauders, invaders, and rogue vampyrs. And their ultimate nemesis—Vlad the Impaler.

"Summers is a master of seduction, horror, and suspense, mixing history with fantasy. I strongly urge you to delve into the world of the Scarlet Order. I promise you, you are in for a ride you will never forget or want to end." Giovanna Lagana, author of *With Black and White Comes the Grey*.

Join the Scarlet Order Today!

Available at Amazon.com and iTunes.

Learn more about the Scarlet Order Vampire series at
http://dlsummers.wordpress.com

Draystone's Secret
Story by Simon Bleaken
Illustration by Kathy Ferrell

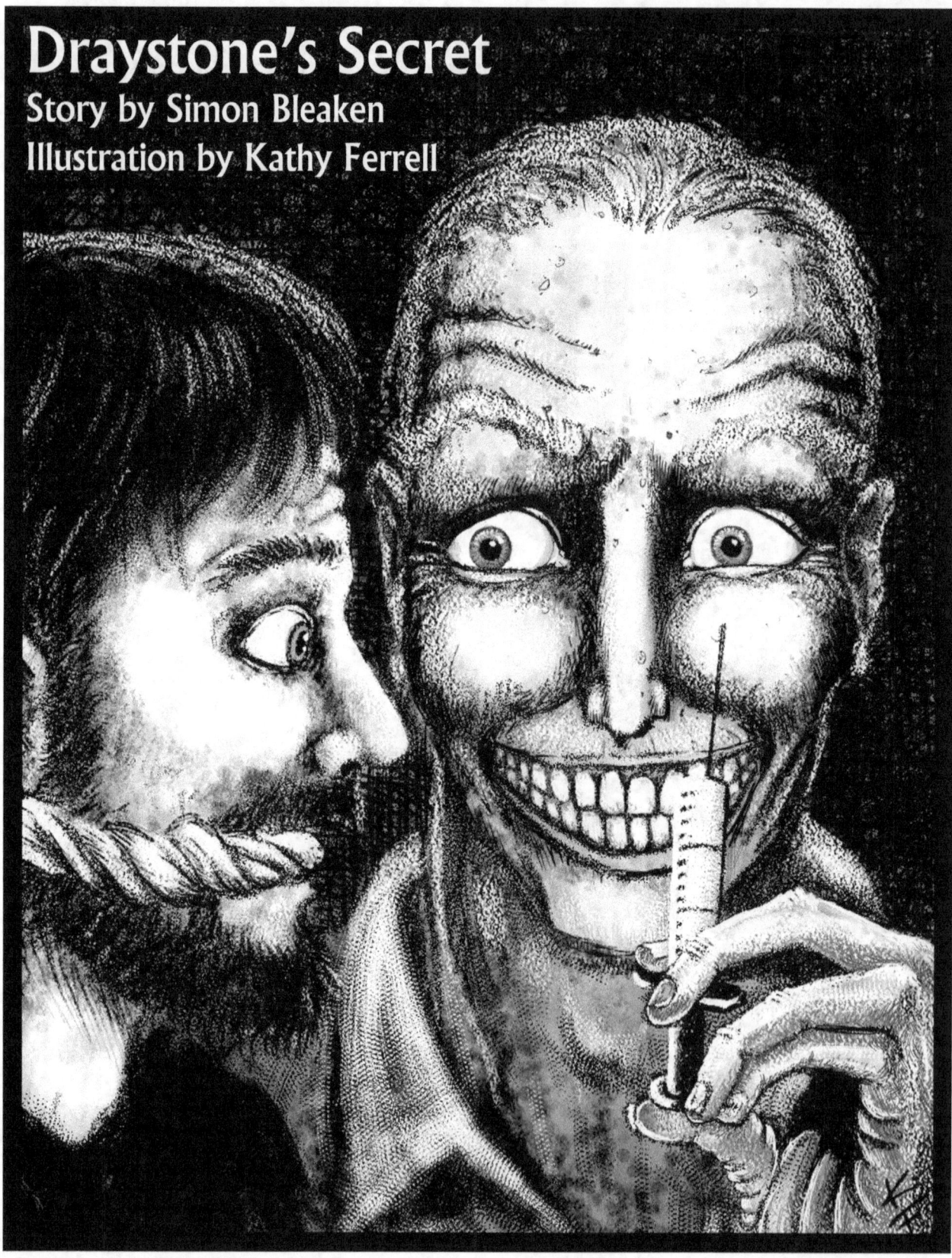

There had always been unsettling rumours connected to the old Draystone building, but I doubt anybody ever could have guessed the truth about it. I certainly couldn't have, and wish I could still count myself amongst the ignorant. It's been just over six months now since I got out of that place, and thinking back still brings a cold terror over me and a nervous tremor to my hands. The building itself, a large old bookshop with the words DRAYSTONE'S in faded gold writing against a dusty green background, looked unassuming and run-down from the outside. It sat on a quiet corner of Savernake Avenue in the old part of town, and was the sort of place most visitors passed by without ever noticing. Inside, the floor above the shop was a sprawling warren of winding linoleum hallways and doors to numerous apartments, all nestled beneath sagging ceilings speckled with damp spots, filled with an air of age and general neglect. An oddly disquieting place, it comprised too many strange corners, odd angles and awkward steps in random places, as though the structure somehow had been deviously co-designed by H. P. Lovecraft and M. C. Escher.

I knew it well, having had the dubious fortune of being the lone tenant for the past nine months. That hadn't always been the case: others had come and gone in my entire three years there, but nobody stayed long. Whether it was the single shared toilet, the damp and leaky ceilings, the bad wiring or just the odd atmosphere, I couldn't say. But it seemed I was always returning home up that narrow staircase to find another room vacant, and Draystone moving silently through it like a ghost, readying it for a new tenant.

Draystone himself was a strange man, thin and gaunt, with pale haunted eyes and a distinctive limp in his left leg. You could hear him creaking his way slowly up from the shop below sometimes. He seemed lonely and distant, and gazed through you when speaking. I had heard a few things about him before moving in: how he had lost his whole family in a terrible house fire years before, that he was a devoutly religious man, though nobody ever seemed to see him at church, and that he had become something of a strange recluse in the past few years. But it wasn't until two days after I had moved in that a neighbour had revealed a darker side to the history.

"Don't you know?" she said, a bright conspiratorial spark in her eyes as she leaned against the doorway of her room. "Apparently, his wife had a breakdown, so they say. She went completely insane. Years of abuse, or something like that. Anyway, the story goes that she tied all the children to chairs around the dining room table and torched the place, herself with it."

"That's horrible."

"They say it was her final act of revenge against him."

"Does he really seem *that* bad, Lorraine?" I folded my arms, trying to reconcile my impressions of the man with the character she was describing. "I mean, you've been here a while now, right?"

"Four months or so, and I don't know," she shrugged, "there's something odd about him. Not sure all the screws are in tight, if you get me. He makes me squirm. And then there's *the room*." She lowered her voice and gestured down the hallway. I followed her gaze but saw only the turn in the corridor. "Follow that along, go past all the other rooms, and you'll come to a door all alone at the very end of the hall."

"And?" I prompted.

"He never rents that room out, and nobody lives there. But every now and then, always at night, you'll hear people sneaking in there. It's not just the same people either, as far as I can tell from the voices—but it's always couples," she added with a wink.

"You're pulling my leg."

"Give it a few nights, you'll see. I call it the *sex room*."

I was staring down the hallway in surprise, and glanced back at her.

"It's not often I'm lost for words."

"I know, odd right? He won't let unmarried couples live here, and always wears a cross, yet he has that going on up here."

We were interrupted by the uneven tread of heavy shoes creaking their way up the old narrow stairs. Lorraine shot me a wickedly impish grin and slipped back into her room. I returned to mine, making a mental note to catch up with her again and find out more. But I never got the chance. Three days later she was gone, her room empty when I trudged home from a tedious day at the office, and Draystone was quietly surveying it, as though scrutinising every speck of dust and mark on the wall. He turned and watched me as I searched for the key to my door.

"Mr Jameson," he acknowledged softly. Watching me from the doorway in his dark suit, gaunt face locked in a motionless gaze, he was the epitome of silent menace, and I fought hard to get the image of an undertaker out of my head.

"Please, call me Michael." I pointed at the empty

room. "Has Lorraine gone?"

"Moved out this morning," he nodded, fingering the small silver cross that hung around his neck. "Gone to look after her mother, I believe."

"She never said she was leaving," I still pretended to look for my keys, though in reality I had them hidden in my hand. I seldom got to speak with Draystone—rarely wanted to in truth—but Lorraine had seemed settled here, and I was curious to find out more.

"Short notice," Draystone said, then turned and limped away towards the stairs without another word. It was a year before he got another tenant in the room next to mine.

That was the strange thing about the whole situation, Draystone certainly didn't need to rent out any of these rooms on the upper floor. He clearly wasn't short of money, and the rent he asked for was so ridiculously low he must actually have been making a loss from it.

I had the cheapest room in the whole place—but also one of the largest, with a ceiling that bowed alarmingly, a floor that felt less than level, a window that didn't lock or shut properly and an intrusive CCTV camera fixed to the building opposite that looked right into my flat as it surveyed the street. I didn't mind too much, it actually made me feel a bit better about the dodgy window, since my landlord seemed in no hurry to fix it. I had considered asking to move into one of the other rooms, but they were all a lot smaller, so I decided just to grin and bear it. I was, after all, saving a small fortune by living there.

The strange couples came and went throughout my three years' tenancy. I would hear them in the evenings, at least once a week, whispering and giggling as they scurried down that twisting hallway to the lone door at the far end. In time, I kind of stopped noticing them. And one by one the tenants all moved on, until I alone remained with the whole floor of locked empty rooms, and the strange nocturnal visitors, all to myself. It wasn't long before I forgot how bizarre the whole set-up was, it slipped into normality, that curious mix of tedium and comfortable familiarity that very quickly becomes your everyday world. I busied myself with work, multiple attempts to salvage my ailing love life, and a determined effort to resurrect some progress with my paintings during the evenings. A local gallery had shown some interest in displaying some of them, but I had allowed myself to let my passion slip into a mere hobby, and was finding it harder than I expected to scrape the rust of several years away.

And that was how I made the final discovery about that mysterious room at the end of the hall, on a stormy September night, when the pattering of the rain against the ill-fitting window and a nasty bout of insomnia had threatened to drive me to distraction. So I kicked off the covers, put on some Fleetwood Mac, and armed with a paintbrush, a pack of cigarettes and a good supply of cold gin and tonic, I determined to paint myself to sleep or greet the dawn with a screaming hangover and a finished canvas.

I had just taken a long drag on the third cigarette, paintbrush poised in hand, and was exhaling slowly as if searching for inspiration in the smoke, when there was a heavy thud from somewhere outside my door, hard enough to shake it.

I paused the CD, cutting Stevie Nicks off in mid-flow, a crime for which I vowed someone would be made to pay, and listened for a moment. For a second there was only silence, and then I heard another weighty thud and a strange sound, like a bizarre mix between a choking cough and a whimper. Then I remembered the mysterious couples that came and went to the sex room.

Keep it down you two, I sighed, reaching out for the CD remote. But something stayed my hand. I had never heard noises like that before, and instinctively knew something wasn't right. I walked to my door and pressed my ear against it, holding my breath, but the hallway beyond was silent now. Gently, I slid the lock on my door and peered out. All seemed still and normal, and I was about to turn back when I noticed something glint on the edge of the rectangle of light thrown by my open doorway.

It was an earring.

I quickly located a pair of jeans and a crumpled t-shirt before making my way back out, flicking on the dim hall light as I did. The hallway was always cold at night, even in summer, and the weak bulb only served to showcase the many nooks and shadows that surrounded me—too many doorways and alcoves for comfort. The place was a mugger's paradise. I shivered as I walked quietly over and picked up the lone item of jewellery. It was partially crushed and twisted, as though it had been torn out and trodden on. My curiosity getting the better of me, I followed the corridor all the way around to the sex room.

The door was ajar.

The whole time I had lived there, I had never seen it open or even unlocked. I had often wondered just how Draystone advertised it and how he passed on the keys—not that I had any interest in using it, only that I didn't know of anyone outside the former tenants who had heard about it.

The lure of seeing inside, even for a second, was too much to resist. The door swung inwards at my touch, revealing a lone double-bed sitting in the middle of a room with a thick cream carpet and white-painted woodchip walls. Dark red curtains hung over the windows, and a box of batteries lay tipped on its side on the floor next to an open tube of cherry-flavoured lubricant. Clothes, both male and female, were strewn clumsily on the floor, and the bed sheets were crumpled and twisted. The smell of sweat and passion was heavy on the air, mingled with a faint whiff of perfume. I moved closer to the bed as I looked around, disappointed that it was so plainly decorated. After all I had heard of it, I had half imagined whips, chains and a glistening PVC gimp suit to be hanging down from the walls. The only curious object in the room seemed to be a strange kind of copper funnel that was set in the middle of the ceiling. It looked more than a little out of place, and had no obvious function that I could discern. It was then that I remembered that I hadn't heard anyone leave, and suddenly felt uncomfortably voyeuristic. I tried to tell myself that I hadn't done anything too terrible by sneaking in here. It wasn't like I had actually tried to spy on anyone in the midst of carnal passion. But my conscience was kicking in and I knew I should get out fast before somebody came back.

As I turned to leave there was a faint creak from behind me, and I realised that a small section of the wall seemed to have come away from the rest. It was only when I reached out and the whole panel shifted, that I understood it was a concealed doorway.

I really should have got out then, and I knew it. Should have turned tail and retreated to my room at these bizarre signs. I've seen and laughed at enough horror movies where people blunder stupidly ahead instead of turning back, but a perverse curiosity had taken hold and compelled me to move forward, instead of heeding the voice of reason and sanity. Besides, this was reality and not some cheesy Hollywood flick. My heart was in my throat as I pulled the door open, knowing at any second I might be discovered, but that made this all the more enticing somehow. Beyond the doorway, a flight of steps rose steeply up into darkness past a wall of bare brick, and I climbed them as quietly as I could. The steps underfoot were polished from use and free of dust, and I paused when my hand ran out of banister, allowing my eyes to adjust. Gradually, I realised I was standing in a narrow attic hallway that stretched down past two padlocked doors to a third at the far end which was partly open and spilled a narrow strip of light across the floor.

I hesitated then, common sense marching back and ordering me to turn around and go back to my room before I was discovered and evicted. I was about to obey, when from that door at the end of the hall there issued a terrified shriek, followed by what could only have been a sudden choked-off gasp and abrupt silence.

Genuine fear finally seized me then, standing in the darkness, heart beating, sweat tickling down my back, staring at the steps that would take me back down to my room as I wondered what to do. I should have slinked away, crept back to my normal life and shut this unusual strangeness out. But I couldn't. I had gone too far and seen too much, and curiosity burned within me as strongly as the fear I felt. But I would have been lying if I didn't also admit to a growing sense of guilt. If somebody was hurt or in pain beyond that door, how could I just turn away and leave them to suffer?

My hands and legs physically shook as I walked down that passageway, treading lightly. In the back of my mind was the notion that I might just be about to intrude on some strange kind of twisted sex game, but I knew that this was something darker and more serious.

I peered gingerly around the door into a large attic cluttered with old bed frames and mattresses, strange glass bottles, boxes of assorted junk, and other items of furniture shrouded in dust-sheets. It was as though a mad hoarder had been accumulating items from house clearances. But a clear path ran through the middle of it all, and the attic branched off to the right up ahead, following the odd shape of the building. As I made my way forward, I noticed the pungent stench of formaldehyde in the air, and as I rounded the corner and the rest of the attic opened up before me, I stopped in shock at the sight that met my eyes.

Ahead of me, sitting around a long ornate dining table and looking for all the world like a demented mannequin's tea-party, were the preserved remains of several of the previous tenants. They stared sightlessly down upon their empty china plates, glasses and silver cutlery, their mouths twisted into grisly smiles with wire, and strange symbols were daubed on their flesh in long-dried blood. I baulked as I recognised Lorraine's corpse among them. There were a few unoccupied chairs, but even these had place settings prepared before them. Resting in the middle of the table was a large milky crystal, covered with the same curious glyphs that were daubed onto the bodies. It sat within a crudely made copper dish which also bore the same bizarre markings and which seemed to have a long tube that extended down through the table and into the floor below.

On the floor next to the table lay a young woman. She was dressed only in her underwear, and her body was spattered in blood. There was a ragged tear to one of her earlobes, a deep gash on her forehead, and red marks on her throat revealed where she had been strangled. Near to her, their hands almost touching, lay a young man, also dressed only in his underwear, the side of his head bloody and bruised.

It felt like I stood there for hours, staring in shock and disbelief at that macabre scene, though it could only have been seconds. I can still see them now, every detail, etched vividly into my mind whenever I close my eyes. What snapped me away from that awful sight was the sudden realisation that one of the dust sheets off to my right was moving, just in the periphery of my vision. As I turned to look, something slammed heavily against the side of my head. I felt myself hit the floor, and everything went dark.

* * *

"Welcome to the family."

The voice that spoke was all-too familiar, and I opened my eyes groggily to see Draystone watching me. He was sitting in one of the previously unoccupied dining chairs across the table from me, holding a long hypodermic needle in his thin fingers. I tried to stand up, but felt ropes bite into my arms and legs.

"I wanted to wait until you were awake. It seemed only fair."

"Come near me and I'll scream," I warned him, hoping the tremor in my voice wasn't too apparent.

He laughed at that. "Go ahead and scream—others have. The building is old and the walls are thick, and at this time of night anyone sober enough to care is home in bed."

"Please! For God's sake, don't do this!"

"God?" he laughed, reaching for the silver cross around his neck. "I wear this to remind me of what I once was, what I once believed in." He stood up and moved around the table towards me, the needle glinting in his grasp. "But where was God when my wife stole my family from me? Where was God when I screamed and prayed for a miracle until I was hoarse?"

I shook my head, tears stinging my eyes and fear crippling my tongue.

"Nowhere," he hissed as he crouched beside me. "I gave him devotion, and he gave me nothing but ashes and grief."

I tried to speak but no sound came out. My arms and legs were shaking now, and my heart felt like it was going to explode from my chest.

"But you know what?" he whispered, leaning in close, the glinting needle tip easing in toward my eye. I tried to flinch away but Draystone's hand shot around to the back of my head, holding it in place. His breath assaulted my skin as he leaned in, and I squirmed as the needle drew closer. "There are other powers in this world. Beings so old we no longer have names for them, but they are still here. They were more than willing to help."

He drew back, taking the needle away, but I felt no relief. I twisted my hands against my bonds and strained my arms and legs as best I could without making it obvious what I was trying to do.

"And, do you know what they revealed to me?" he continued, a wry smile on his lips as his gaze turned to the crystal. "The solution was all around me, bound up in something I once deemed sinful and unclean. How blind I was."

He turned and gave me a sideways glance, and I knew he was daring me to guess. But I could only shake my head.

"Sex," he laughed. "Of all the things."

My right arm was slowly working loose, a mix of sweat and my frantic wrenching and twisting.

"Sex has a power, and it has energy. Oh, you wouldn't believe what that energy can do if you tap into it. It's potent and regenerative. It's pure life energy, filled with that spark of creation and passion. It is that magical moment when life moves from a potential to a reality." He ran a hand gently over the large crystal in the middle of the table. "This is right above the bed below, and all that life energy is directed right up into it. And when I have enough stored up, I can bring them back. I can channel back the spirits of my family into these empty vessels of flesh and bone and bind them there with life energy. It takes years to get enough to bring back so many—but soon I will be with my children again, and I shall settle a very old score with my wife."

"You're crazy," I finally whispered, my voice hoarse. "Totally mad."

"But these two," he shot a disdainful glance down at the body of the prostitute and the young man lying in a heap at his feet, "were like you." He gestured at me with the needle, then angled it to point at Lorraine's corpse as well. "You all couldn't leave well enough alone. Had to go peeking and snooping where you weren't meant to, and saw what was private. But it doesn't matter—spare vessels are always useful."

"I've got friends, and family," I said quickly. "People who'll come looking for me!"

"You don't think she did too?" he nodded at Lorraine. "They all did. But did you see anything in the papers? Did the police come asking questions?"

"No," I whispered, a chilling realisation suddenly dawning on me. There had been nothing—no investigations, no questions, no news stories.

"The ones I summon, those forgotten ones I discovered, are very good at making sure people forget the things I want them to. You'll be forgotten too, just as they all were."

The rope around my right hand seemed to be working loose, and it felt like the chair was on the verge of giving out too, probably riddled with woodworm, but I feared moving too much while he was looking at me, and I was already afraid that the beads of sweat on my face and brow might give the game away. My mind was racing now, desperately trying to find some way out of this—from the cutlery on the table that might serve as a crude weapon, to wondering how heavy and solid that crystal might be if I swung it against his head.

And then I saw the young man on the floor stir—his arm lifted and his eyes flickered open, and I held my breath, terrified that he might make a sound and draw Draystone's attention.

"You're forgetting," I said quickly, hoping to keep Draystone's gaze fixed on me, my voice trembling, "the bodies here—they're older than your children would have been."

"I don't care about the shells," he waved a hand dismissively, "only the souls within. The body is just flesh. They will be my children whatever their outward form might be."

"But how will you know it's really them? How…"

Draystone shot forward then, the needle glinting toward my face once more. "I think you need to be *quiet* now!" he hissed, his eyes blazing furiously as I recoiled from him. Then he blinked and looked down at the needle in his hand, and a faint smile flickered over his thin lips. "Now, where were we?"

From behind Draystone I saw movement as the young man rose shakily to his feet, then slammed into the back of his attacker with a cry of rage. At the same time Draystone pitched forward and the needle flew from his grasp and struck the surface of the table next to me.

Without stopping to see what happened next, I did the only thing that I could think of—I pushed with my feet as hard as I could, tipping the old chair up on the back legs, then let it slam down against the floor whilst trying to keep the back of my head from hitting along with it. The shock was still jarring and I failed to keep my head from smacking against the floorboards as I struck. But I heard the chair break at the same time, and felt the bonds loosen a little, and rolled onto my side as I managed to pull one arm free, my head ringing.

I could hear the sounds of a struggle behind me, but couldn't see what was happening—my legs were still coiled in rope and one of my hands was still bound tightly at the wrist. I clawed and tugged at my bonds, and finally felt them all giving way.

I staggered to my feet to see the two men wrestling with each other over the table. The young man had one hand around my landlord's throat and the other clamped around his head, whilst Draystone himself was struggling to reach the needle that was rolling across the table just out of reach of his fingers. Then he changed tactics, and drove his elbow back into the young man's stomach, before lunging again for the needle.

But he hadn't seen me. In a panic I snatched up the hypodermic—and as he turned I stabbed wildly at him with it, a cry of anger and horror bursting from my lips.

It plunged straight into his left eye.

Draystone froze, his jaw dropping open in surprise as he stared at me with his right eye. He seemed to be trying to blink.

I think the look of horror on his face must have mirrored that on my own. I jumped back, and then everything seemed to happen in slow motion. Draystone swayed like a tree in a storm, pawing ineffectually at the needle embedded in his eye with trembling hands—then he crashed down onto the table as his legs buckled under him, and I heard the awful sickening crunch as hypodermic went fully in as his face slammed against the tabletop. For a second his whole body trembled and twitched, and he seemed to be desperately reaching for something with his right arm. I saw his shuddering fingers fumble at the milky crystal—and then he just went still, his hand coming to rest atop it.

I also went still, staring in mute horror at the sight before me.

What have I done?

Then I felt a hand touch my shoulder. The young man was watching me, his hair matted with blood and his face pale and frightened.

"Are you okay?" he asked, his voice as unsteady as mine had been earlier. I nodded, but I didn't trust myself to say anything. Then he saw the woman lying on the floor and knelt beside her, touching her face with a trembling hand.

"Oh God."

I just watched blankly as he closed her dead eyes. It didn't even feel real to me—it was like watching events on a screen. I just stood there, staring.

"Can you move?" he said at last, looking up at me. "Let's get the hell out of here and call the police."

"Yes," I managed finally. "Yes, we should."

I dimly remember following him down out of that attic space, pausing only to allow him to get dressed before making our way through the twisting hallway of the building that I had once called home. It all felt different now, unfamiliar and unwelcoming, and I wondered how I had ever allowed myself to stay there. How had I let all those little odd occurrences over the years become so familiar and normal?

We called the police from my cell phone, standing in a shop doorway across the street from the old bookshop. I couldn't face going back into my room, not just yet. And I wondered what would happen when those cars with their wailing sirens finally drew up. I had just killed a man—and the worst part was, I didn't know if I had meant to or not. It had all happened so fast, and I had acted instead of thinking. I wasn't sure looking back just what I had intended to do with that needle—had I really meant to aim it for his face, or just to scare him back? The fact that Draystone had been a killer and had planned to murder me didn't seem to make what I had done any less terrible.

The police arrived soon after, cordoning off the road as they went into the house and we were taken away to the station. To be honest, most of what happened after was a blur. All I could see was Draystone's face with that needle sticking out of it, and I kept hearing that awful sound over and over as his face struck the table. I must have been half out of my mind with guilt and shock. It was only some time later, while I was anxiously making my confession down at the station, and seeing looks of confusion on the faces of the officers there, that I learned they hadn't

found Draystone's body in that attic, nor had there been any sign of the milky crystal we had described to them. They did, however, find the corpses around the table just as we had reported, with my landlord's fingerprints all over them, along with enough taxidermy equipment to preserve several elephants.

The story was in the papers for weeks, and with it came the overdue outcry from friends and relatives of Lorraine and the rest of the victims—as though they had somehow just resurfaced in their memories. I don't pretend to understand it, and the more I think about it, the less I feel able to sleep at night.

They never found Draystone, despite an ongoing manhunt. Sometimes I wonder just how he survived, and how he's managed to elude capture these past six months. And I keep thinking about what he said about finding older forces that were willing to aid him.

Barrie, the young man who escaped that attic with me, kept in touch with me following that awful night. He was the only one who knew what truly happened, and he was a great support in helping me through my ongoing grief and guilt, just as I know he appreciated having someone who understood what he had been through. It was funny how that horrible event changed us both, turned two strangers into the closest of friends.

Barrie even managed to shed some light on just what had happened that night, and the look on his face as he recounted it to me has never left my memory since.

"I found out about it on Craigslist, good place for a hookup, apparently," he'd confessed over coffee one afternoon, the drone of traffic outside forming a comforting backdrop of normality against memories of a night that was anything but. "I met her across the street outside. Said she had a deal with the landlord, and had the keys to the room. I thought the place looked like a dump, but she was hot, so what did I care? Anyway, it was all going great until we found that staircase. I guess he hadn't shut it properly. We thought we'd check it out, for a laugh, but he was up there—sitting at that table, watching that crystal. When he realised we'd seen those bodies, he went crazy. I tried to stop him, and that's all I remember until I woke with a splitting headache to see him coming at you with that needle."

But everything changed three nights ago. I had just got in from work and flicked on the news when I saw the report. Barrie had been found dead in his home, just across town from where I now live. He had been tied to a chair in his kitchen, with strange marks daubed in blood on his body and his left eye gouged out. The truly strange thing is police have no idea how the killer got inside the property—there was no sign of forced entry or any damage to the house. I must have watched that report over and over again as the news repeated it throughout the evening. I couldn't believe what I was seeing. It still doesn't seem real.

I try to tell myself it wasn't a message for me, and that I'm not now in terrible danger. Sometimes I can almost make myself believe it.

Most of the time I know full well that Draystone was just plain crazy. Just a lonely old man lost to his own mad delusions. But other times, usually just after dusk when the character of the world changes and those things that seem laughable by day suddenly take on a different, more solid reality, I sit inside, afraid to go near the windows for fear he might be standing outside, a knife or needle in one hand and that milky crystal in the other, and I wonder.

Spinning the Threads

The Fates
Sin the thread
From a mixture
Of fiber strands,
A strand of time
Cob web thin
Wrapped in a strand
Of double helix DNA
Of the intended soul,
Twisted around a plucked
Hair from the coyote
Trickster god's coat
To add interest to the life
And then measured to
The required life span
And snipped with
Golden shears.

— K.S. Hardy

Finally Free

Story by Frances Silversmith
Illustration by Erika McGinnis

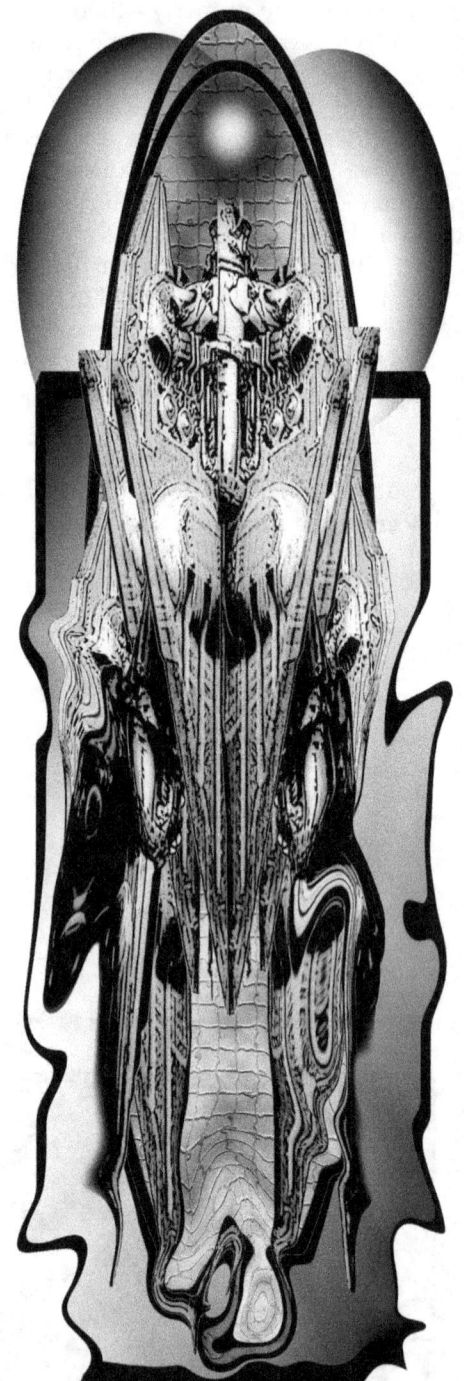

Laira stood in the damp cellar, stared at the narrow bed she had spent her days on for the last seven centuries. Seven hundred years, without once seeing the sun.

"You'll get used to it," they'd said. "You'll love being a vampire."

They had lied.

She turned and ascended the stairs. At the front door, she hesitated.

Seven hundred years. How she missed the sunshine. She opened the door, stepped outside.

Birds sang. The morning sun painted the world in bright colors. She drew in the scent of spring flowers and fresh grass.

For one glorious moment, she was free.

* * *

First published in *Daily Science Fiction*, September, 2013. Reprinted by permission of the author.

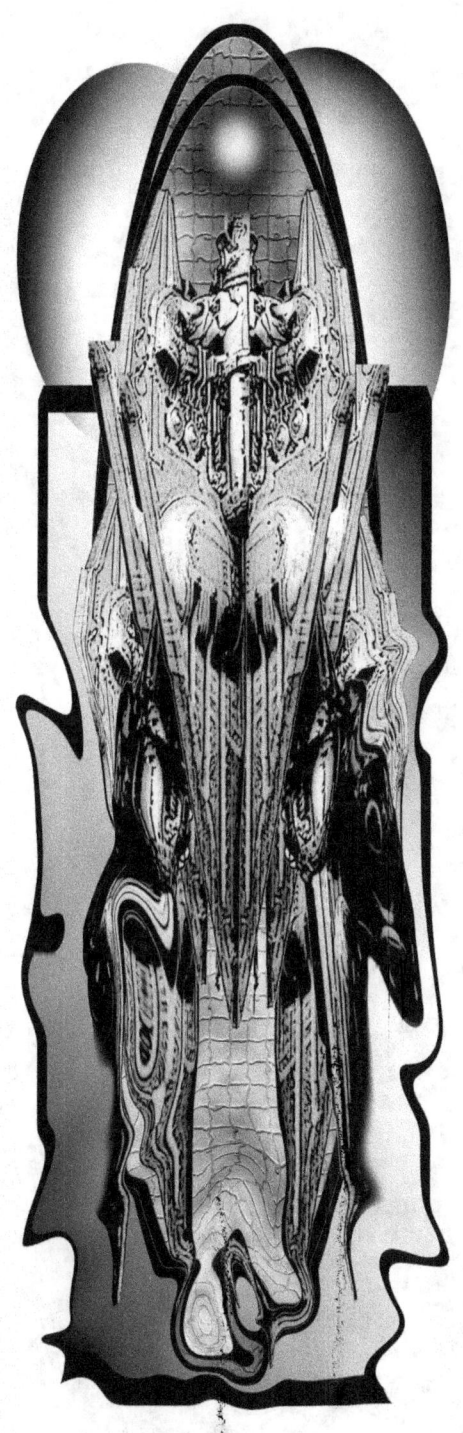

Night Life

Her name was Hannah
She was a waitress
In one of the city's cocktail lounges
I waited 'till her shift had ended
Sometime just after 3
And then we hit some other late night
Early morning bars
An old lover
With dead years in his eyes
Appeared and began to follow us
From place to place
Until she grew tired of seeing
His sad and yearning face
And shooed him
Back into the shadows
From whence he came
A gypsy child in rags and tatters
Selling flowers
Came to our table
Gave her a rose without a word
And would take no payment
In return
When dawn came up
She said she had to go
And buy a pint of blood
From the city slaughterhouse
There was a pallor
Beneath her olive coloured skin
And she could never
Get enough, she said
Of that red nectar
That came rushing free
From a freshly
Opened artery

— William Corner Clarke

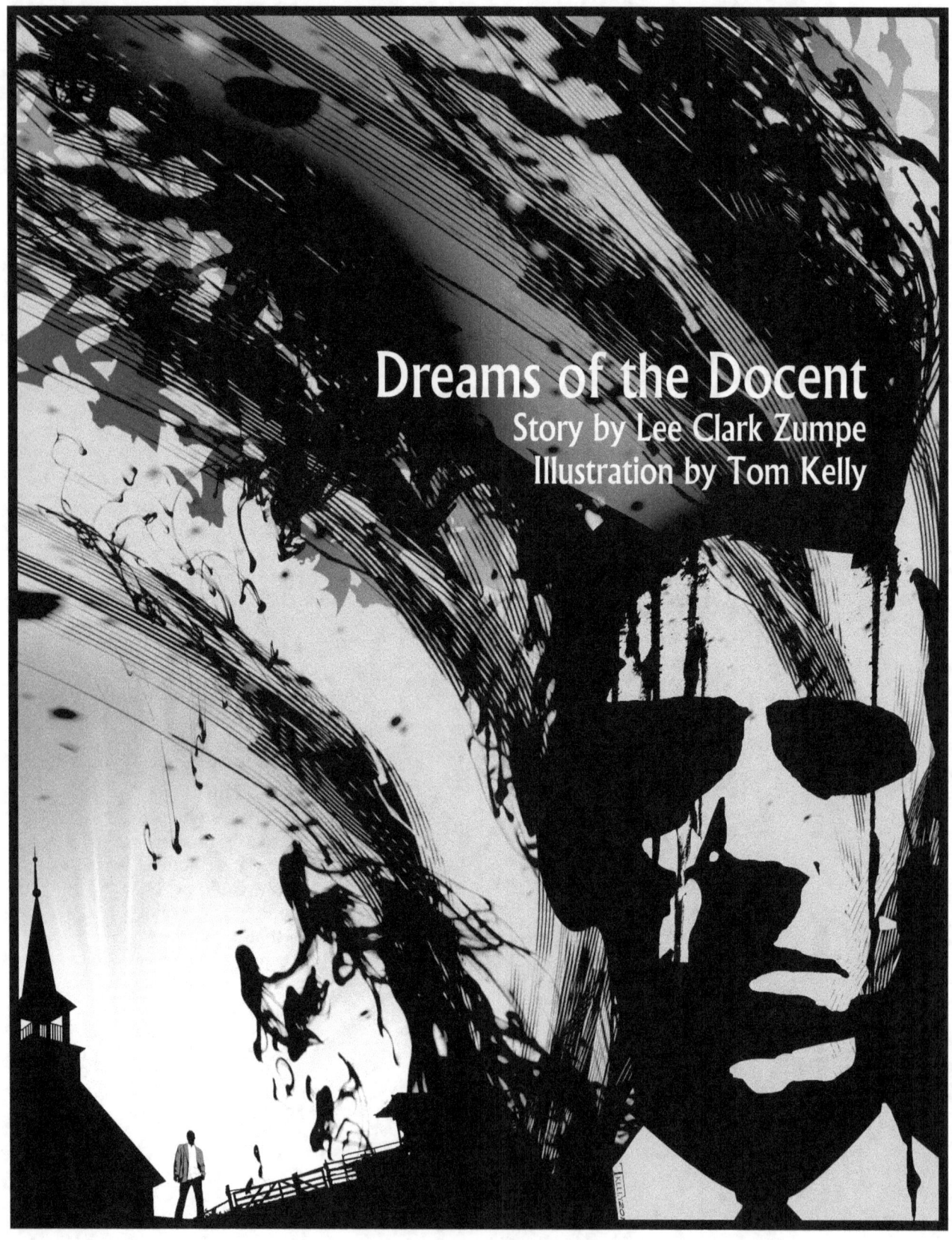

Dreams of the Docent
Story by Lee Clark Zumpe
Illustration by Tom Kelly

American history lingers along forgotten ribbons of asphalt dismembering the vast countryside, on obsolete two-lane highways forsaken by all but the most intrepid explorers. Corridors once teaming with tourists and thriving with commerce sank into dreary decline following the introduction of the Interstate System, depriving whole townships of both revenue and purpose. Amidst the ruins of rundown neighborhoods, the remnants of boarded up roadside attractions and the hollowed-out shells of moribund communities, time languishes and lives fester.

The lure of the unknown drew me onto one such shadowy stretch, an antiquated artery meandering along the spine of peninsular Florida equidistant from the Atlantic and the Gulf of Mexico. Far from the tourist conveyer belts of I-95 and I-75, down a winding tract of pavement skirted by dense oak hammocks draped with Spanish moss and carpeted by ferns, on a rural route paralleled by an equally idle set of railroad tracks, I took an unanticipated detour that offered pastoral produce stands, rustic flea markets, wayside antique barns, sprawling citrus groves and derelict alligator farms.

Ultimately, the diversion delivered me to the uninviting little town of Shady Haven. Late on a Saturday afternoon, I found myself miles from any reputable-looking service station with a dashboard full of flashing red lights and an engine that sounded like something monstrous had taken up residence beneath the hood.

"Not much I can do on the weekend." Nate the middle-aged mechanic pressed his shoulder against the outside wall of the garage. He used a blue shop cloth first to clean his grease-stained hands, then to mop sweat from his forehead. A lifetime of filth had accumulated beneath his fingernails and his smile revealed a mouthful of crooked teeth stained from habitual indulgences with chewing tobacco. "Ain't got the parts to fix it," he said, though he had never actually identified the problem—not that I had the technical aptitude to approve of his diagnosis. "I'll make some calls first thing Monday morning. Nobody's open on Sunday 'round here."

"There a motel in town?"

"Just one." He looked over his shoulder, nodded on down the street where a number of dilapidated old office buildings congregated to form the downtown district. "Mose Lipscomb runs Sleep Tight Inn down on Main Street. I'm sure he's got a vacancy."

Reluctantly, I hauled my suitcase from the trunk and gathered a few things from the backseat before entrusting my vehicle's security to Nate. Shambling over fractured slabs of sidewalk plagued by the unchecked propagation of weeds, I noticed a ramshackle billboard half-enveloped by kudzu in a vacant lot. Roasting in the scorching heat of the central Florida sun, I paused long enough to decipher the advertisement's original message, long-since obscured by both vegetation and the elements:

Mose's Haunted House of Hideous Horrors
See: Poe's Walking Stick!
See: Locks of Lizzy Borden's Hair!
See: Signed Salem Witch Confessions!
See: Voodoo Artifacts from Southern Plantations!
See: A Crucifix used in a Failed Exorcism!
Hear: Your Own Screams!

Though the likelihood that the museum still existed seemed slim, I took consolation in the fact that the motel proprietor might be willing to share some interesting stories and artifacts.

"I sure could use a room for a couple of nights." I spoke loudly, not certain whether the man behind the counter was dead or dozing. After several instants, his eyelids lifted and his eyes rolled anxiously as if he had been shaken from some portentous dream. "Do you have any rooms available?"

"Car troubles?"

"Yeah, how did you know?"

"Mister, nobody stops in Shady Haven intentionally." Mose pushed the guest register across the counter as if submitting evidence to support his assertion. Taking the pen he offered, I scanned the signatures and accompanying dates. The most recent guest had passed through six months earlier; before that, years had gone by without lodgers. "See what I mean?"

As I etched my name across the page, Mose stood and stretched. Just shy of being extraordinarily tall, the innkeeper scratched at his shabby yellow beard while his drowsy, vacuous eyes scanned a collection of keys dangling from tiny hooks on the wall behind the counter. After much deliberation, he plucked one from its place and handed it to me. A tiny chain connected it to a crystal tetragonal trapezohedron. Upon one of its eight faces, the number 8 had been inscribed.

"You can have the best room in the place. Does $20 a night sound reasonable?"

"That's fine," I said, digging for my wallet.

"Don't worry about it now. We'll settle up when you check out." Mose eased himself back into the chair, resting both arms on the desk. His eyelids sagged and his lower lip, shimmering with spittle, drooped and quivered as he panted from the brief exertion.

"Is there a restaurant you could recommend?"

"There's a restaurant, but I wouldn't let my dog eat the pigswill they serve." Mose glanced at a clock on the wall. "Come back down to the lobby in an hour. I'll see what I can come up with."

"I don't want you to go to any trouble."

"No trouble at all. Be nice to have some conversation with a meal for once."

* * *

The Deep South—and particularly Florida— had coined the term "sleepy little town." From the dingy window in my tiny room on the second floor, I could see the entire town of Shady Haven, from the hodgepodge of strewn auto parts torn like tumors from declining vehicles and discarded on the land surrounding Nate's garage to the swarthy steeple towering over the local church and its accompanying burial ground. In between the two landmarks, the town boasted a small medical center, an old-fashioned five-and-dime store, a hardware store, a few dozen aging houses in various states of disrepair and a rustic eatery called Buford's Smoke House.

For an hour, I stared out that foggy glass waiting for the inadequate window shaker to cool off the room a few degrees, watched as trucks hauling citrus or lumber raced through the town without tapping the brakes. Not once did I notice a pedestrian strolling along the avenue, a child playing in a yard or even a raggedy mutt looking for trouble. Nate had disappeared, his bay doors closed, my ailing car left sitting in the precise spot where I had parked it.

The room resonated with the town's former claim to fame. Leftovers from Mose's Haunted House of Hideous Horrors included classic monster movie posters, a stack of old genre pulps on the nightstand and a coffin-shaped coffee table. Rampant cobwebs, bathroom mildew that mimicked blood stains and a warped mirror above the sink unintentionally added to the ambiance

Back in the lobby, I found Mose waiting with a platter full of sandwiches and canned sodas. The old man had shaken his fatigue and seemed interested in talking about the town's former glory.

"Yeah," he said with a trace of sadness. "It was great fun while it lasted. Lots of visitors, kids and adults alike. We always had a good time. No better way to make a living than scaring people."

"What happened?" The question seemed obligatory, though I could already guess the fate of the museum.

"Tourists stopped coming through here. Shut down after a few years. Practically a ghost town now, just a few stragglers too stubborn or too impoverished to give up everything they've always known."

"Why'd you stay?"

"No where else to go. My place is here, with the relics. Just because no one comes to see them anymore doesn't mean that they've lost their relevance."

"So, you've kept everything?"

"Sure—the collection is scattered through the motel rooms, bits and pieces, here and there. In fact, you'll be sleeping on Lovecraft's pillow tonight."

"Beg your pardon?"

"Well, that's not quite truthful, I reckon," he said, chasing the confession with a swig of Nehi Peach. "Long time ago, legend has it, Mr. Lovecraft visited friends or relatives right here in Shady Haven. He slept so poorly that night—plagued with nightmarish visions—that come morning, he shredded his pillowcase in a fit of madness. Peculiar thing what he found inside it." Mose paused, guzzled another mouthful of soda and nibbled at a sandwich quarter. An accomplished storyteller, he knew exactly how to milk the moment, to perch his audience on a precipice and make them sweat for resolution. "Seems there was a tangle of feathers, dead center of the pillow I s'pose, what were all black and bloody. Now, men like the two of us know there's a rational explanation behind it—but townsfolk saw it as something altogether different."

"I don't blame them for turning to old superstitions to explain it."

"Course not, and I'm sure poor old Mr. Lovecraft forgave them for running him out of town," Moses said. The sound of a passing truck interrupted his thoughts momentarily. He stood, shuffled over to the window and peeled down one slat of the yellowed metal Venetian blinds. "Getting dark out there," he muttered, weariness sneaking back into his voice. "Best call it a night."

"Wait," I said, wanting to hear the rest of the story. "What happened? Why did they chase him out of town?"

"Oh," the old man said, stroking his whiskers. "Because, they blamed him. They said his nightmares were so powerful they tainted the pillow, the bed

… maybe the whole damn town." The smile that fractured his expression when he revealed the tale's climax left a stronger impression than the story itself. I tried to dismiss the whole yarn as an old man's last grasp at his glory days, one last shot at spooking a customer. Such luxury would not be mine, though: He saw to that disappointment with the fanatical proclivity simmering in his eyes, the lingering titillation at the macabre recitation as he showed me to the door. "I bought them all, you see, those black, bloody feathers. Thought it was good business. Scattered them all through the motel, one per pillow, one pillow per room."

"It's a good story," I said, trying to mask my embryonic apprehension. I thanked him for both the dinner and the discourse. "I'll do my best to get a good night's sleep."

"Yes sir," Mose said. "Pleasant dreams, sir."

* * *

Admittedly, my acquaintance with the weird fiction of American author H.P. Lovecraft was limited to tales I had perused in various horror anthologies over the years. Since the current high regard afforded Lovecraft by modern scholars had not yet fully blossomed during my college years, I found him on none of my reading lists for English literature courses, including one which examined the influence of Poe on 20th century writers. As Mose's narration permeated the gray matter, my memory dredged up snippets from a short biographical sketch from some nameless collection and I recalled that the Providence, Rhode Island native had, in fact, made several sojourns to the Sunshine State during his short lifetime.

Still, the Lovecraft account seemed senselessly far-fetched. The "fit of madness" seemed a particularly aberrant reaction for an urbane, cultured writer; and the inference of some connection to voodoo ritual played like the subtext of an acutely lurid Southern Gothic novel.

Despite my skepticism, I thoroughly examined the pillow—as well as the bedding—before switching off the lamp on the nightstand and plunging the motel room into abject darkness for the night.

If I am thankful for one thing that happened in the hours that followed it is that my extreme fatigue precluded me from committing every detail of my dreams to memory. The visions I suffered that intolerably long night originated from terrifying realms of unconscious imagery. An endless cavalcade of graphic atrocities paraded through my mind's eye delivering horrors that have no parallel outside of Dante's Inferno.

In the morning, I was left with vivid snapshots of my gruesome phantasmagoria: smoldering cities, toppled towers and thoroughfares lately blackened by emerald waves of flame; disfigured and charred corpses putrefying in the streets, cruelly unheeded by stunned survivors; a blanket of viridescent ashes loosed by churning, sallow xanthic skies; endless dark devastation occupied by desperate and despondent refugees seeking shelter from the omnipresent, unearthly conquerors and their horde of warriors—unspeakable, mute green monstrosities with tentacle-like appendages and dozens of bulbous eyes and greedy, jagged teeth.

It was an apocalyptic vision of some alien world set within the ultimate void of the black planets in an ancient corner of the cosmos—yet it was hauntingly familiar.

In the final instants before I awoke from my unquiet slumbers, I faced the author of this staggering holocaust. It dwelled in an aerie of writhing shadows surrounded by dead civilizations and pallid, spent stars. A graveyard of doomed worlds clustered in folds of darkness, their hooded priests long silenced and their consecrated shrines abandoned. Worship and sacrifice stirred no clemency in the barely sentient, blind and mindless Daemon Sultan at the very heart of Ultimate Chaos.

Its hideous profile exposed its terrible, overwhelming apathy.

I lingered for some time on the shore of dreams, teetering on the precipice of sleep as if eager to steal one last glimpse at the fading horrors. When I finally pushed myself out of bed, I was surprised to find half the morning had slipped away silently.

* * *

Time moves with unceasing tread—but in Shady Haven, it does so with a pronounced limp.

The television in the room boasted a basic cable setup but seemed only capable of receiving six or seven local stations, half of which featured evangelical programming. After a quick shower, I thumbed through a couple of the pulp magazines Mose had placed in the room to generate atmosphere. The March 1949 issue of *Weird Tales* featured novelettes by Theodore Sturgeon, Robert Bloch and August Derleth; short stories by Stanton Coblentz and Thorp McClusky and cover art by Matt Fox. A 1945 issue of *Thrilling Wonder Stories* included the novella "Sword of Tomorrow" by Henry Kuttner.

Though well-written and engaging, the stories

fell short of capturing my attention. With little else to do besides sleep—an eventuality that held both dread and morbid curiosity for me—I slipped on my shoes and went for a walk along the town's main street.

Along narrow avenues lined with sprawling live oak sat modest bungalows with small-paned windows and vacant porches. I hiked up to the town's lone church—curiously untenanted on a Sunday afternoon—which squatted on a central summit overlooking a neglected citrus grove. Its obligatory burying-ground reeked of antiquity with its gnarled old oak and black, unembellished gravestones. From its highest crest, Shady Haven looked deserted and forsaken, the ghost of a forgotten community.

Making my way back to Sleep Tight Inn, a solemn procession of townsfolk encountered me unexpectedly, startling me and forcing me to stagger off the sidewalk onto someone's lawn, cluttered with willow trees and odd, gray standing stones scarred by curious glyphs. The scowling residents neither greeted me nor acknowledged my existence as they passed hurriedly, each adorned in decidedly dark attire and clutching some form archaic hymnal. As the final member of the uncanny throng marched down the avenue, my eye sought his down-turned face.

His ominous countenance revealed an unsettling, alien omnipotence sustained by appalling apathy.

* * *

"Sure, I've seen it," Mose said, offering me a warm cup of Earl Grey tea. Clouds had overrun the sky during my afternoon walk heralding an unseasonable drop in temperature. Shady Haven had been besieged by an aberrant burst of Arctic air. "'The thing that crouches in shadow,' they call it. Or 'The thing that haunts the darkness.'"

"You mean everyone in town has the same dream?" I spoke hesitantly, not certain whether my reluctance sprang from disbelief or fear. I questioned the sanity of my host—and in doing so, found myself forced to examine my own mental stability. "How can everyone dream the same dream?"

"Not everyone," he said. "Maybe one in four."

"So one out of four people living in Shady Haven have the same dream every night?"

"That's just it, though" Mose explained, showing the first signs of impatience. "It's not *our* dream. It's that thing's dream. It's as if those visions are being transmitted from some place outside space and time, rerun over and over again in our heads."

"So all that nonsense about Lovecraft was just gibberish you use to spook the tourists?" I could not help but feel somehow violated, though I did not believe Mose intended any harm. "The voodoo feathers, too?"

"Well, the voodoo feathers I made up," Mose said, smiling at some unuttered yarn. "But Lovecraft did visit Shady Haven. That's when all this started. Fact is, townsfolk blame him for it. Think he fiddled with the dial on the cosmic radio, so to speak—opened the channel and initiated the transmission."

"But what about," I mumbled, but I stopped myself short of finishing the question. The churchgoers fit into the equation in some manner that defied logic. The phenomenon itself challenged common sense. "I saw a group of people heading to the church on the hill."

"Best not ask questions about those folk," Mose said, his mood souring once more. "Some don't understand it like I told it to you. Some think that its two-way radio, that they can talk back to that thing. Don't know why anyone would care to attract his attention, myself. Seems like a bad idea all around."

* * *

I put off sleep as long as I could, but eventually succumbed to exhaustion—and to curiosity.

The dreams returned, more vivid than the previous night. I found myself assailed by sickening and indescribable reflections of horror. The disorienting, nightmarish landscape punctuated by forgotten and neglected graves spread beneath grim alien skies. The ghastly mountains of tangled, mutilated bodies had worn away into mounds of glistening bones. The emerald waves of flame had been extinguished, though the viridescent ashes still drifted amidst the rubble.

Refugees found themselves subjugated by the pitiless mute monstrosities who crowned themselves priest-kings and demanded endless sacrifices in rituals of unutterable depravity.

As the dream continued, I found myself standing at the black doorway far beneath the swarthy steeple of the nearby church, gazing out across the town of Shady Haven, watching as a blight spread inexorably across the landscape. Doom seemed to radiate from the small central Florida town, enveloping the unsuspecting Earth in a fulvous yellow shroud as flashes of emerald flames ignited from beyond space and time.

I saw the architect of this inevitable cataclysm for only a single instant: His three-lobed burning eye displaced the Earth's moon as its cities crumbled and condemned denizens articulated a single plea for amnesty which went unacknowledged.

* * *

I stirred from my fitful sleep some time after noon on Monday. I spoke not another word of my dreams to Mose as I settled my bill and set out to find Nate the mechanic to determine the status of the repairs on my car.

"Don't let it gnaw at you," Mose said as I turned to go. "Awake, you see the pretense of reality. Asleep, you see all the horrors evolution has taught us to dismiss."

Much to my delight, Nate had managed to get the car running.

"It'll get you up to Jacksonville," he said. "I'd stop by the dealer and have them run one of them fancy diagnostics on it before you go further, though."

"I'll do that," I said, presenting a credit card.

An hour later, I sat in the driver's seat of my car just outside Shady Haven. I had pulled off onto the shoulder of the road for one last look. Intermittent traffic sped by on that antiquated artery tracing the arching spine of Florida.

Some people see the world differently. Whether their vision is a gift or a curse is debatable. Either way, their dreams can be so powerful that they become imprinted upon their surroundings and their possessions.

I told myself that the dreams would not follow me home from Shady Haven. *Dreams are dreams, nothing more.* No matter how many times I repeated that mantra, I did not believe it.

Two hours later, I reached the outskirts of Jacksonville. As I approached, a broken, splintered moon lighted up a ghastly scene, and the aspect of an alien sky with its swirling, anomalous constellations, pulsating comets and fiery falling meteors offered stark contrast to a landscape littered with festering corpses and ruins.

I rubbed my eyes and the façade of reality mercifully reemerged from the shadows.

Under the Cancer Tree

At the foot of the Cancer Tree
is a cave where reside three women:
one sews, one rips, one chooses.
They pass a single eye and ear
between them. At any one time
only one can see, one can hear:
one ear to hear the silent prayers,
one eye to see the broken.

Only the one both deaf and blind
will choose—
A committee's lack of responsibility
for the fallen.
No one can meet them
and come away unshaken.

— Sandra Lindow

Angel Comfortings
Story by Douglas Empringham
Illustration by Paul Niemiec

Colby touched the rail again and still felt no tremor while the pernicious sun continued to drain night from the eastern horizon. Unlike phoenixes, his kind did not arise from their ashes. But, train or no train, a forest surrounded him. In it he was sure to find a cave or hollow tree that offered refuge. Though swifter than a deer, he could not outrun light.

It was only then that he remembered Tall Ann and her Night Owl Diner. Soon after, from the crest of a knoll, he was looking down on a neon sign welded to a vintage railroad dining car attached to a Pullman sleeper.

He noted the changes as he descended the slope. No trace of the siding remained and the cars now had a redwood rather than a cinder block foundation. Scrub behind the diner had given way to a fenced kitchen garden. And the formerly rusty cars had been painted a metallic ebony.

There were now only steps to the diner. Those of the sleeper had been removed and the space between cars enclosed. Any wishing to reach the sleeping compartments had to go through the diner.

Colby knew there had been a change in ownership when he entered and failed to see Tall Ann in the kitchen alcove. The new cook was a closely shaven young man with regular features and brunet coloring. Another young man—taller, paler and thinner but also wearing silver-gray cotton tunic and trousers—was pouring coffee for three truckers.

When he saw the cork bulletin board outside the kitchen alcove he immediately noted something missing from the menu.

"No more roadkill stew?" Colby asked. Tall Ann had been partial to it.

"Board of Health fined the previous owner when they found out it wasn't a joke."

"A fresh kill is a fresh kill."

"Try our omelet with bacon ends."

"My immediate need is for a bed in the Pullman," he said, dropping two crumpled U.S. Grants on the counter.

The cook took a long moment to reflect upon Colby's attire: blue suede half-boots, a chartreuse velvet coat, fuchsia silk shirt and pink satin trousers. One of what the vampire thought of as a "bully-bait" combination.

"You've passed this way before," said the cook, taking his money.

"And will again. A comet of sorts."

"'Twas a time when comets were dread portents."

"Only to the ignorant and superstitious." Referring to himself as a comet opened fewer questions than using the term *ange d'mort*.

The key to compartment three in hand, he went on into the enclosed space between cars, now housing a freezer and cabinets. The sleeper itself, rather than smelling of dust and mold, reeked of cleaning products. An odor made more tolerable by that of rose incense.

As they are not Asian, he reasoned, they are probably Catholic.

From the window, seeing that the sun was brushing the forest canopy, he drew the shade. The lower berth had been made up but he chose to open and spring into the upper. A cozy *billet du jour* with a small pillow, a thin blanket and a flock mattress.

When night made its return, Colby decided to prowl the nearby town. The shortest way was to follow the railroad tracks, and he was almost to the embankment when he heard a freight approaching from the south. Then he heard and saw a helicopter closing from the west and shining a powerful beam into the woodland below.

He stopped short of the gravel ballast and crouched behind an infant pine. After the diesel engine had rolled by, someone appeared in the door of a boxcar, dimly backlit by the helicopter's searching beam, They did not jump, though, till that car had passed Colby. And their leap became a tumble down the steep incline, arms gyrating.

It was only after the freight had rattled on north and the helicopter beat eastward that Colby heard bitter curses, groans, and other cries of baleful distress. But he could only guess by the jumper's bad luck until he reached the pit of woe and the full moon had emerged from cloud cover: the other lay entangled and struggling in coils of rusty barbed and razor wire.

There was near equipoise between how much the other's pain and hardship amused Colby and how much the sweet fragrance of blood excited him.

The other, struggling to escape the wire's thorny grasp, was peeling away clothing and spreading the pieces to form a bridge over the barbs: a high collared cape, a slouch hat and a frock coat. Each move and shift in weight was marked with a curse or a grimace. His wounds were many even if small, though no artery had been punctured or torn.

"You aren't the Phantom of the Opera," Colby observed. "He wears a mask and rarely strays from his sewer."

The man held himself motionless and stared—

though even with his enhanced night vision and a full moon it was difficult to see the eyes overcast by long hair and beetling brows. Then the other said:

"Listen! Bring dead branches and help me get free and you'll be paid."

"First you tell me why you're hunted. Jaywalkers and litterbugs don't rate a helicopter chase. And don't forget to mention if there is a reward."

The other bared costume fangs and hissed. "Do not mock or trifle with me, mortal!"

"Are you practicing for Halloween? The feast of Samhain?"

The other raised up and lunged toward Colby, and his desperate grab nearly succeeded. But while he failed, a coil of razor wire slashed his white dress shirt and lay open a *Dia de los Muertos* skull tattoo on his forearm.

Colby smiled. He liked nothing better than biting through body art. And in a feat of vampirish strength, he lunged and seized the bleeding arm, jerked the man nearer, and drank.

The other was overcome by spasms of disbelief, of outrage, then frenzy. *"The asylum doctors LIED!"* he howled. *"All the doctors lied! Vampires are real—REAL!!"*

Then, crazed with bitter resentment, he twisted and became further tangled in the cutting wire—without ceasing to rant about Colby's unworthiness: "You are a nothing, a loser punk kid! Unworthy of such grandeur and majesty! *I am the one who deserves to be a vampire!"*

"You may now take pride in having fed a vampire."

"Leave my sight you—*you clownish abomination!"*

Colby now heard a helicopter circling back and working its way along the railroad tracks. He reacted by springing onto the other's chest, rendered him unconscious, then levitating into the dense canopy of an oak and settling on a branch.

Little time elapsed before the airborne searchlight discovered the costumed vampire in his tangled web. The sounds of ground pursuit followed apace, with armed police rushing in from the major compass points. Relieved to find him alive and helpless, positively delighted when he revived to pain.

Colby listened as credit for the capture of the Full Moon Vampire was parceled out to fate, karma, personal gods, and sound police work. Some found humor in his being "wired" but others stayed angry, mindful of the serial killer's eleven known victims.

Another helicopter came with planks. After the fugitive had been tranquilized, EMTs stood on these boards to stanch and patch the worst of his punctures and lacerations. Then he was secured in a harness and flown away.

He revived long enough to return to his earlier theme: *"The shrinks lied!* You will cover up the truth with lies! *Vampires are real!"*

The costumed vamp, Colby told himself had given himself something to mull over while in prison. Before his appeals run out and they strap him down and bite him with a needle.

"He's sure to have a fan club," he said aloud.

* * *

Colby approached the diner with caution—though the police were clustered about their vehicles, consuming coffee and donuts or babbling into their cell phones. He assumed that media professionals had followed the captured fugitive.

Just inside the door a pair of female truckers had tea and vegetarian chili. The only other customers inside were a young couple in frock coats who had night vision goggles dangling about their necks. Open at their feet was a gladstone bag holding the de rigueur vampire hunter's kit: wooden stakes, a mallet, a string of whole garlics and vessels of holy water.

"Steampunk vampire-hunters?" he inquired. His silent judgement was: another pair from the League of Ordinary Wanna-bes.

They looked up from their meal of fried chicken, onion rings and Pepsi to tout that they had spotted the Full Moon Vampire first. Only to be shoved aside by the police.

"Did the media respect your claim?" Colby asked, sweetly.

"Oh yeah, they're respectful like cops!" said the shaggy-haired young man with a wispy beard. "But our phone pix show time, so screw 'em!"

"They held us back *for our own safety!"* said his companion. But her Kewpie doll face was more given over to pique than snarling resentment.

"Did he seem the formidable menace of myth and graphic novels?"

"Poser dressed like a Halloween Dracula." Then he added, with a greater sneer. "Jumped off train and landed in buncha barbwire. Talk 'bout a lame-ass loser!"

"Phonies are disgusting!" But her smirk did not hide a trace of disappointment.

"Do you want to slay a vampire," Colby asked, "or date one?"

The young man nudged the gladstone bag with his foot. "You show us one that's a real deal an' stan' back! You'll see."

When Colby reached the kitchen, the cook said, "I sense that one is only role playing. His companion, though … she hopes of actual contact."

Colby had not become a vampire by choice, but he would've had no quarrel with the change if … he'd looked nineteen when bitten. Instead, now as then, he was a half-inch short of sixty inches and was so adorably angelic that no one guessed his age at more than 14.

"Their 'lights' are drab, sickly," said the waiter. "In each grows roots of wickedness."

Only now, glancing slantwise at them, did Colby perceive that both cook and waiter had pale ghostly wings. *They are fallen angels!*

Instead of venturing a comment on that, he asked, "Tall Ann used to get Coca Cola syrup by the gallon. Mixed her own with added flavors."

"That hasn't changed," the cook said. "We have truckers who swear by Coke syrup. It's their cure-all."

Over the years Colby had found that it improved his guests 'blood to have them drink Coca Cola syrup and eat sugary cake with cream filling. The antipodes of holy water and communion wafers. And at that moment his gaze strayed to packages of Cane Boy Cupcakes.

"Killer sweet," said the cook, with a laugh. "Über sugary sponge cake filled with honey-flavored whipped cream."

"Perfection. Say no more. A liter of syrup and a dozen cakes."

"You're one of those," said the waiter, "who does not mind each cupcake shortening his life by an hour."

"Being my own pardoner," Colby said, "I am post liberal with indulgences."

The team of vampire-hunters came just then to pay for their meal.

"If you've fully embraced the steampunk ethos," the waiter jested, "why not travel in a steam-propelled vehicle?"

"Steampunk's only a cover story, dude," the young man told them, reaching under his frock coat for a 9mm automatic. "Now let's see how much yeh took in durin' th' vampire hunt."

"Just commonplace thieves," Colby said. "How dreary."

The barrel was pressed into his chest. "If you're aimin' f'r Goth, runty *poser*, y'only got t' feeble wanna-be."

"Even vampires can be eccentric."

The other snickered until Colby extended his canine teeth, at which the other's face sagged and his eyes bulged.

His companion was excited: "Oh Clyde, he is one…! *He truly truly is!*"

"Clyde?" The vampire was tickled. 'Named after the famous Clyde Wheelbarrow?"

Clyde blinked, swore, and put a shot into the diner ceiling. "Jus' more Halloween crap, Bonnie!" he shouted. "Them teeth's either wax or plastic."

"Stand still and I'll give you a bite."

"I ain't scared, I got th' firepower!"

"Am I afraid? I'm not even impressed."

"Guns can't hurt him, Clyde!" Bonnie squealed giddily.

"Yeah? You watch, Bonnie," said Clyde, jerking the trigger.

The deafening report stung Colby's ears and forced him a step back. Then, examining the tear, he rapped: "You put a hole in my silk shirt, moth-boy!"

"Armor—he's wearin' armor," Clyde babbled. "Chest protector!" Unable to convince even himself, his bladder emptied and the gun slipped from his fingers.

When Colby unbuttoned his shirt to catch the slug being rejected by his pale smooth chest, Bonnie inched toward him. When she was nearer, she held out her hand. When he dropped the bullet into her hand, she held it reverently, as if a precious relic. Trembling, she begged:

"Please, take me, please! Initiate me into the Blessed Dark Mystery! I'll be your slave. All I've ever wanted is to stay young forever!"

Her words enraged and outraged the waiter. "But your soul! Has it no value to you?"

"My soul?" she sneered. "It's nothing but a phantom, a spook." She spit the last word into his face, turned away, and renewed her plea to Colby.

"Then you believe eternal youth is worth dying for?" the vampire asked.

"*Yes! Oh yes!*"

The waiter, gripped by fury, twisted her head until her spine snapped. At which Clyde swore and moved to recover his handgun—but Colby forestalled and entranced him.

In the same moment the defrocked angel, horrified by his deed, folded in upon himself, fell to his knees, and began to sob. The cook came to embrace and comfort him.

"'Was it anger that caused your fall from grace?" Colby asked.

"Anger rooted in despair. We could no longer believe in human goodness."

"Humans are rather given to admiring evil," admitted the vampire.

"'We were able to stand against great evil," the cook said. "What wore us down was the trivial and quotidian cruelties … the petty and picayune selfishness."

The fallen angels moaned and held each other closer.

"Why don't you turn off your neon sign and close shop? I'll take out the trash."

"Were you sarcastic and cynical before you died?" asked the cook.

He nodded. "They may not qualify as virtues, but they keep me sane."

"Even as gallows humor has long helped Jews remain resilient."

* * *

An enthralled Clyde carried Bonnie to their dented black Mustang. The vampire drove to an overpass to nowhere, a span left unfinished due to graft and shoddy construction materials. The nominal barrier closing the road was decrepit and easily shattered. Then Colby stopped, put Clyde in the driver's seat, and told him:

"At my signal it's peddle to the metal, desperado! Up the high road to glory."

Onto the unfinished concrete roadway they went with Colby astride the Mustang's hood. At the top, where the arc ran out, the car vaulted toward the full moon and the vampire levitated. And from that perspective he visually drank the crushing of Bonnie and Clyde.

Yellow, Orange, Red

Yellow, orange, red.

The sun goes down
against the peaks.
Timeless signs of rock:
each sunrise new, each sunset old.

Sit, watch, and wonder.

Close your eyes on all you love,
then open them inside
and keep on watching.
Come in, enjoy, bathe into bliss.
It will go on, be sure, farther than you imagine,
far beyond the point you think you'll never reach.

The shades ascend
upon your walk.
Others will take over
and you'll be right where their footsteps fall.

Yellow, orange, red.

Then the deepest blue:
light slips into darkness,
letting stars appear
to greet more walks.

Be calm, do not despair, do learn:
despite the end
you will go on
in what begins then ends again.
And on, and on, and on,
after you have gone and afterwards.

Again the snow will come, again will go.

Thus life and everything you know,
along with all you don't.
The sun, the shades, the stars,
and each and every walk.

Yellow, orange, red.

— Alessio Zanelli

Bound

Story by Timothy Bastek & Taylor Packer
Illustration by Kathy Ferrell

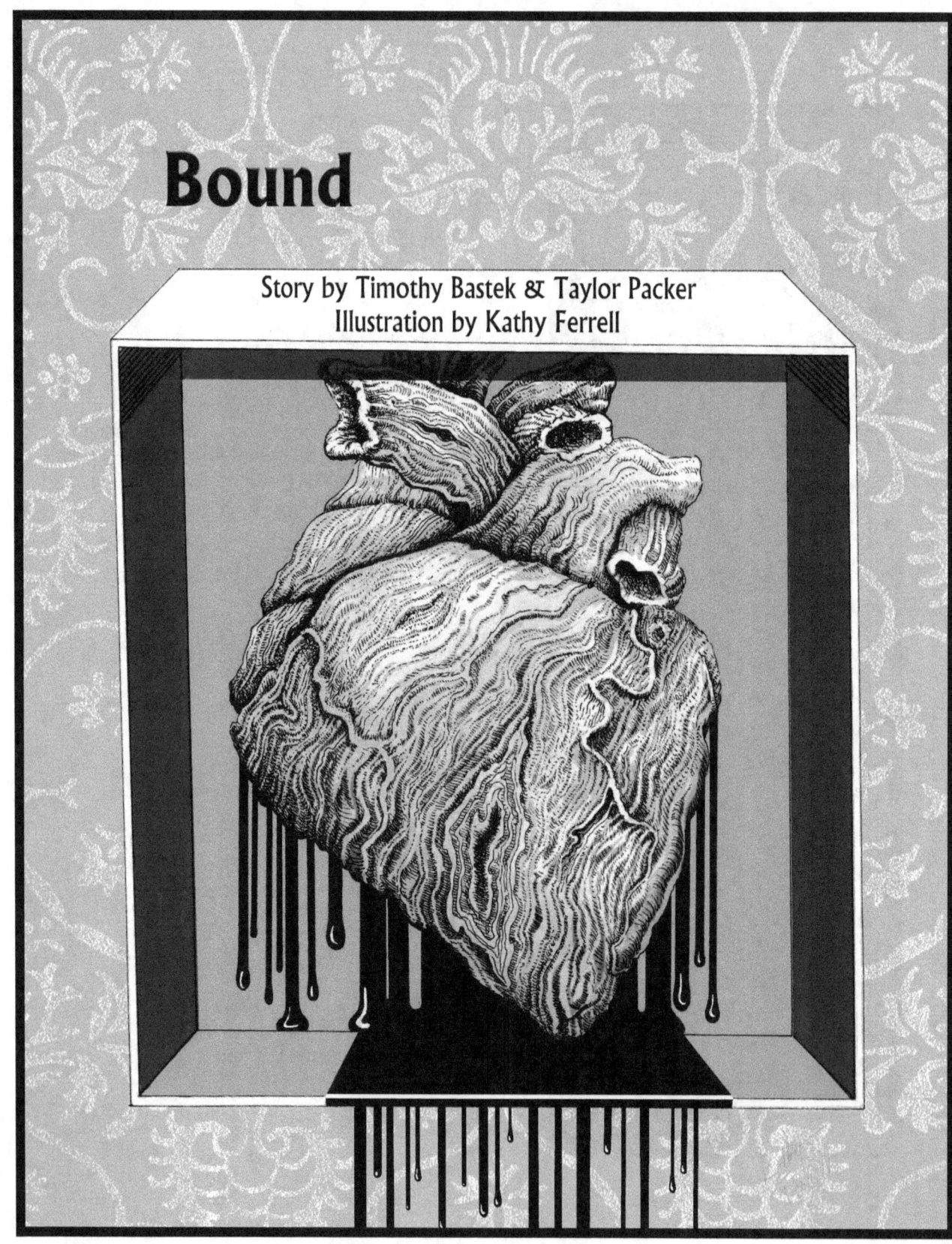

I

The woods were dead. The leaves that once hung from the branches had long since fallen to the ground and lay rotten and black, curled at the ends like the flaking skin of some great beast. Fierghus sat under a skeletal birch, wrapped in his heavy cloak. He pulled his hood up to shield his head from the light flurries of snow. He held his map of the Oakbourne Region and traced his route with his finger.

He had left Noradia two weeks ago and struck off through Oakbourne by ways of the old trade routes. No one used them anymore, so they were difficult to follow, but according to his map, they were the fastest way to Agornea, which was said to be home to the last living necromancer in the entire empire.

Fierghus put away the map and picked up the urn he had brought with him. As he held it, he could feel a pulse. Her pulse. He caressed the coarse surface and whispered condolences to the soul trapped inside. He longed to be with his betrothed once more; to see her, to touch her, to hold her in his arms.

He resumed his journey through the silent woods. He soon saw the towering plateau with Agornea's dark fortress perched at the top.

Some time later, he stood outside the abandoned village at the foot of the plateau. The houses were made from logs strapped together, many of them nothing more than black shells, remnants of a fire long forgotten. Maybe that's why the village was deserted. No one knew for sure. Fierghus remembered hearing stories about the place from his father, while he and his siblings sat around the evening fire many years ago. Stories about the Navari, fire demons, who invaded the village and slaughtered its people.

Once, when he had manned the merchant stalls in his hometown, Fierghus witnessed a story-teller in the town square who claimed the Four Divine had sent angels to purge the land of the necromancers' evil ways, and an old beggar on the road had said the necromancers had summoned some supernatural force that took all the people away.

Despite how different each tale was, they all agreed on the same thing: the village is cursed, and whosoever enters it never leaves, for the last remaining necromancer steals their soul and locks it deep within his fortress.

Fierghus remained at the entrance and told himself they were just stories. A sudden wind blew through the eaves and made a sound that reminded him of tortured prisoners. Other tales claimed demons prowled the woods and ghosts lurked in the empty homes.

Fierghus shuddered. "Come on; we're almost there," he said to the urn and stepped into the village. The only sounds he heard were his own footsteps and the screaming wind.

Whoever built Agornea didn't seem to follow any set plan. A single road stretched through the village, yet the houses on either side were placed at various distances from each other. A stone archway marked the trail to the fortress at the village's far end.

The stones were dark grey. They looked almost black in the pale light. The trail wove its way through the woods and up the plateau. Snow and ice covered the trail the higher he went and made the climb long and difficult. Fragments of a low wall stood at the outer edge of the trail. Where large chunks of the wall were missing, Fierghus held the urn with one hand and used the other to hang on to the large rocks protruding from the cliff's face. The wind whipped at him and threatened to push him off. The cold bit into his exposed flesh like burning steel. He gritted his teeth and pulled himself one-armed up the trail.

His foot slipped on the ice. He fell forward and struck his knee against the ground and slid backward on his stomach. He flung his free hand out and tried to hold onto something, anything, but found only ice and snow. The next moment he felt his legs pass over the edge. He grabbed a piece of the crumbling wall. Pain shot through his shoulder as his body jerked to a halt. The urn teetered in the crook of his arm and then it was midair and falling toward the woods below.

"*No!*" Fierghus screamed. He threw his free hand out and grabbed the urn and hurled it up the cliff. He watched as it soared through the air and landed in a small pile of snow. He sighed.

He dragged himself up over the edge and attempted to stand. His foot slid again and he grabbed the wall once more to prevent himself from sliding down the trail. He pulled against the wall and flung himself at the pile of snow where the urn had landed. He picked the urn up with both hands and stood slowly.

Near the top, the trail turned to the left and a long staircase ascended through a tunnel cut into the cliff. Fierghus entered the tunnel and slumped against the wall, glad to be out of the wind. He rested a few minutes and ate the last of his food: a piece of dried beef and a stale chunk of bread. He had depleted his water supply the day before and resorted to sucking on dirty ice to stay hydrated.

When his food was gone, he continued his climb up the stairs. The sun was setting as he emerged from the tunnel and stepped onto the top of the plateau. In the fading light, the snow turned a deep shade of grey and the woods looked as if they were covered in ash.

The fortress stood at the very edge. It had been constructed from the same dark stone that made up the archway. A wall with a large, iron door enclosed a small courtyard. The door hung open, as if inviting Fierghus to step through. He accepted the invitation.

Some of the towers had been built below the edge and around the cliff and clung to the plateau. The keep sat at the very back and was the tallest structure of the fortress. If the legends were true, the necromancer would be found there. Another door, this one made from wood, stood at the entrance to the keep. It was closed. When Fierghus approached it, he wasn't sure if he was supposed to knock or if he could just walk through. He went to open the door and found it unlocked.

Inside, a long, wooden table stood in front of a large fireplace. Three candelabras sat evenly spaced along the table's surface, each bearing three candles. Tall shelves lined the walls and were packed with books and scrolls. A fire had been lit and cast a warm glow throughout the room. A small cauldron sat on top of the fire. The smell that drifted through the air told Fierghus it contained stew. A spiral staircase stood to his left and wound up behind the wall. It was the only indication that the keep possessed more rooms.

Fierghus was the only one in the room. He attempted to call out, but all that came out was a hoarse whisper. He cleared his throat and attempted once more. His greeting echoed up the stairs and through the keep. When no one came, he called out again.

"Why have you come, traveler?" said a voice behind him. Fierghus spun around and saw a tall man at the door. He held a bundle of firewood in his arms. Deep red hair hung past his shoulders like a curtain of blood. He wore long, grey robes, the color of the necromancers from long ago. He was a lot younger than Fierghus expected. Fierghus didn't place him much older than he was himself.

"Are you the necromancer?" Fierghus asked.

"I am the one who resides in the fortress," the man said. He strode over to the fireplace and set the wood on the floor. He glanced at the boiling stew and grabbed some heavy cloths and heaved the cauldron off the fire. He dipped a wooden ladle into the stew, drew it toward his mouth, and blew on it. Tasted it. Smiled. He began scooping stew into two wooden bowls.

"Please," Fierghus said, "you must help me."

"Let me guess," the man said as he worked. "Someone close to you has died and you want me to bring them back to life."

"It's my betrothed."

The man glanced at Fierghus. "Where's the body?"

"Excuse me?"

"The body. Or at least part of it. In order to resurrect someone, you need a piece of or the entire body for the process to work."

"I didn't bring her body. I couldn't."

"Then how do you expect to be reunited with your dearly departed?" His tone held the note of mockery.

Fierghus drew back his cloak and revealed the urn. "I brought her soul."

The man's eyes flashed, yet Fierghus didn't notice.

"I figured we could find a new body and you could put her soul into that. That should work … shouldn't it?"

"In theory, yes," the man said. He motioned Fierghus to come to his side and offered him one of the bowls. "Come, eat. I know the climb up the cliff is no stroll through the woods. Then tell me how you managed to get a hold of your betrothed's soul."

Fierghus ate in silence and stared at the floor. It wasn't until the man prodded him with more questions that he told how he met his betrothed, how she had been taken from him by a powerful druid, and how he enlisted the help of another druid and his apprentice to rescue her. All the while, the man listened intently and shot glances at the urn by Fierghus' side.

"He turned her into a tree," Fierghus said, his tale drawing to a close. "The evil druid who took my betrothed turned her into a tree to prevent her from leaving his side. And when she uprooted herself and crushed him, she died. I looked over at the other two, but they had abandoned me. I didn't know what to do. I was lost. I was alone. Then, I remembered the tales about this fortress, about you, and knew I could be with my beloved once more."

"Yes, but her soul," the man said and leaned forward. "How did you get her soul?"

Fierghus paused, startled by the man's impatience. "I carved it out of her, with my sword. At the very center, I found her heart, a gnarled mass of wood, which emitted the same black sap that had poisoned the forest and the town. I knew her tortured soul was locked therein."

The man reached out. "May I see it?"

Fierghus clutched the urn with both hands. He saw the man's manic grin, his wild eyes. He became suspicious and afraid.

The man noticed and calmed himself. "You want to be with your beloved once more, do you not?" he asked.

"Yes."

"Then trust me and give me her soul."

Fierghus reluctantly handed the urn to the man, who took it in both his hands. He sighed and caressed its sides. He tried to pry the lid off, but it refused to budge. "What's sealing it?"

"The heart never ceased emitting the sap," Fierghus said. "It sealed the lid shut."

"Yes..." He fingered the black stains and sealed cracks where the sap attempted to break free. He held it carefully as he wrapped his cloak once more around his shoulders. He headed towards the door. Fierghus asked where he was going, but he ignored him. Fierghus followed as he stepped outside and wondered who this man could be.

II

His name was Thanasis. He was a diplomat-turned-thief from the southern country of Viran, a land populated with bogs, lakes, and low, sloping hills. He had been convicted of stealing a book said to contain powerful, yet dangerous, magic. The king of Viran wanted to use this magic to restore his kingdom to its former glory. Only Thanasis saw the folly in this plan, and stole the book and fled from justice. He made it as far as Agornea, in Erihelm, where he collapsed from exhaustion, but not before the Viranese officials who followed him wounded him, reclaimed the book, and left him for dead.

When Thanasis awoke, he found himself unbound and naked in a bed with the covers pulled up over his chest. A dark shape hovered over him. As his eyes focused, the shape transformed into a withered face with a long, white beard and hair.

"Ah, good, you're awake," the old man said. His voice was soft and calm.

"Where are my clothes?" Thanasis asked.

"I burned them. They were so torn and filthy, there was no way to mend them, and I'm terrible with a needle, so it's all for the best in the end. I laid out some of my robes on the chair next to you. They may be a bit too big, but at least you won't have to go running around in the nude." The old man smiled

and patted Thanasis on the leg.

"Who are you?"

"Lysandor is my name."

Thanasis noticed the old man's grey robes. "You're a necromancer ... aren't you?"

"That I am, and the last one in the Empire, as far as I'm aware. And who might you be? I detect from your accent you are not from the Imperial proper."

Thanasis introduced himself and told Lysandor about his homeland and the troubles it faced. As he spoke, Lysandor just sat and smiled, his eyes sparkling with delight. When he finished, Lysandor invited him to come to the keep when he felt strong enough. "I've prepared stew for you. I know it's too early in the year, but I figured you would want something easy to eat after your excitement in the village."

Once Lysandor left, Thanasis lay back and looked around the room. Beds lined the walls on either side, each accompanied by a writing desk and a wooden chest. A massive fireplace stood against the wall behind him.

He put on the robes Lysandor had given him and discovered the old man had spoken true. The sleeves hung past his hands and he had to hold the hem off the ground to avoid tripping.

Once they finished their meal, Lysandor took him back to the bunkhouse. "Unfortunately, my room is the only one with a bed in the keep, so you'll have to stay in here," he said. "It's where the necromancers-in-training slept. If you get cold at night, feel free to light a fire. There's a room beside the fireplace where you'll find wood."

"I'm not staying," Thanasis said.

"But, you must."

"No, I have to return home. My people are in danger and I'm the only one who realizes the king must be stopped before he opens that book and releases who knows what darkness upon the land."

"Thanasis," Lysandor said calmly, "you need your rest. You've been up for only a few hours. You are in no shape to travel all the way back to Viran. Stay and rest."

Thanasis sighed. He knew the old man was right, but the thought of the king opening that book terrified him. "Fine," he said, "but the moment I regain my strength, I'm leaving."

He helped Lysandor with small tasks around the fortress to keep himself busy: tidying up the keep, cooking meals, and cleaning the bunkhouse. By the end of the third week, he was splitting firewood. He was ready to leave.

That night, Thanasis thought the old man entered the bunkhouse and approached his bedside, but when he woke in the dead of night, the room was empty. He passed it off as a dream, despite how real it seemed. He had felt Lysandor clasp his hand in both of his. The old man whispered something, but Thanasis wasn't able to hear the words. Lysandor let go with one hand and reached into his robes. He pulled something out that rattled in the air. Thanasis didn't see what it was, but by the sound, he thought it was some sort of chain. Lysandor muttered to himself, and again, Thanasis wasn't able to hear what was said. The rest of the dream escaped him.

The following morning, Lysandor came into the bunkhouse as Thanasis packed his few belongings.

"You're leaving," the old man said.

"Yes."

"Won't you stay? Please? I've thoroughly enjoyed your company." He wrung his hands together.

"I can't."

"Aren't you a wanted man?"

"My people are in danger. I can't just abandon them, even if that means I am walking into the arms of my enemies." He thanked Lysandor for his hospitality and left.

When he reached the foot of the plateau, a wave of fatigue washed over him. The closer he approached the village's border, the more it felt as if a great weight was pressing down on his shoulders. He repositioned his pack and continued on his way, but it didn't seem to help. Once he reached the edge of the village, Thanasis could go no further. He attempted to put one foot in front of the other, but his body refused to move. The invisible weight on his shoulders increased to such an extent that he could hardly breathe. The only option left to him was to turn around and go back the way he had come. The further he walked from Agornea's border, it no longer felt like he was being crushed from above.

Once he returned to the fortress, he marched into the keep and found the old man sitting by the fireplace preparing dinner. Lysandor looked over and smiled.

"What did you do to me?" Thanasis dropped his pack and crossed the room so he was face-to-face with the necromancer.

Lysandor's smile vanished. "You have to understand," he said, "I couldn't allow you to leave."

"Tell me what you did." He grabbed Lysandor's robes and pulled him in close. "Answer me, or by your precious Four, I *will* kill you."

Lysandor bowed his head. "Your soul," he murmured.

"What?"

"It's your soul. I bound it to the fortress to keep you from leaving."

Thanasis stared at him for a moment, his eyes glaring into Lysandor's. He screamed in rage and pushed the necromancer against the wall. "You have no right!" He paced around the room with his hands burrowed in his hair. "Release me!"

Lysandor pushed himself from the wall. "No, I won't."

"My country needs me."

"Oh, damn your country, and your king! They don't want you. They don't need you. Not like how I need you. After all the years of silence and solitude, I finally have someone to talk to. Someone real." He approached Thanasis and reached out to touch his face.

Thanasis slapped his hand away. "Stay away from me."

Lysandor recoiled, his shoulders hunched.

A month passed. Thanasis spent all his time in the bunkhouse and refused to speak with Lysandor, and when he finally did emerge, Lysandor treated him like a pet. He would brush his bony fingers through Thanasis' long hair or rub his hand along his back in passing. Each time, Thanasis struck his hand away and Lysandor would shrink back then scold him like he was a misbehaving dog. And Thanasis would beg to be released, and every time, Lysandor refused.

At night, Thanasis would sneak into the keep and read the books on soul binding, yet even though he understood the language, the words were cryptic. Lysandor caught him in his research and yelled at his prisoner and rained blows against his face and chest. Then, he knelt and took Thanasis in his arms, sobbing and apologizing. From then on, the necromancer kept those books locked away.

One day, Thanasis sat outside, skinning and gutting a rabbit for dinner. He paused in his work and stared at the knife, then glanced up at the keep. In many stories about curses, the heroes were able to break free by slaying the one who bestowed the curse upon them. Did they hold any truth? Could it work? He finished with the rabbit, then slid the knife into his robes.

He crept into the keep that very night. He quietly ascended the stairs and slowly pushed open the door to Lysandor's room. Moonlight poured in through the window and spilled across the room. Lysandor lay on his back. His white hair and beard shone in the pale light. Thanasis stood in the doorway and drew the knife. His heart pounded in his chest and echoed in his ears. He clutched the knife in a bone-white fist and approached the bed. He stood over the old man for a moment, then raised the knife and plunged it into his chest. The blade slid through the flesh and bone with a startling lack of resistance.

Creaking laughter drifted through the air behind him. Thanasis turned and saw Lysandor standing behind the door, his beard and hair considerably shorter. "Did you honestly think I didn't see you hide that little knife of yours?"

Thanasis stood dumbfounded. He glanced at the figure in the bed. It was nothing more than a man made from grass and straw. "No," Thanasis murmured. "No." Then he screamed the word, his voice cracking with the strain. He gripped the knife tighter and charged at the grinning necromancer.

"Stop!" Lysandor said. His voice boomed across the room and Thanasis could feel it reverberate through his entire body and he stopped. "Put the knife down."

Beyond his control, his knees bent and he knelt against the floor and dropped the knife. He buried his face in his hands and broke down in sobs. "No," he said. "No. No. No."

Lysandor knelt beside him, wrapped his arms around him, and pulled him in close. "Shhh," he said. "Everything will be okay. Don't cry, my son." He kissed the top of Thanasis' head and smoothed back his hair. "Shhh."

Thanasis looked at the knife. He reached out his hand, but Lysandor said, "No. Don't pick up the knife." His voice carried the same power, and once again, Thanasis found himself obeying the command. He cried all the harder. He attempted to grab the knife again with a single image in his mind: the blade sticking from Lysandor's corpse.

"Stop!" Lysandor demanded.

Thanasis' hand inched closer to the hilt.

"Thanasis, stop this at once!" His voice grew more frantic.

In his mind, he saw himself drive the knife into Lysandor's heart. He finally grasped the hilt.

"Stop, Thanasis! Please!"

He stabbed the blade into the old man's chest. Lysandor gasped. His words no longer dominated his body. Thanasis stabbed him again. And again. And again. He finally stood and let the knife clatter to the floor. Lysandor's body slumped to the side, his eyes and mouth wide open in shock. A dark stain grew along his chest. Thanasis resisted the urge to vomit, then turned away.

He looked down at himself, almost expecting to see a change. Had it worked? Was he free? He didn't feel any different, but then again, he hadn't noticed when Lysandor first bound his soul. Not until he tried to leave.

He ran from the keep and fled down the trail. He didn't bother to pack food or water. All he cared about was putting Agornea far behind. As he ran through the empty village, the ever familiar crushing weight descended on his shoulders. He continued to push forward, almost in denial, until the weight forced him to halt. He fell to his knees and let out a long moan.

All hope was lost.

There was no escape.

He buried his face in his hands once more and collapsed in the dirt as heavy sobs shook his entire body.

The months that followed were long and lonely. He found the books Lysandor had hidden from him and spent his days researching. He finally began to make sense of the words. According to the books, his soul would in fact be bound to an object, which would in turn be bound to a portion of the fortress. In order to free himself, he would need to find another soul to replace his own and command the second soul to stay.

Thanasis searched the entire fortress until he found a chamber located in a tower below the edge of the plateau. Inside, wooden shelves towered overhead. They were all filled with empty lanterns, each intricately designed, each with broken glass and dead candles. What they had been for was beyond Thanasis' knowledge. On the floor, in the very center of the room, lay a pair of iron shackles. The very same shackles Thanasis had worn when he stumbled upon Agornea. He attempted to pick them up, but they refused to budge. No more than he expected.

He sat next to the shackles and stroked them. "Soon," he whispered. "Soon. I promise." But where would he find another soul? Nobody dared to approach the haunted village. Nobody was foolish enough.

III

Night had fallen. Flurries of snow lashed at their faces as the wind howled around them. Fierghus drew up his hood and pulled his cloak tight around his body. Thanasis marched forward, oblivious to the cold. They descended a flight of stairs and arrived at the chamber of lanterns. Thanasis held Fierghus back.

"Wait here."

"What do you intend to do?" Fierghus asked.

"Patience." He took a key from his pocket and unlocked the door.

"Please, I can help. I've done research. I know the theories."

"No," Thanasis said. "I must do this alone."

Fierghus forced his way past as Thanasis opened the door. Thanasis ordered him to leave the chamber, but Fierghus refused. He was not going to leave his betrothed alone, not after everything he went through to bring her here.

"As you wish," Thanasis said. He strode to the center of the room and smashed the urn against the floor.

Fierghus let out a cry of horror. He rushed toward Thanasis. "What are you doing?"

Thanasis shoved him back and commanded him to be silent. He glanced back at the wooden heart that now sat next to his shackles. A thick, black sap oozed from the cracks in the heart. Thanasis smiled. Fierghus had spoken true: a soul rested inside the heart, for only a soul could emit such a powerful substance. A twisted, tortured soul, yes, but it was still a soul.

He paced the floor, unsure of how to proceed. He tried a variety of commands, altering his tone, his inflection, yet nothing seemed different. He raked his fingers through his hair and took in a breath of frustration. The books were never clear on how to make the command.

Fierghus watched in confusion. "What are you doing?"

"Silence!" He thought back to when Lysandor commanded him to release the knife, thought back to how the old man shaped the words, how they sounded, how they carried power. Thanasis stood before the wooden heart and tried to imitate Lysandor's voice. He commanded the woman's soul to remain in the fortress. He felt resistance so he said the command with a stronger voice.

A low wailing crept into the air. It came from the center of the room, where the heart sat, and grew louder and louder until it became almost too much to bear. Fierghus added his own voice to the wail and attacked Thanasis. He grabbed Thanasis' arm and pulled him away from the heart.

"Stop!" he said. "You're hurting her!"

Thanasis shoved Fierghus back and shouted for Fierghus to stand down. Fierghus released his arm and remained where he stood, confused. He hadn't meant to cease his attack.

Thanasis turned away from Fierghus. "Release me from my imprisonment," he said to the heart. "Remain here and rot!" Thanasis felt a shift in the air. He ran forward and picked up his shackles. He smiled in triumph.

The next moment, Fierghus struck him in the jaw and knocked him to the ground. Before Thanasis knew what happened, the other man was on him, raining blows and demanding him to bring back his betrothed. Thanasis attempted to command Fierghus to halt, but his words no longer held power. He strained to break free from Fierghus' grip, but Fierghus was too strong. Thanasis drew his knife from his belt and slashed the blade forward. Fierghus clutched at his face and screamed. Thanasis kicked him back and stood. He grabbed his shackles once more and fled from the chamber.

The storm had picked up and he had to fight his way through knee-high snow once he reached the village. As he struggled his way toward the border, he kept expecting to feel the crushing weight. Yet, it never came. Closer and closer he stepped, until he finally broke free of Agornea's border. He stared down at his body, then back at the village. An uncontrollable giddy laughter possessed him. He was truly free.

Thanasis wrapped his heavy cloak closer around his body and fled deeper into the woods. Not once did he look back.

IV

Inside the chamber of lanterns, Fierghus knelt on the stone floor and clutched at his bleeding face. Sobs ripped from his body and echoed up through the tower. He crawled toward the heart and placed both hands around it, unconcerned about the black sap that continued to pulse from the haunted soul within. Fierghus attempted to lift it from the floor, but it would not budge. All he could do was kneel before the poisoned heart of his betrothed. He had failed her again.

Fried Okra

with a wave of her hand
Mama made magnolias bloom

at the 4th of July picnic
she held back a lightning storm
by a steely upheld fist
giving us children time
to race for cover

when Mama McGregor's AC failed
she murmured her incantations
until cool air caressed our faces

but Mama's best magic was Sunday dinner
fried chicken, mustard greens,
and the sizzle of fried okra
hot golden balls cornmeal-crisp
a crunch and gush between my teeth

all the rest of the magic
it just happened, but this
was something we made together
Gramma's oil-speckled recipe
our cantrip
my hands gloved in cornmeal
the oil scent so heavy
it still weighs on my tongue

— Beth Cato

Metamorphos

Story by Kathryn Yelinek
Illustration by Teresa Tunaley

A crunching sound behind the collection tent startled Norah to her feet. The automata Terra motored round the corner, her wheels scraping over the pebbles and seal bones that made up the beach.

Norah's stomach cramped. "It's okay," she whispered to the ptarmigan she'd been trying to feed. It wasn't, though. She never knew what to expect by a visit from one of her husband Dr. Reynolds's automati. The ptarmigan, a plump brown and gray bird, cowered in its cage.

Terra rolled to a stop. She had a rigid metal face, a barrel chest, and stubby hands with three fingers each, which she wiped clumsily on her shapeless dress. She looked quite out of place with the beautiful slate gray waters and elegant icebergs of Spirit Sound behind her.

"You have been summoned." Her voice grated from a box in her throat.

"What does he want?" Norah asked, fighting to keep her voice steady. A summons from Dr. Reynolds—she could think of him no other way—rarely ended well.

In reply, Terra creaked at her, a noise that could mean *Don't ask stupid questions* or *Hurry up, you* or *Look what I have to put up with.* Maybe all three. She jerked up the ptarmigan's cage. The bird panicked, throwing itself against the bars, wings thrashing, feathers flying.

Alarmed, Norah reached for the cage. "Let me—"

A grinding noise from Terra stopped her short.

"Metamorphos do not leave the tent," Terra said.

"My apologies." Even though Norah itched to pluck the cage back, she bowed her head and kept her hands by her sides. It was, she'd learned quickly, the only acceptable response in Dr. Reynolds's world.

Terra clanked, a scoffing noise, but she released the cage when Norah took it. Norah hurried into the collection tent before Terra could say anything else. "It's okay," she murmured, half to the ptarmigan. "We're going to be okay."

Inside the tent, dozens of eyes watched her slide the ptarmigan into its place next to a raven and a snow goose. Loons, snow buntings, and sandpipers shifted in their cages. From behind a curtain came the stirrings of gyrfalcons, snowy owls, gulls, and hawks. Further back, butterflies and mosquitoes, foxes and wolves, lemmings and hares, seals and walruses, paced or fluttered in their cages. Now, during the day, each looked like a normal animal, but dusk was coming. As soon as darkness fell, each one would change, and the tent would be filled with all manners of fairies, pixies, gnomes, griffins, and nixies.

Norah patted the ptarmigan's cage. "You eat something, all right?"

The ptarmigan lunged, beak open.

Norah stumbled back, yanking her hand away from the cage, lucky to have escaped a bite.

"Dr. Reynolds called for you," Terra said from the doorway.

Norah pressed her hand to her chest. She could never be sure how the metamorphos would act this close to their changing time. Their restlessness seemed to be catching, and it made her even more nervous about this summons from Dr. Reynolds. With unsteady fingers, she combed her hair and smoothed her parka. Then she pocketed a few nails that lay on the table by the cages, to use on the trip to his tent. "I'm coming."

She took the long way, past the cook shack and supply pile, where Dr. Reynolds's Esquimaux packed nets, traps, and cages into wooden boxes. Stones and bones crunched under her boots. The air smelled of ice and brine, and she breathed deeply, filling her lungs with sky and sea and tundra, and for those few breaths the knots in her stomach eased. She'd been a country girl before Dr. Reynolds bought her, and she wished for a few more days before the whaling ship would carry them back to Philadelphia, a few more days before the city swallowed her up in its noise and smoke and cramped, close salons.

Terra creaked, and Norah walked faster, skirting the half dozen unicorn horns laid out by Dr. Reynolds's tent, causing his guard automatum Spiro to bark at her. Little more than a rolling box with jaws on top, it snapped at her until she tossed her handful of nails behind it. It whirled and set on them, sharp teeth crunching.

Even in death the unicorn horns shone faintly. They had been provided by the Esquimaux, for Dr. Reynolds had never caught a unicorn, barely even caught sight of one in its daytime narwhal aspect, though not for lack of trying. Norah let herself linger by the horns. How could drab old Philadelphia compare to the many sights she'd yet to see here?

At the door to Dr. Reynolds's tent, Terra surprised Norah by bowing low to her. "Goodbye."

Norah blinked. "What do you mean? He's not getting rid of you?"

In reply, Terra swiveled and rapped on the wooden box that served as a door knocker.

"Enter."

At that crisp voice, sweat coated Norah's palms. "Terra," she whispered, "what's going on?"

Terra rolled back and gestured Norah inside. "Dr. Reynolds called for you."

So Norah stepped inside with her mind working furiously. It was a large tent, almost as large as the collection tent, with a curtain that screened the back sleeping section. She half expected to see a scientist from the scientists' outpost ten miles up the Sound, because their visits always put Dr. Reynolds in a black mood, and she could imagine that Terra had meant he intended to trade her to the scientists. But he was alone with his automatus Ignis.

As usual, they ignored her as she entered. Walking softly, careful not to step on any of the crucibles or beakers or wadded up papers that littered the floor, Norah took up her usual place in the corner. She bowed her head, clasped her hands in front of her, and kept her ears open.

"It will work," Dr. Reynolds said as he leaned back in his chair. His face beneath his beard was baked red from the Arctic sun, and he wore black gloves, the two smallest fingers of the left one stuffed to hide where he'd lost the fingers to frostbite. "The Esquimaux insist one is there. They won't lie to me. I've made sure of it."

Ignis shook his head. He had a fully expressive face and wore a woolen suit. His lips moved as he spoke. "I don't like it. We should have tried four days ago when the moon wasn't in Aries."

Dr. Reynolds glared at Ignis. By far the most sophisticated automatus that Norah had ever seen, Ignis had been specially designed to serve as a valet and assistant to Dr. Reynolds, probably, Norah thought, because no human would want the job. Certainly Dr. Reynolds didn't seem to appreciate him.

"The sun and Venus are both in Leo. We're fine. I got the griffin under worse signs, remember. I'll get this, too, and dare any scientist to call me a failure."

Norah squeezed her hands together. A collection trip? Did she really get to leave camp on another collection trip? A final day under the wide tundra sky would almost be worth trapping more animals.

"We only have tonight," Ignis said, "and maybe tomorrow. Captain Williamson won't hold the *Magus*."

"Then we stop yapping and get out there." The front legs of Dr. Reynolds's chair thudded to the floor.

Ignis handed him his parka. "You sure the girl is the right bait?"

"Why do you think I've kept her like this?"

Norah flushed. Ignis might be only an automatus, but she still didn't like him knowing her private life. Dr. Reynolds had married her because his academic reputation would have suffered if he'd been caught traveling to the Arctic with an unmarried woman, but he hadn't touched her since he shoved the ring on her finger.

Ignis squinted at her. She kept herself from glaring back. "She's gotten bony. Aren't you feeding her?"

"Terra takes care of that." Dr. Reynolds strode to his trunk and threw it open. "Get the bear gun. We're leaving."

Norah froze as Ignis rolled to the gun cabinet. The bear gun? That was a weapon to tranquilize a polar bear, not a hawk or a lemming or even a caribou. What could Dr. Reynolds possibly expect her to catch this late in the expedition?

"Terra said that some of the seal meat has started to turn." Ignis's voice echoed inside the cabinet. "Should we take some in case the ogre doesn't like girl?"

Ogre? They liked their meat fresh, preferably still kicking.

Norah bolted. As she darted through the tent flaps, Dr. Reynolds shouted. She spun right and leaped over the unicorn horns. Spiro charged her, barking, but she ran past him, out of his range, and the barking fell away. She dashed out of their camp, towards the stream where she drew water each morning. Automati were terribly fast, but they had trouble crossing water. If she made it—

A whirring sound rushed up behind her then a yank on her parka hood jerked her back.

She fell, landing on her bottom, the jolt rattling up her neck and jaw. Ignis hauled her up, but not before she'd grabbed a handful of grass. Then Ignis had her, she was captive in his metal grip, and as they raced back to camp she could only hope that she'd managed to grab something poisonous to ogres.

Ignis set her on her feet in front of the tent as Dr. Reynolds came out, three guns slung over his shoulders and a bag in each hand. Ignis kept a grip around her arms and over her mouth.

"That was stupid," Dr. Reynolds said. He frowned, obviously upset that Ignis had to restrain her rather than carry some gear.

"Do you want her tranquilized?" Ignis asked.

"No."

"It would be kinder. For her."

"I'm not wasting my supplies. Come on."

Dr. Reynolds headed west along the shoreline, lugging his supplies, and Ignis trailed, dragging her behind. She was on her feet, with the plants in her pockets, and that was better than being carried like a dead seal. On her feet she could try to run, if only she could incapacitate Ignis.

But first they turned inland along the banks of a slow, wide river. Here the ground turned to tundra of low grasses, lichens, and ground-hugging shrubs interspersed with little white flowers, and Norah's heart sank. She didn't want to go this way, didn't want to be dragged along this river. They had taken this path a week ago when they moved to the beach camp. A two-day hike up the river led to the natural philosophists' research station, where they had over wintered, and where, for a few days at a time when Dr. Reynolds was away, she had been happy. She didn't want to die along this path.

She stumbled over a particularly rocky patch of ground, throwing herself against Ignis, trying to tip him over. But he didn't falter. He pulled her up, his fingers maintaining an iron grip around her wrist. She stumbled again, slamming harder against him, and he slowed, stooping to help her up, tutting over her banged knees, shifting their path a little so they avoided the rockiest spots.

Norah cursed under her breath. Did he have to be so nice? The third time she stumbled, Ignis yanked at her hand, twisting her wrist.

"I'm trying to make this as easy on you as I can. But try to knock me over again, and I'll break your ankles."

She scoffed. "I'm supposed to feel grateful to you?"

"Feel whatever you want. Just don't do that again."

She tried to pull her hand back, but that must have been the final negative in Ignis's calculation of her. He pulled her arm up and lifted her, carrying her pinned to his chest. It was more uncomfortable than before, even after Norah decided to save her strength and laid still. She rested her check against the locked door in his chest, behind which lived the metamorpho whose nightly transformations provided the energy to run him. What it was, she couldn't say—something a bit larger than usual to account for his intelligence and emotions. A sphinx, perhaps, or a dwarf dragon, creatures she hadn't known existed before she came to Dr. Reynolds. Right now, she would have preferred ignorance.

What horrific machines could he run on the energy of an ogre?

She tried not to think about the possibilities as they traveled for another hour, while the temperature dropped and the sun slipped below the horizon, bringing on the twilight that was the only night the tundra saw this time of year. She fished in her pockets, pulling out the plants she'd grabbed by the camp. But she'd snatched all grasses and lichen with none of the poppies or buttercups that were supposed to repel metamorphos. She tossed them away in disgust.

Then Dr. Reynolds stopped.

Ignis rolled to a halt. "Here?"

"Yes." Dr. Reynolds knelt, dropping his bags to the stunted grass.

Norah, cold and stiff, stirred enough to see that they had stopped beside a small falls. The river ran narrower and faster here, the water rushing down a series of small cascades. It was a wild, desolate place, lonely and hard, the kind of place where no one wanted to die.

Ignis knelt and set her down. She twisted to get away from him, but she was chilled and slow, and he pinned her to the ground.

Soon Dr. Reynolds crouched at her shoulder, pulling aside her parka hood. "Hold still."

She caught a glimpse of what he held in his hands: a locket-sized metal box that could only be a shock box. She yelled and tried to throw herself sideways, but Ignis held her in place.

Dr. Reynolds pressed the box to the left side of her neck. It seemed to burn against her skin. Then a collar snapped around her throat, holding the box in place. She heard the key click that locked the collar closed. Fear clawed at her heart.

Ignis let go, but she lay frozen, dread weighing her down. Already he and Dr. Reynolds had retreated further upriver, to a rocky shelf that overlooked where she lay. They erected their blind, a misshapen mound that could just pass as a boulder amid the smaller rocks. Not extravagant, it would still be a comfortable location to watch her being eaten.

She sat up gingerly, rubbing her bruised arms, and turned her back on the blind. The river churned below her on her left, a black, burbling ribbon that cared only about reaching the Sound. Yellow still banded the western horizon, darkening overhead to a grayish blue that was not dark enough for the encouraging lights of stars. In the east, the waning gibbous moon hung like a ghostly light. It was a strange, in between kind of time, not quite night but no longer day.

She fingered the box and collar around her neck. Dr. Reynolds had used the same kind of device on his sled dogs at the research station. In the box was a tiny pixie, one half of a bonded pair. Somewhere nearby he would have left another box containing the pixie's bonded mate. If she tried to leave the vicinity, the distressed pixie around her neck would shock her with an agonizing, debilitating jolt. It made an effective invisible fence, and after she'd seen what it did to the sled dogs, she had no desire to test it.

Nor did she want to be dinner. Where had Dr. Reynolds hidden the other box?

There were no large rocks suitable for hiding it, just a scraggly carpet of matted grass and low-lying shrubbery. He must have buried it quickly when he put down his bags. And she hadn't thought to mark the spot.

Cautiously, alert to any warning buzzes against her throat, she moved to where he might have set his bags. The ground didn't appear disturbed, but Ignis and Dr. Reynolds had left tracks. Perhaps they had tramped down the box.

She blew out her breath, frustrated that she had to search for a box rather than preparing defenses against an ogre, but set to work. Systematically she scoured the area where Dr. Reynolds might have knelt, prodding the grass as far as she could reach before sliding sideways and starting over with a new patch of earth. She poked at flowers and clumps of dirt and bits of lichen, pocketing any decent sized stones that her fingers found. They would make minimal weapons against an ogre, but she would take what she could get.

She'd just seized a black stone the size of her fist when it struck her that she'd been at these falls before. Dr. Reynolds had brought her here in September and again in late May, instructing her to sit out on the rocks to attract a unicorn. She sat back on her heels, wondering. If she had caught a unicorn for him, would she now be here? Or was this more than a punishment? Maybe he had always meant to set her out like this, no matter what she caught for him.

A scrape sounded behind her. Norah started and swung around, flinging the black stone. It smacked Ignis square in the chest, thudding with a deep echo. He rocked, nearly tipping, and Norah scrambled to her feet. She zinged off another stone as he surged forward, grabbing her under the chin and lifting her to her toes. One moment she was on her toes, swinging at him, then he'd turned her head and something cut her high along her left cheek.

He let go. She stumbled back, and in that moment, the pain came, searing the length of her cheek bone.

Ignis leaned down and wiped his knife along the grass. "Dr. Reynolds says to stop nosing about, to sit still and bring him an ogre. This should help."

Norah pressed her hand to her cheek. Tears pricked her eyes, and she wondered if the blade had been poisoned. She was bleeding freely, the blood hot against her fingers.

"There are two here already."

Ignis froze in mechanical confusion. Then he whirred back to life and snapped his knife closed. "Very witty."

He rolled back to the blind, and Norah sank down on her haunches, utterly lost as to where she'd stopped her hunt for the box. She pressed both hands to her cheek, rocking in pain and shock and cold. Which would be worse? That an ogre came and devoured her, or an ogre didn't come and Dr. Reynolds left her here to starve? He wouldn't take her back to Philadelphia, not now.

The donors would fall over themselves, fêting the natural philosophist who had tragically lost his young wife. His next expedition would be paid for before the ravens finished cleaning her bones.

Movement caught the corner of her eye, something moving along the riverbank. She tensed and palmed a stone. It was cold and hard and falsely reassuring in her hand.

A flurry of movement brought a unicorn gliding over the bank. Norah gasped, and it stopped twenty feet in front of her, gleaming, glittering, its mane rippling, its tail streaming, and its horn a silver spear in the twilight. It turned its head, eying her, snaking its neck back and forth, evidently trying to decide if she was worthy enough to approach.

Norah felt herself shaking, mostly in awe, but also at the nearness of that horn—a weapon, the only real weapon that she might have at hand. Dr. Reynolds had always wanted to collect a unicorn, and she had no doubt that he would take this one, either in addition to or in place of an ogre. That meant he'd expect her to draw it in. As a plan formed in her mind, she wiped her palms on her parka and carefully tore up a handful of grass.

"Here you go, girl." Respectfully, she held out her palm of grass, as she might have done for one of the mares on her parents' farm too many years before.

The unicorn snorted and backstepped, its ears laid flat.

Norah knelt, her heart thudding. The unicorn had to come to her. Her whole plan depended on its approach. She had no idea how like a horse unicorns were—this one was wilder, more fey than any horse could be—but the language of horses was the only way she knew to communicate with it.

She held the grass out, balanced on her palm, as the unicorn advanced a single step, its tail switching. "Come on," she said, urging it on its careful, alert way. At the sound of her voice, it stopped, tossing its head. She kept quiet and ripped up more grass, adding one of the daisies that grew along the river. After a silent, still moment, the unicorn glided forward two steps, its cloven hooves making the shadow of a sound against the earth.

Finally, its lips brushed her palm and plucked up the grass with the delicacy of a queen selecting pastries.

"Good girl."

Its ears flicked, but it stayed in place, and slowly, slowly, Norah rose to her feet, sliding her hand up the unicorn's neck. It felt like silk, like the dresses her mother had kept wrapped in paper. It shivered under her touch, its skin rippling, and she realized it was shaking, trembling, just as she was.

She gentled it, stroking its nose and neck, but it continued to shake until she understood that it was feeding off of her emotions, reflecting back to her her own fear and nervousness. She breathed in, breathed out—the unicorn smelled like honey—and tried to calm her fluttering heart, but her heart would not be calmed. They would have to fight through her nerves.

A whirring made her jump. Beyond the unicorn, Ignis aimed his small game rifle. He cocked his head, urging her to step aside.

Norah's fingers knotted in the unicorn's mane. Dr. Reynolds had schooled her carefully. She must hold the unicorn in place until such a time as Ignis was ready to shoot. Then she should abandon the unicorn, retreating so it might be tranquilized without fear of harming her.

Apparently, Dr. Reynolds didn't want her damaged so that she might still catch an ogre.

The unicorn blew, picking up the increased tension in her body. "Listen," she whispered in its ear. "We have to time this carefully. On my mark, you charge them both, all right?"

One ear flicked, and she wondered if the unicorn *really* understood her, any more than a ptarmigan did.

Ignis crept closer, finger on the trigger. His head twitched, shouting at her without words.

Footsteps sounded behind her. Dr. Reynolds. He had come to pull her back so Ignis could bag the unicorn.

Norah held her breath, her head turned just enough to see Dr. Reynolds creeping up behind her on her left, keeping himself out of the line of fire. His black-gloved hand crept out, ready to grab her arm. His face was cold, his lips pressed together in annoyance. The unicorn trembled, its muscles taut under her hands.

When Dr. Reynolds was nearly at her elbow, she lunged at the unicorn. "Now," she shouted.

It screamed. Whether it responded to her words or to the prey instincts of a horse, she didn't know. Norah threw herself back just in time to miss the horn swinging like a lance. Someone—Dr. Reynolds—shrieked. Then Norah was on the ground, rolling as far as she dared, stones digging into her hands, the cut in her cheek stinging. Hooves pounded, and she huddled facedown, her arms over her head, seeking what protection she could.

A man's voice shouted, high and piercing, sounding neither human nor automatus. Then there was a gurgle, the thump of a body on the ground. Metal screeched, and shots fired, one, two, three loud pops.

Something punched her right hip. She grunted, and as hooves thundered and metal screamed, pain blossomed down her leg.

Silence.

She took a shuddering breath then pulled her hands away from her head and touched her hip. Already it was wet with blood. She'd tended cuts and burns and frostbite, but never a bullet wound. First, though, she had to see what else she faced.

A body sprawled on the ground, face up, gloved hands open at its sides. Dr. Reynolds. A dozen steps away, Ignis lay in two pieces. His head rested beside him, a deep dent stamped under his ear. The unicorn was nowhere to be seen.

Norah dragged herself towards Dr. Reynolds, one hand at her hip, tears pricking her eyes at every jostle. But she had to know.

A wide hole punctured his chest, black blood staining his parka. He breathed still, the air whistling in and out of his lungs, but his breaths only prolonged the inevitable.

She gazed down at him, trying to feel anything more than pain and weariness and a faint wooziness at the stench of blood. She'd heard that the dead looked smaller, wizened, but he looked no smaller to her, and she hesitated before she pulled up his parka, revealing the bag he wore on his belt. Inside she found the key that opened Ignis but not the key to the collar around her neck. She slumped down, breathing with the pain, before crawling towards Ignis. Perhaps he would have her key.

The box buzzed against her neck before she reached him. She threw herself back, sprawling on the ground, the right side of her body throbbing.

Her head spun, and she sank her face in the grass. How long would she last here? Before an ogre came at night, or a polar bear in the day, or the cold and the blood loss brought infection?

She pushed herself to sit up. One thing at a time. Care for her hip then worry about the collar and how she might crawl away from here. She leaned back so she could lift her parka and rip off a strip of her undershirt for a bandage. As she did, her leg pressed into something sharp and square and metal. The other box. She snatched it up, barely believing, hardly thinking that the buzz had come from excitement over the pair's nearness. The box was bent, maybe from a hoof, but that didn't matter. It meant she could leave, drag herself from this horrid place.

A whinny brought her head up.

A dozen feet in front of her, the unicorn shied away. Blood stained its horn, and its eyes were wild. Perhaps it didn't recognize her under all the blood.

But she needed the unicorn, spooked or no, because that horn could heal as well as kill.

She couldn't stand, but that might have been just as well. She tucked the box and key in her pocket and held out her hand, her fingers stained red. "Come here, girl."

The unicorn tossed its head, flinching back several steps, but it didn't flee, and its gaze never left her.

Norah lifted the edge of her parka and rolled down the waistband of her wool skirt, then the top of the caribou trousers she wore for warmth underneath. The unicorn flared its nostrils as her hip came into sight.

"I need your help. Either help me, or go on your way."

The unicorn blew as if offended, but pain made Norah resolute, and the unicorn knelt beside her, pressing the tip of its horn against her hip. She hissed, for the horn was unexpectedly cold. Then the shock died away, and a soothing, pain-deadening warmth flooded her side. She closed her eyes, sinking into the bliss that came with the cessation of pain. After a few moments, the unicorn lifted its head.

Norah's skirt and trousers were still wet with blood, but the skin on her hip showed smooth, no sign even of a scar.

"Thank you," she whispered. As the unicorn rose, she scrambled to her feet. There was no pain anywhere, not in her hip, or her cheek, or her bruised arms and knees.

The unicorn swung its head towards Dr. Reynolds. He was dead already, wasn't he? But no, his chest still rose and fell, if only a little. The unicorn reared back its head, its skin pricking as at something unpleasant, but it started forward, its mission apparently not yet done.

She grabbed its mane. "No! No—don't—"

The unicorn dragged her forward a few steps. She didn't have the strength to hold it back.

"No." She made her voice strong. "Not him."

The unicorn swung its head back to look at her. Was there condemnation in its eyes? Or was there nothing at all, merely a reflection, a mirror, into which she could read her own human emotions?

"He's evil," she said. "He'll never stop hunting you, even if you help him now. Your healing is not for him."

The unicorn turned and left her. It picked its way to the riverbank, its hooves making the softest noise on the stones. It disappeared over the side. When Norah peered down, she saw only water and rock and a flash of white rounding the river bend.

She blew out her breath. Her legs felt shaky, and though she felt a rawness like grief at the unicorn's leaving, she didn't regret her choice. She skirted Dr. Reynolds and went to what remained of Ignis. Fiddling with the key, she opened the door in his chest and lifted out what was inside. A phoenix, red and orange, no bigger than a sparrow. It stirred and opened yellow eyes on her.

"Come on," she said, tucking it into the warmth of her parka hood, "we're going home, but we don't have much time."

The whaling ship would arrive soon, and there were dozens of metamorpho cages to open before then. She set off the way she'd come, yellow lighting the eastern horizon, the phoenix singing in her ear.

Echo Canyon

they come the canyon down
    they ride the wind
we hear the mother drown
    we know we've sinned

we know there is no god
    we do not care
they well may think us odd
    they may well dare

we look to find an end
    they look away
we know we have no friend
    they cannot say

— Neal Wilgus

We Call Them the Gods

There are men in the sky, and we call them the gods. Their beards shine with the light of rejected stars, harbor failed empires and the wailing souls of extinct hominids. Always their dark, playful eyes are hot with mischief. They delight in a belief that the goddesses are impressed by their creations, amused even. Surely they got a kick out of *Homo sapiens*, that inferior clay fumbling wildly over the layout of design. Such fodder for comedy. But in dull pockets of timelessness, when the bearded ones are idle, the goddesses—because it is their way—have been known to nurture Earth's fetal spirit, to channel love there, to fire-open seeds of art and philosophy, to spark the ambitious theories we never prove. Myriad tasks are assigned to fairies, mystics and angels; demons too, if it should lead to a truth. Much then becomes nurtured in the hidden spectrums of our souls, in the heart of posterity. There are men in the sky, and there are women. These are the gods.

— Jason Sturner

The Sphinx &
The Signet

Story by
Courtney Floyd

Illustration by
Paul Niemiec

Albuquerque was shrouded in dense gray clouds the day Billie stumbled into my office, hair braided in an elaborate Dutch style and fire-truck-red lipstick slightly smeared at the bottom of her lip. She had dark hair and tan skin and she smelled of the dampness of the day, a bit like rain and a bit more like the steam of the streets.

Billie wiped her face dry with the sleeve of her charcoal cardigan, further smearing her lipstick.

I waited.

If first impressions are important in day-to-day life, they are even more so in the world of private investigation, so I drank in every detail.

She was dressed stylishly, but there was a slipshod feel to her demeanor that suggested a thrift store lifestyle. Her worn shoes and generic makeup marked her a trailer-trash debutant right down to her long acrylic French-tips.

Having spent the last decade hopping from trailer park to trailer park, I've got what you might consider first-hand experience with all of the many iterations of trailer park society. Hell, I'm one of them.

Plus, I'd seen her coming and going at my current residence and place of business, Enchanted Trails RV Park, for the past several weeks.

I live and work out of the '63 Winnebago I inherited from my great aunt, Sophie. It's a convenient arrangement.

"Are you Sara Phix?" Billie asked, finally.

"The one and only."

I've googled it. I know.

Billie collapsed into the small, 70's style cushioned armchair on the other side of my tiny desk.

She held the bridge of her nose, as if holding it was the key to holding herself together. A couple of mutinous teardrops escaped from her heavily mascaraed lashes despite this precaution.

I watched them roll down her cheeks with suspicion. This line of work has really honed my cynicism.

"I need help finding something," she said, snagging my attention away from the authenticity of her tears.

I inclined my head, willing her to continue. The tears had me expecting a murder, a kidnapping, or something equally emotionally traumatic. A lost or stolen item didn't seem worthy of so much emotion.

But I kept listening. Might as well give her the benefit of the doubt until it came time for contracts and signatures.

"A ring," she said, "I need you to find a ring."

She paused, and I leaned back, skepticism skyrocketing.

The mention of a ring puts me on immediate alert: awooga, awooga, stereotypical investigation ahead.

Still, a ring didn't necessarily mean a romance. It could just be a family heirloom, a treasured piece of jewelry, a personal bauble of great significance.

I'd hear her out before giving her the boot.

"A ring and the man who's wearing it," Billie added. "His name is Alex Smith."

I sat up straighter. Sure, missing persons cases involve their own set of difficulties. But they're a whole heckuvvalot more interesting.

"It's a signet ring," Billie said, leaning forward.

I shook myself into attention while she continued, "which is why I came to you. I hear that you specialize in this sort of thing…"

She left the sentence hanging, implying something that I definitely do not advertise.

And, in case you're wondering, I do not specialize in the recovery of lost signet rings or the men who wear them.

I specialize in the supernatural.

Well, that's not quite accurate.

I am the supernatural. I specialize in dealing with the supernatural.

* * *

Billie looked honest enough, a bit naive even, but there were three things weighing heavily against her. One, I don't advertise my specialties, and it takes a certain class of person to hear about them. As a detective, I tend to work with people who *need* a detective. Usually, that means they've mixed themselves up in something shady.

Two, although Billie seemed innocent enough, her aura was radiating guilt like a sidewalk radiates heat in the middle of July. Auras aren't an exact science by any means; they're kind of like mood rings, giving vague indications of what a person might be thinking or feeling at any moment. Some people even learn how to control their own auras, much like the masterminds who know how to manipulate lie detector tests. Billie's guilt might be entirely unfounded, but the fact that she was feeling enough of it to turn her aura a deep, silky grey was troubling.

Three had little to do with Billie, but it's something that I tend to keep in mind. Thing is, the last time someone came to me for my special kind of help, I was a bit too open and, long story short, I won't be returning to New Orleans any time soon. Or ever, probably.

See, I am the direct descendant of the original Sphinx.

I read people. I solve riddles. I guard treasure. I prevent or right injustice. And I do all of these things in whatever form necessary. Sometimes I'm a P.I., sometimes I'm a psychologist. Other times ... well, let's just say that I prefer not to dwell on the other times.

I made a promise to myself after New Orleans that I would stick to strictly mortal problems. They could be less interesting, sure, but they didn't have an ugly tendency to get me driven out of town.

"A signet ring that does what?" I asked.

Half of me was busy hoping against hope that this was just some generic signet ring, crafted at the whim of some hipster with a passion for jewelry making.

The other half was hoping that the subliminal message she'd sent had not, in fact, been a figment of my imagination.

What can I say? It's been a boring couple of years.

Billie took the precaution of glancing around my office, eyes narrowed, before she replied.

"I think," she said, forcing the words out despite a sudden crack in her voice, "it's the Seal of Solomon."

Her eyes fluttered and she gave me an uncertain half-smile, just like the kind a toddler might flash when she knows she's done something very, very bad.

I blinked.

The mother-fracking Seal of Solomon?

Not possible.

No way. Uhn uh.

I knew for a fact that one of my great, great ancestors had destroyed it during the Crusades, inspiring Tolkien to write his world-famous trilogy by hauling the thing to Mount Vesuvius and throwing it into the fiery depths of the volcano.

And good riddance.

Much like Tolkien's One Ring, the Seal of Solomon was no laughing matter. In fact, it was more of a screaming and tearing your hair out while running in circles, flailing like a dying fish kind of matter.

According to legend, the thing could be used to summon and control demons and genii, to do whatever the heck it is alchemists do, to transmogrify anything or anyone (for you supernatural laymen, that means shape shifting), and to literally and completely steal the identity of any living person.

I blinked again.

"Couldn't be," I said, out loud, because Billie was looking at me with a mixture of concern and dismay, her eyebrows quirked at different angles.

I looked away.

"It was destroyed," I said, shuffling the papers in front of me into a better semblance of order.

Billie shook her head, holding up a finger before rummaging in the tattered knit bag she used as a purse.

"I thought you might say that," she said, "which is why I brought proof."

She pulled a wad of photos from the bag and shoved them toward me.

"Here, look," she said.

I hesitated. In the unlikely event that she was right, this was not something I could turn away from. It was part of my responsibility. My familial obligation.

If I didn't see the pictures, I didn't have to follow up on this. I could go back to my life as an ordinary, everyday P.I. and pretend I'd never met Billie or heard about the Seal of Solomon. I could deny culpability.

My hand inched its way forward, despite my misgivings.

That annoying little part of me that misses the supernatural world and hates sticking to its resolutions squeaked in joy at the prospect of a "respectable" case, one that involved something besides hotwired BMWs or stolen jewels.

"You took these yourself?" I asked, grabbing the photos before I could dither with myself anymore.

Billie nodded.

"A week ago. The night we bought the ring."

"Did you have the ring inspected by a jeweler or a professor or anyone who could actually authenticate it?" I asked, as I turned my attention to the pictures.

Fortunately, paranoia and skepticism are part of the job description. I turned toward the pictures with a cool eye and a mostly clear mind.

Unfortunately, one glance at the photos and my skepticism was beginning to desert me. Something—probably the bean burrito I'd eaten for lunch—churned deep in my gut. I had a bad feeling about the case, the girl sitting across the desk from me, and the state of the universe in general.

The ring *looked* like the Seal of Solomon, at least as the Seal is described in all of the lore. There was a faint engraving visible in the grainy pictures, with what looked like a six-pointed star (also known as the Star of David) and various scrawlings in what looked remarkably like ancient Hebrew.

Oh, and one more thing.

The ring had an aura. An aura strong enough that it showed up in the photos, even though they were just normal mortal-camera photos.

Gulp.

"Okay," I said. "Say I believe you, how did *you* end up with the ring in the first place? And what makes you think that your boyfriend is missing? Isn't it more likely he ran off to keep the ring to *himself?*"

Billie listened with almost perfect passivity; the muscles around her bright red lips twitched, a mere fraction, when I mentioned her boyfriend.

She folded her hands in her lap and took a breath before replying.

"My *fiancé* has no idea what the ring is. I bought it as a sort of engagement ring for him and I didn't realize what it was until a few days later."

She gulped air.

"I wanted to be absolutely sure before I took it back. I mean, from his perspective, what would it look like if I took back the symbol of my love?"

I scrunched my nose in sympathy, even though I wasn't sure whether or not I bought the story. Your average shmuck doesn't know enough about folklore or legend to suspect a ring of being an ancient and magical seal.

For now, I'd let it slide. But that did not mean I trusted Billie. Puppy dog eyes notwithstanding.

"I'm going to need the name and address of the person who sold you the ring, an account of your activities on the day Alex went missing, a list of people who might have something against you or Alex…"

I thrummed my fingers on the top of my desk, thinking.

"Oh, and a picture of Alex might be nice."

* * *

I drew up a standard contract for Billie and sent her on her way, telling her to check back with me in a day or two, after I'd had some time to nose around.

After days of inactivity, I finally had a to-do list.

Now, all I wanted was a pint and a burger. Not necessarily in that order.

I sighed and jotted down my list, unwilling to leave it to the roulette that is my memory.

First thing's first, I needed to check with the street vender who'd sold Billie the ring. If I could trace the ring's ownership, I could determine whether or not it was, in fact, the Seal of Solomon.

That meant a trip to Santa Fe, so I stepped into the rain, heading for my Jeep.

* * *

After about an hour of driving, I parked behind the St. Francis Cathedral Basilica and wended my way through middling Wednesday afternoon crowds and into the thick of the Plaza.

Although it was the tail end of summer, tourists were still plentiful and the street vendors were taking full advantage of them, hawking authenticity from wool blankets spread underneath turquoise panted awnings.

According to Billie, I was looking for a middle-aged woman named Gus, whose goods included jewelry and sketches of cats arrayed in various historical haberdashery.

After about twenty minutes of fruitless meandering, I caught sight of an 11x14 calico in a stovepipe hat and headed toward it, figuring there couldn't be too many artists who painted cats in costumes.

The vendor, a pasty-faced redhead whose head was almost completely enveloped by an enormous, floppy straw hat, looked to be somewhere in her forties.

I paused to look at a particularly intriguing, by which I mean to say disturbing, oil tableaux of a poodle dressed as a dandy, ala Oscar Wilde, while the vendor settled accounts with a peppy tourist couple.

When they'd finished and moved out of earshot, I stepped up and caught the vendor's eye.

"Are you by any chance Gus Winsham?" I asked, throwing on my most touristy smile.

Probably-Gus hesitated.

"Why do you ask?" she asked, her voice a mousy tenor.

"A friend of mine keeps raving about this ring she bought about a week ago. She loves it so much I thought I'd stop by and see if you had another like it," I said, pasting on another smile.

"I see," she said. "Well, in that case, I am Gus Winsham. But, I'm afraid I'll have to disappoint you, all of my jewelry is unique. No two pieces are alike."

She smiled and set to work straightening her goods, assuming that I'd fall to browsing or leave, I suppose.

"Excuse me," I said, again.

She turned, impatience flickering across her brow before she shoved it down with a polite smile.

"Could you tell me where you got the ring, if I showed you a picture?"

She hurried over as I sifted through my bag for a photo.

"I really like this particular style," I said, when she crossed her arms with renewed impatience.

I fished out the photo and handed it to her,

watching her face carefully for any sign that she knew the ring's significance. I doubted she had even the smallest inkling, since she'd sold it for such a small price, but maybe she was a sadist and the chance to inflict pain on unsuspecting innocents outweighed the prospect of a fortune worthy of Forbes status.

There's a huge black market for these kinds of things, and the people who know about it have usually been around for centuries. Theirs are the Marianas Trench of deep pockets.

"You know," she said, "I don't recall purchasing this piece. I do remember selling it, but I have no idea where I picked it up." She puckered her lips in thought.

I shifted from foot to foot, trying not to let my exasperation show.

Clearly, I wasn't going to get the information I needed as a tourist.

I pulled my P.I. license out of my back pocket and presented it to her.

"Ma'am," I said, pulling on my official-business voice, "I'm investigating a missing person's case, and the disappearance seems to be linked with this ring."

Gus's hand fluttered to her more-than-ample bosom as she squeaked in surprise.

"Oh," she said, eyelids fluttering, "I'm sorry to hear that. I just, I can't see how I could be involved."

I stuck to my official-business guns, voice stern.

"That's not information I'm privileged to share, ma'am," I said, taking my cue from the series of B-rated action flicks I'd watched earlier in the week. "I just need to know where the ring came from. Is there a logbook you can check?"

Gus nodded and dropped to her knees, digging in the boxes beneath her table.

Technically, I had no official capacity to demand the documents. The stern, official-business voice can be hit or miss because of that. Some people fall for it, some don't.

This time, it panned out.

Gus climbed back to her feet, a tattered three-inch binder in hand.

"It may take a while," she said, waving at the book as evidence. "I may have sold the ring a week ago, but I have no idea when I acquired it, so I'll have to go through page by page.

I nodded, eyeing the book with a twinge of guilt.

"Why don't I give you my information and you can call me if you find anything," I suggested.

I pulled out one of my business cards—"Have a puzzle you just can't solve?" it reads, "Call Sara Phix,

P.I."—and passed it across the table to her.

She swallowed, and her Adam's Apple bobbed visibly, a bulge pulsing down her neck.

"I'll let you know if I find anything," she said.

* * *

Back in Albuquerque, I set about interviewing the trailer park residents on Billie's list.

I trudged over to the rusty airstream in the lot next to mine, taking a moment to button the top button on my blouse.

Ray, the airstream's rather amorous inhabitant, is about seventy years old and makes frequent requests to hold my hand. It's not the most suggestive request that's ever been made of me, by any means, but it's definitely changed the way I think about hand-holding.

Putting on my sternest and hopefully most off-putting expression, I knocked on the airstream's battered metal door.

Somewhere inside that tin can masquerading as a mobile home, Ray belched and shouted a slurred, "Coming!"

"Have you seen Alex lately?" I asked, as soon as he opened the door. It's best to take an aggressive tack with Ray, keep him unbalanced so he doesn't spew inappropriate suggestions and obscenities.

Ray's aura is a rusty red, much like the oxidized bits of his airstream. A redneck red, if you will. It's volatile but not psycho-killer volatile. Put a couple of beers in him and it either fades to a reasonable orange or bubbles into a brilliant, volcanic red. Really, it depends on the day and the company.

Ray opened and shut his mouth, a sign that my tactic had worked.

"Well, hello to you, too," he said, letting loose another belch and patting his beer belly.

"Well?" I asked.

Our relationship is straightforward. I'm direct and usually rude. He's either flirtatious or brutish. Despite everything, I have a soft spot for Ray. He's dependable in a very cantankerous way.

Tonight, he was running in brutish mode.

He scratched the underside of his belly and thought about my question.

"Nope," he said, cracking a tobacco stained grin. "Can't say I have."

He scratched the stubble on his chin and waited for further commentary.

"When was the last time you *did* see him?" I asked.

He turned and waved me inside, crumpling his

beer can with his free hand.

I sighed and ducked into the trailer.

The inside was surprisingly tidy. Sure, the curtains were actually towels and the entire place smelt of stale beer and smoke, but the floors were clean and had obviously been swept and mopped recently. A stack of folded laundry on the tiny kitchen table boasted of actual housekeeping, as did the tidy sink—there was nary a dirty dish in sight.

Ray yanked his fridge open and grabbed a couple cans of Pabst.

He offered one to me and popped the tab on his own.

I followed suit and took a swig before pressing on.

"Well?" I asked, again. Using the word to mask the hint of a burp.

Ray caught it and winked at me.

"Last I saw Alex, he was headed to the campus to talk to some professor-type about a ring his lady bought him. He had the idea he could sell it and buy her a diamond, if I remember right. Looked like a piece of junk to me, but he was convinced."

Ray leaned against his counter and chugged the beer, pulling away after a few seconds and wiping his mouth with the back of his forearm.

"When was this?" I asked, feeling suddenly impatient.

"Must've been Thursday? Maybe Friday," he said.

I nodded, thinking. If that were the case, the professor could very well be the last person who'd seen or spoken to Alex.

"Did he mention a name?" I asked, a surge of excitement coursing through my veins. Gus had most likely been a dead end, although she still might prove useful. But this, this felt like an honest to god lead.

Ray titled his head back, thinking.

"Might've been Gold" he said, still straining in thought. "Sorry, Sara. That's all I've got. Now how 'bout you and me head back there," he said, nodding toward his bed, "and play footsie?"

And here I was thinking Ray had turned over a new, and more helpful leaf.

I did my best not to gag and excused myself, mentioning my long list of names. I had a lot of interviewing left to do.

Outside, I took a few deep breaths and headed back to my own trailer. I'd talk to the other park inhabitants if this lead didn't pan out, but for now, all I needed to continue my investigation was a laptop, an internet connection, and the UNM website.

* * *

Dr. Celia Gold turned out to be an associate professor for the UNM English Department and the Anthropology Department. The website listed her specialties as Classic literature (including Greek and Latin) and Early Modern cultures.

I emailed her to request a meeting and, at seven-thirty the next morning, she replied, suggesting we meet for coffee around ten.

We met at the Starbucks on Central, near the university. Dr. Gold, a young-looking forty with long brown hair and gray eyes, had already ordered by the time I arrived.

I grabbed my usual and joined her at the corner table she'd chosen.

"Thank you for meeting with me," I said, extending my hand.

"No problem."

She held up a tall drink and flashed a rueful smile. "I have to get my fix."

I joined her in a sip of coffee and then dug through my bag for the photos.

"I'm looking into a missing person's case," I said, "and I have reason to believe you may be the last person who saw and spoke to the individual."

I placed the photos on the table.

"A man named Alex was supposed to see you in regard to this ring," I said. "Do you remember seeing him?"

Her aura pulsed at the question, sending swirls of black into what had been a calm blue cloud.

She pondered the photos, shaking her head slowly.

"No, I don't recall speaking to an Alex. Or looking at this ring," she said, running her finger over the photo, "and trust me, I'd remember seeing this. It looks quite rare."

The black swirls in her aura hardened and spread, overtaking the blue like an invading army.

The woman was lying. She'd seen the man and the ring. But why lie? Unless she knew what the ring was.

But that would mean…

As a Sphinx, I can do much more than see auras. I can see into people's souls, read their very beings. And it was looking like I'd have to do that now.

All I needed to do was pose a riddle. But despite seeming simple, reading a person's psyche—or looking into a soul—is a messy business.

If she got the answer wrong, I'd be able to

psychically nudge her into doing what I needed her to do: answer my questions honestly.

That, and her entire life would be an open book to me. There are no privacy settings for my particular talent, which is part of the reason I avoid using it. It's easy to take advantage of people when you know literally everything about them.

If she got the answer right, she'd know who I was and what my intentions were. Which meant she'd make a scene or try to kill me. Or both.

These things tend to get ugly.

Still, if the Seal of Solomon was wreaking its havoc nearby, it would be foolish of me to waste time chasing shadows when I had a viable lead right here.

I took my time, sipping coffee and swapping small talk, while I formulated my question.

You've heard of the riddle of the Sphinx? Well, legend only recorded part of the story. We Sphinxes aren't limited to a single riddle. We can ask whatever riddle we want, the trick is asking one that gets an answer we can use. My great, great, great, great, great, great grandmother went wrong when she accepted help from the muses while composing her riddle, thereby violating the rules of fair confrontation and forfeiting her life to Odysseus.

The rules are important, unfortunately.

So, I stewed over the wording, because it's important to get these things just right or they tend to backfire.

Finally, just as the professor was getting ready to leave, I had it.

I reached out and touched her sleeve as she was standing.

"Just one more question," I said.

She sat.

"Of course," she said, a false smile creeping over her lips, belying the swirling blackness of her aura.

"What binds two people together, but touches only one?" I asked.

When a Sphinx poses a riddle, the individual to whom it was posed is literally compelled to consider the question and then attempt an answer.

Professor Gold smacked her lips a couple of times and took a sip of coffee, leaving me in horrible anticipation. My heart thudded like a prop out of an Edgar Allen Poe story as I wondered whether or not she'd come up with the correct answer.

"Love?" she asked, after a second sip of coffee.

I smiled but didn't respond—the moment I gave her the correct answer, her soul would slam shut and my influence would be severed.

Professor Gold's soul opened up before me like a thick, musty book, pages flipping by in a calliope of images, her life story flashing before my eyes.

A few things became quickly apparent.

She'd been adopted at the age of seven, and she never quite accepted her new parents.

She had an obsession with mincemeat pie.

And her biological father was part Golem, a mythical protector of the Hebrew people, because of which she'd seen the ring and recognized it immediately as an artifact from her own heritage. An artifact she wanted, desperately. She'd attempted to take it from Alex who, under its influence, had balked.

But she was still trying to get it.

And she knew where Alex was staying.

* * *

Having discovered what I needed, I shook my head.

"No," I said. "A ring."

Her eyes narrowed, considering the answer. She shrugged again.

"Are we done here?" she asked.

I nodded.

"Thank you for your time," I said, as she swished through the glass doors and disappeared into the intense late-summer sunlight. The black swirling of her aura hovered in the air a few seconds after she left, menacing the entire room.

Under that menace, I got the feeling she'd known the answer to the riddle, an unsettling possibility.

That's the other iffy part of soul-reading. If a particularly conniving and in-the-know mark gets the answer right, she can still choose to say the wrong answer. It is possible, if you know what you're doing, to peek into a Sphinx's soul while she rifles through yours.

My stomach plummeted at the thought. I tossed the remainder of my latte into the nearest trash bin and headed for my Jeep.

* * *

Professor Gold headed down Central, away from the University and through increasingly ramshackle neighborhoods. I stayed a few cars back, darting in and out of lanes to keep up with her.

Wherever Alex was hiding, it couldn't be very pleasant. In this side of town, you think twice before stopping at a gas station—whether or not you have supernatural powers to swing around in a fight.

She pulled into the Botanic Gardens parking lot and scurried in through the front gate, tossing the fare at the attendant without even a glance.

So, Alex was hiding in the Botanic Gardens?

I couldn't claim to understand, so I turned my attention to parking. A sneaky bastard in a Volvo tried to edge me out of a space, but I blared my horn and floored it.

Civility is underrated, especially in the face of impending doom.

And don't think I wasn't kicking myself about the impending doom bit. Why had I decided to be clever? Why had I chosen a riddle that was related to the case? Why couldn't I have given her a hard one, like: What English word has three consecutive double letters?

I'm a Sphinx with a B.A. in English and it took me days to figure that one out.

I sprinted from my car to the gates, practically forcing my credit card into the attendant's hand, and then bolted into the gardens.

I'm pretty sure I'm the most eager customer the place has ever had.

Sadly, Professor Gold was nowhere in sight. But the gardens are pretty big and there are lots of places to hide, which I decided to take as a good thing, even though it meant that the whole situation could be, and probably was, an ambush.

For all I knew, Professor Gold could be planning to unleash a maelstrom on me amidst a small field of poppies, cackling like the Wicked Witch of the West.

I pushed the thoughts aside and forced myself to consider the place rationally.

Sure, it was big. Sure, I couldn't possibly cover it all and keep an eye on the exit at the same time. But there were only a few really good hiding places: a couple of buildings and a couple of play structures for kids.

The play structures were closer to the exits and, as public schools had just gone back in session, probably suffered much less foot traffic than other areas of the Gardens at this point in the day.

If I was on the run and delusional enough to take refuge in a Botanic Garden, I'd hide there.

* * *

Deep in the heart of a giant pumpkin, I caught sight of Dr. Gold.

She stood at the other end of the pumpkin, whispering to someone, or something, I couldn't see in the gloom.

I slowed, measuring my breath until the sound was almost nonexistent.

My vision adjusted to the low light and as my brain interpreted what I saw, my own actions seemed to be stuck in slow motion:

The professor handed Alex a wad of cash.

Alex handed the professor the ring.

I shouted and hurled myself toward them.

The professor slipped the ring on and waved at Alex, sending him flying into the fiberglass wall of the pumpkin.

Then, she turned her attention to me with a smile, spouting indecipherable words as she stalked toward me.

To my dismay, the snatches of words I caught sounded like Ancient Hebrew.

I crouched into a fighting stance.

But the professor just flicked a dismissive hand at me, and suddenly pumpkin vines with the strength of steel pinned me to the wall and wound themselves around my arms and legs.

She pulled a mean looking letter opener from her handbag, waving it around in the dim light, mincing her way closer and closer to me and my tender flesh.

Too bad I could only read a soul once. I could've bought myself some time with a riddle, otherwise.

I looked around the pumpkin, searching for a way out—magical or otherwise.

The flickering of the ring's aura, reds and blacks and bursts of neon purple and gold, filled the room. It made my skin crawl. With it, the professor could summon demons or steal my identity, neither of which would be good for the world. Demons would rip the world apart for fun. But with my knowledge, the professor wouldn't even need demons. She could destroy the world or shape it to her own will with barely a thought.

But, as far as I knew, the ring didn't make her invincible.

There was only one option left, and it was one I'd vowed never to use again.

I had to become the Sphinx, physically as well as mentally. I grimaced, looking from Professor Gold to Alex to the vines wrapped around my very human arms. Unless a shower of options rained down on me in the next few seconds, this was going to be my best bet whether I liked it or not.

So, I closed my eyes and breathed deep.

It's hard to explain the change, except to say that something a lot like pure gold and obsidian flow through my veins, and when I open my eyes I know that I can fly and leap and maul and protect. Because protecting is all. It's just a tiny matter of who and what.

I could feel the vines snap and sag, tickling my limbs as they fell.

I could smell the surge of blood in the professor's veins, the rapid thumpa-thumpa-thumpa of her heart as it leapt from her chest to her mouth.

I could see her eyes widen in that slow-motion horror that usually only happens in movies.

And I was strong and circling: first slow and firm, then faster and with anticipation.

The professor was no longer a human, at least not as I saw her. She was a mouse, or a deer. Something small and timid and weak.

And it had been so long since my last feast.

* * *

Mercifully, the rest was a blur. I woke to the beeping of a hospital monitor. At my bedside, Billie and Alex waited with clasped hands.

Alex couldn't quite look me in the eye.

I stared at them for a moment before turning to more pressing matters, such as my humanity.

A quick lift of the coverlet revealed two human legs, the right one swathed in an enormous, blood-tinged bandage.

My right thigh throbbed in response to the attention, and I lowered the coverlet with a grimace.

Satisfied, I croaked something resembling a hello.

"Hey," Billie said, her smile accentuating a dimple. She stood and held out her hand, tiptoeing toward the bed. "We thought you would know what to do with this," she said.

I held out my hand and she plopped the Seal of Solomon into it.

She shook her head, blinking back tears.

"Thank you for finding him," she said.

I nodded, waving away the thanks. I still needed to know what had happened.

"The professor?" I asked, before they could leave without filling me in.

"She's alive. In ICU, but alive. They said a lion escaped from the zoo and mauled her."

Billie narrowed her well-mascaraed eyes.

I mustered a weak smile.

"Oh, and Gus called," Billie added, her voice fading, "she said to tell you she has no record of the ring's purchase."

I mumbled a response, just cognizant of the fact that the information mattered, somehow. But my pillows were the essence of cashmere and feathers. And whatever they had me on for the pain, it was good. I could barely feel the wound. I was floating on purple clouds while swirls of opalescent rain danced around me.

The Seal of Solomon tingled in my palm and I knew in a few hours I'd have to break myself out of the place to take the ring somewhere safe and secluded, but for now I was content.

I'd survived, I could stay in town until I was ready to leave on my own terms, and the apocalypse hadn't come tumbling down on all of our heads.

By all accounts, it was a good day.

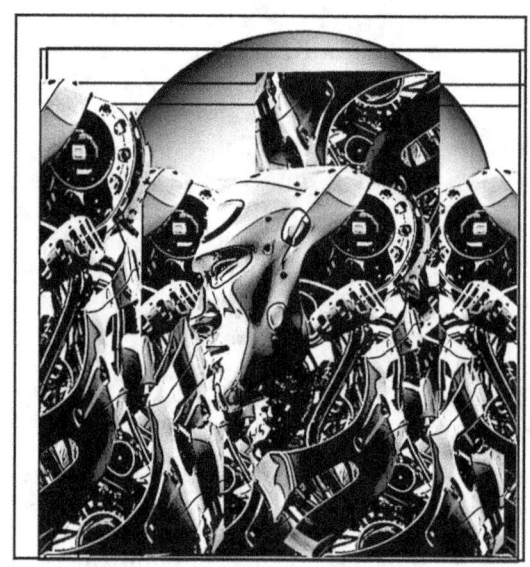

Fairy Moon

Grandma loved her rocker.
Sipped her dandelion wine
and crazy rocked at the end of every day.

When she passed
Pa had them dig a right deep grave
Buried her, rocking in her chair
her diamond on one finger
her ruby on another.

I wanted them rings.
I cast my runes
they bode me wait for the second fairy moon
in the seventh year following her death.

I suffered those long years
until the foretold night
When I hurried to her grave
and watched my grandmother rise
rocking madly in her chair
on the hardened ground
beside her stone.
Margot Walker, 1830-1910.

I stoop
pick a yellow dandelion
place it in her skull.
She grasps the flower
in her skinless hand
shoves it in her mouth.
Spits yellow onto the ground.
I pull the diamond from one finger,
the ruby from another.
I tell her, "Now. You go on back to earth."

"I'll stay right here.
I hate the lonely dark and cold.
My bones need bleaching in the morning sun."

I shove her back into the hole.
She grabs my ankle as she falls
trips me into her grave.
"No," I scream. "I'm not dead."
Her bones wrap around my body
she yanks the diamond from my hand
scribes on her stone.
"On March 10, 1917 my grandson
came to end my empty nights"

— John Hayes

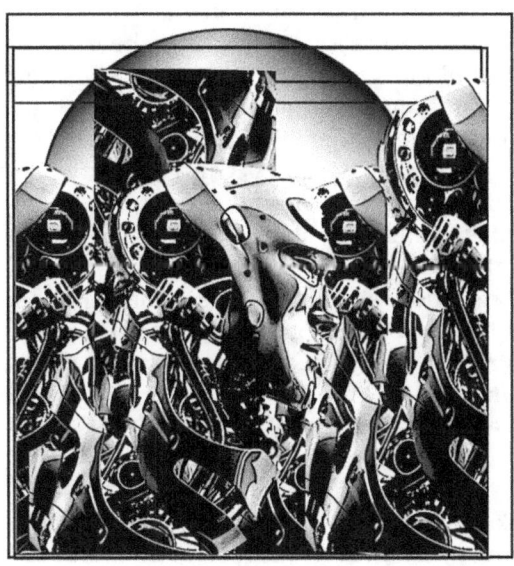

Book Reviews

The Automation
B.L.A. and G.B. Gabbler
S.O.B. Publishing
$11.74, Trade Paperback
$0.99 Ebook
362 pages

The Automation tells the story of twins Odys and Odissa Odelyn. When Odissa visits their late father's attorney to pick up their inheritance payment, Odys must walk to work and meets an odd fellow named Pepin who looks as though he's on his way to a steampunk convention. Pepin gives Odys a coin, then promptly commits suicide. The coin proves to be the resting state of an automaton named Maud forged by the god Vulcan. She becomes a genie-like servant to Odys—the only catch, she now possesses his soul. We soon learn that Maud isn't the only automaton. Other automata and their masters are very interested in Pepin's suicide. As it turns out, there's a master who would like to control all the automata and the one way an automaton may be passed to a new master is through the death of the old.

In essence, the plot is Odys and Odissa learning about this past, their connection to the automata, and their connection to the villainous master. In the meantime, they're being manipulated by the other masters who are, in turn, being manipulated by the gods themselves. All of the characters are being manipulated by the author and the editor, who break the fourth wall in a running commentary that bounces between the text and the footnotes.

One thing that did get a bit old was the author's insistence on replacing characters in trademarked names to avoid spelling the name—for example +@rget for Target. It's just not legally necessary and it was distracting. Also, there were a couple of points where I was shown actions but would have liked a little more insight into the characters' thought processes. All in all, though, these were minor quibbles in a book I thoroughly enjoyed. I felt the narrative structure was innovative and, for the most part, the characters engaged me.

I liked the idea of bringing an epic tale of the gods into the modern world and like any good epic tale, it might touch a nerve or two, which I do consider a good thing.

— David Lee Summers

Rarity from the Hollow
Robert Eggleton
Dog Horn Publishing
$20.84 Trade Paperback
$5.95 Ebook
284 pages

Lacy Dawn resides in the back woods of Appalachia with her poverty-stricken family. Although a bright girl, she suffers abuse at the hands of her father. Her best friend, who also has an abusive family, is killed early in the book. Aside from her intelligence, the only things in Lacy Dawn's favor are her ability to talk to trees and the alien android who took up residence 'Roundabend,' who is enhancing her intelligence for his own purposes.

Although this could be the setup for a rather dark and frightening novel, it soon explodes into satire. The android, named DotCom, turns out to be an employee of the distant planet Shptludrp, which is a giant shopping mall. Lacy Dawn has been bred throughout humanity's existence to save the mall, which is the hub of all civilization. As Lacy Dawn matures, she convinces DotCom to heal her family so they can help her. This ends the abuse and they go on to establish themselves as champion traders, getting the best deals at the mall and selling their strange intergalactic wares in a big yard sale and online as "Rarity from the Hollow." This positions Lacy Dawn and her family to do what's necessary to save the universe. All the while, she's coming of age and bringing DotCom right along with her.

There's a lot to like in this novel. Lacy Dawn is a clever and engaging character, who overcomes her difficult family situation, and her blossoming sexuality with homespun, common sense wisdom. She's equally at ease talking to alien androids, her classmates, the trees, and ghosts. Eggleton makes an admirably smooth progression from the grim realities of Appalachian life to the broadly satirical look at the "alien" economics of consumerism and how a smart kid can find solutions to problems entrenched management have made for themselves.

Unfortunately, I felt Eggleton undercut these strengths with an over reliance on potty and drug humor. Also, the full omniscient head-hopping became dizzying at times, especially with the occasionally interspersed first-person thought, not set apart with italics or helpful punctuation.

The novel is like the residents of the Hollow, imperfect but worth knowing. Lacy Dawn, her family, and friends go on a journey that is both fun and thought-provoking. What's more, Eggleton is donating the novel's proceeds to a child abuse prevention program operated by Children's Home Society of West Virginia.

— David Lee Summers

The X-Troop
Clay Davis
Self-published
$4.99, Ebook
155 pages (estimated)

In 1876, President Ulysses S. Grant faced many problems including economic crisis, corruption and keeping a nation ruptured by civil war from falling apart again. According to Clay Davis, he also faced terrorist plots and renegades who would do anything they could to lay their hands on the top-secret weaponry for their own nefarious aims. To that end, Grant commands General Phillip Sheridan to create an elite cavalry unit called the X-Troop. Sheridan's choice to lead the team is Colonel Orsen Ritter, an army officer falsely accused of graft and corruption.

With Sheridan's help, Ritter's name is cleared and he assembles a team of officers to lead the X-Troop. His team includes the best men for the job,

regardless of race and background. It even includes the best doctor he can find who happens to be woman. Meanwhile, an outlaw band called the Locusts under the direction of masterminds called the Four Horsemen are working to steal a new secret weapon—trains that roll on treads and don't require rails.

In essence, *The X-Troop* is the stuff of speculative western adventures such as *The Wild Wild West* and *The Adventures of Brisco County, Jr.* The top secret military unit offers a lot of storytelling potential and in this first novella, we certainly see a mix of espionage, political thriller, and plenty of western action. For the most part, Davis has a good grasp on the history and politics of the period, which lends this fantastical tale an air of authenticity.

There were some formatting glitches in the edition I had that hopefully can be fixed in a later release, but generally the story held me enough they didn't distract too much. What I did wish for was the opportunity to know these interesting characters a little better and a little more time seeing the fantastical gadgets in action, which might have added to the sense of menace.

The X-Troop was an enjoyable debut from Clay Davis and I hope to see more of Colonel Orsen Ritter and his cavalry unit in the future. If you enjoy classic TV and movie westerns of the 1950s and 60s, especially those with a science fictional twist, then I suspect you'd enjoy *The X-Troop*.

— David Lee Summers

About the talisman scale:
Books are ranked on a scale of five talismans with five being the most recommended and one being the least.

Please note: We are no longer accepting books for review. Thanks to all the authors who have kindly provided books for our perusal.

Journey to Wasteland
Austin Miller
Self-published
$7.99, eBook
228 pages

Mesha P. Winebottom grew up on his father's thrilling stories about the exploits of the wizard, Arcadia. But when Mesha loses his parents in an accident, the stories are all he has left of his father. As Mesha grows more and more disgruntled with life as a shepherd on his grandparents' farm, Mesha's grandmother encourages him to leave and seek the magic his father believed in.

Mesha embarks on a quest to find the fabled Wasteland where rumors say a cabal of powerful wizards banished the legendary Arcadia. Along the way, Mesha collects a band of allies, including siblings Driggs and Piper, and the mysterious Fang and his wolf, Luna. The group encounters numerous friends and foes during their journey, and each confrontation solidifies Mesha's belief that Wasteland is real, and he's on the right path to find it.

Mesha is strong willed and generally likeable, but is often derailed by a tendency to throw temper tantrums. Driggs and Piper are fairly consistent characters, but their motivations for following Mesha are underdeveloped. Fang has the potential to be a dark and enigmatic character to balance Driggs's and Piper's congeniality and charm, but he remains mostly two dimensional throughout the story.

Journey to Wasteland is a classic quest tale, and Mesha's group encounters a few conflicts along the way, but these struggles are often quickly and easily resolved. More often than not, Mesha confronts random and usually benevolent situations, as if his universe aligned to aid him on his quest. Many of these encounters echo the strange yet usually innocuous events that Alice confronted in her journey through the looking glass.

The story of Arcadia weaves in and out of Mesha's narrative, always presented as fairytale told by Mesha's father. Until the end, it is unclear if Arcadia's story is mere fable, or if Arcadia's deeds will affect Mesha's life in any way other than to inspire him to leave home. This lack of a clear, overarching conflict leaves *Journey to Wasteland* without a strong sense of urgency or imperative and tends to make the pacing drag in places. Whether the crew finds Wasteland or not seems to have little import to anyone other than Mesha. Throughout the story, the consequences of Mesha's failure appear inconsequential, and only at the end, in the last few chapters, do the stakes of success or failure really matter.

For an indy-published book, Miller did a good job of proofreading, but the story lacked the polish and finesse a good editor could have provided. However, a young audience looking for a relatively simple tale of magic, adventure, and mild romance, should find plenty to like about *Journey to Wasteland*.

— Karissa B. Sluss

Codex Jermyn
Cardinal Cox
Starburker Publications
Poetry pamphlet, no price listed
12 pages

If the title begins with "Codex" chances are it's British poet Cardinal Cox doing H.P. Lovecraft. Codex Jermyn is the eighth such pamphlet by Cox—nine rhyming poems loosely based on the Lovecraft short story "Arthur Jermyn."

The HPL story is one of his lesser efforts and involves eldritch doings in the Congo by several generations of Jermyns mating with apes. Fortunately, Cox doesn't dwell much on such horrors, but generates poems about other ape-like creatures such as the apes of Djehuty in Egypt, Hanuman of India and the Voormis of Hyperborea. There are also appearances by Lord Greystoke and that critter from the Rue Morgue, and references to the "ape-like Edward Hyde" and even the Yeti. As usual, what Cox doesn't cover in verse, he comments on in notes at the bottom of each page.

Copies of the Codex pamphlets are available from Cox at 58 Pennington, Orton Goldhay, Peterborough PE2 5RB, United Kingdom. I'd suggest sending a dollar or two (cash) to cover postage. Don't monkey around!

— Neal Wilgus

About the Contributors

Linda Maye Adams is originally from Southern California, transplanted to Washington, DC on the military plan. Least likely to be in the military, she served for twelve years in the Army Reserves, the Army, and the National Guard. Her tour of duty included Desert Storm, when it was still a strange thing for women to be at war. She has been writing since she was eight years old, and has been published in *Fabula Argentea* and *Enchanted Spark*. For more about her, visit linda-adams.com and garridon.wordpress.com.

Timothy Bastek is from Chandler, Arizona, where he has lived all his life, except back in 2012 when he got the crazy notion of studying for a year in Sweden. While in Sweden, he managed to survive the winter, became lost in the woods, was sniffed by a moose and relentlessly pursued by a herd of cows. He now works as an aide at the Chandler Public Library. "Bound" is his second story to be published in *Tales of the Talisman*.

Simon Bleaken is a long-time fan of the Sci-fi, fantasy and horror genres. His fiction has appeared in several magazines and chapbooks, including: *Lovecraft's Disciples, Strange Sorcery, Night Land, Beneath the Moons of Zandor, Weird World of Zandor* as well as in previous issues of *Tales of The Talisman*. He has also appeared in the anthologies: *Eldritch Horrors: Dark Tales* and *Space Horrors: Full-Throttle Space Tales #4* and will also appear in the anthology *Best Gay Romance 2015*. He is a supporter of Greenpeace, the World Wildlife Fund and the Stonewall charity, as well as a member of OBOD and British Mensa. He lives in Wiltshire, England.

Bruce Boston's poetry and fiction have appeared in hundreds of publications, including *Asimov's SF, Amazing Stories, Realms of Fantasy, Strange Horizons, Weird Tales, The Pedestal Magazine, The Twilight Zone Magazine, Tales of the Talisman, Year's Best Fantasy & Horror*, and the *Nebula Awards Showcase*. His poetry has received the Bram Stoker Award, the *Asimov's* Readers' Award, the Rhysling Award of the Science Fiction Poetry Association, the Balticon Poetry Award and the SFPA's Grand Master Award. Boston's fiction has received a Pushcart Prize and twice been a finalist for the Bram Stoker Award (novel, short story). He holds the distinctions of having appeared in more issues of *Asimov's SF* than any other author, and of coining the word "cybertext."

Mark Anthony Brennan lives off the west coast of Canada on Vancouver Island. He is a member of SFWA and SFCanada, with numerous publishing credits to his name. In addition to pursuing his master's degree at the University of Victoria, he is also a music critic and journalist.

Beth Cato is the author of *The Clockwork Dagger*, a steampunk fantasy novel from Harper Voyager. Her poetry has been published in *Apex* Magazine, *inkscrawl*, and *The Pedestal* Magazine. She's a Hanford, California native transplanted to the Arizona desert, where she lives with her husband, son, and requisite cat. Her website is BethCato.com.

William Corner Clarke was born an Englishman, but is now a U.S. citizen. Most of his published work has been in British anthologies and magazines including *Palantir, Ammonite,* and *Fire*. More examples of his work can be found online at the poetry magazines collection of the British Arts Council's poetry library. The website is: www.poetrymagazines.org.uk. One of his poems can also be found in the science poetry anthology *Dreamers on the Sea of Fate* edited by Steve Sneyd.

Douglas Empringham has had fiction accepted by *Black Gate, Space and Time, The Lamp-Post, Leading Edge, The Armchair Aesthete, Rosebud* and other genre and literary magazines including both *Tales of the Talisman* and *Hadrosaur Tales*.

A frequent contributor to both *Tales of the Talisman* and *Hadrosaur Tales*, **Gary Every** is the author of the science fiction novella *The Saint and the Robot*, which is based upon a medieval legend concerning the youth of Thomas Aquinas. *Shadow of the OhshaD*, a collection of the best of his award winning newspaper columns about Arizona's Native Americans, history, and environment is also available at Amazon.com or his website www.garyevery.com

As a child, **Kathy Ferrell** refused to share her crayons, preferring to eat them all herself. Today she is an artist and writer working from her decidedly sinister 19th century home, nestled deep in the backwoods of Appalachia. When not creating, she can be found wrapped in a shawl, drinking tea and wondering what on earth could be making that incessant creaking on the stair. She also uses the internet, in spite of being warned.

Paintings: cuposwank.carbonmade.com
Words: cuposwank.wordpress.com

Livia Finucci is a cat lover and a seagull admirer. She likes to read fairy tales and mythology from various countries. In her free time, she practices botanical painting. She has had short stories and poems published in several anthologies and magazines. One of her haikus published in *Tales of the Talisman* was chosen for the *Dwarf Stars 2014* anthology for the previous year's best short poems.

Neil T. Foster is a freelance artist who lives in Australia. He has penciled and inked various comic books, recently completing an online comic—*Beware the Beast*—for the official International *Planet of the Apes* Fan Club. He has done illustrations and painted covers for various SF fanzines, CD booklets and computer games. His work includes everything from illustration, cartoons, logos and comic strips to artwork for action figure packaging. His illustrations and painting have also appeared in *The Corpse* and *Black Petals* Magazines.

Courtney Floyd is obsessed with parenthetical commentary and em-dashes (perhaps and intervention is in order—perhaps not). She loves rain, coffee, and books; all is right in her world when these things converge. When she isn't writing, she's likely to be found with her nose in a book. In fact, she's about to begin a PhD in English, studying Victorian Sensation Fiction and Penny Dreadfuls. You can keep up with her writing, as well as the chaos and madness she calls her life, at her blog: www.synonymsandsuch.com

Laura Givens is a Denver Based author and artist. Her art has graced the covers of numerous publishers' books and magazines. She has provided illustrations for *Orson Scott Card's Intergalactic Medicine Show, Jim Baen's Universe, Talebones, Science Fiction Trails* and *Tales of the Talisman*. Her work may be viewed at www.lauragivens-artist.com. In 2010 she naively decided she could probably write stories as good as many she had illustrated. She has sold works ranging from zombie stories to space operas. She was co-editor and contributor to *Six-Guns Straight From Hell*, a weird western anthology, and is art director for *Tales of the Talisman* magazine.

Morland Gonsoulin is a traditionally trained artist and avid science fiction fan living in Colorado Springs, Colorado. He has done artwork for various publications before, including *Tales of the Talisman* Magazine.

K.S. Hardy's fantasy poetry has appeared in *Dreams and Nightmares, Blood Bond, Mythic Delerium* and *Not One of Us*. His short stories have been in *Tales of the Talisman, Frost Fire Worlds*, and *Lore* (which received notice from Brian Lumley) amongst many others. His first children's book *Her Best Trick or Treat, Ever* is available around the world, most recently in New Zealand.

John Hayes gives poetry readings, acts, and directs in Community Theater. He exhibits sculpture anywhere he can find an outlet. He was a scurvy looking corpse on *Homicide* and a shopper on *WIRE*. Seven of his one-act plays were produced. *Wily Writers, The Meadow, Whitefish Review, Tales of the Talisman, Liquid Imagination, Welter, Premonitions*, and *Big Pulp* are some of the magazines that have published his work.

Tom Kelly received a degree in Graphic Design from Lycoming College and holds a master's degree in Sequential Art from the Savannah College of Art and Design. Tom has worked for several years producing graphic design and illustration for numerous design and production companies. As a freelance artist, Tom has produced illustrations and cartoons using a wide variety of classical and electronic techniques. Tom focuses on creating dynamic visuals by fusing together a wide variety of elements into one thought-provoking illustration. Tom's sequential work focuses on the power of bold black and white elements as well as the power of graphic design to relate a narrative.

Jag Lall works in both the comic book industry and book illustration field producing bold, atmospheric artwork. The former is his lifeblood and he is currently working on a project to raise awareness of different cultures.

Sandra Lindow lives on a hillside in Menomonie. Wisconsin, where she teaches, writes, edits and competes with wildlife for the pleasure and sustenance of her various gardens. Her book, *Dancing the Tao: Le Guin and Moral Development* (Cambridge Scholars, 2012) focuses on the development of moral maturity and was a finalist for the 2014 Mythopoeic Award for Scholarship in the Study of Myth and Fantasy.

Recently she coordinated the SFPA 2014 Dwarf Star Poetry contest and edited the contest chapbook anthology. She was a finalist for the Rhysling Award twenty-one times. She has seven books of poetry. The most recent is the *Hedge Witch's Upgrade* (2012).

Lauren McBride finds inspiration in faith, nature, molecular biology (a former researcher) and membership in the Science Fiction Poetry Association (SFPA). Twice nominated for the 2014 SFPA Dwarf Stars Award, her work has appeared in various speculative, nature and children's publications including: *Dreams and Nightmares, Star*Line* and *The Magazine of Speculative Poetry*. She shares a love of laughter, science, and the ocean with her husband and two children.

Paul Niemiec plays guitar in a swing band—atomic pablo. Check it out at myspace.com. Paul's first job in high school was an art job doing safety filmstrips for hard-rock miners. After that, the office situation—smooth jazz radio, and chain-smoking co-workers—really put him off commercial art.

After a long hiatus, he got back into drawing. Paul was trying to figure out which way a camel's front legs bent, and he decided to go to the zoo to draw camels. Later, he met some of the Squid Works guys at a figure drawing class.

Taylor Packer is from Chandler, Arizona, where he lives peacefully and causes no amount of ruckus. Ever. In addition to writing, he is an aspiring film director. He is in the middle of directing and producing his own short horror film entitled *The Color of Hunger*. He now works in retail. "Bound" is his second story to be published in *Tales of the Talisman*.

David B. Riley is the editor of numerous horror and weird western anthologies. He is also the author of four novels and more than 100 short stories. He writes horror, science fiction and steampunk and is an active member of the Horror Writer's Association. He also is publisher of *Steampunk Trails* Magazine. David lives in Colorado and works in the hotel business when he's not working on literary endeavors.

W. C. Roberts lives in a mobile home up on Bixby Hill, on land that was once the county dump. The only window looks out on a ragged scarecrow standing in a field of straw and dressed in W. C.'s own discarded clothes. W. C. dreams of the desert,

of finally getting his first television set, and of ravens. Above all, he writes, and has had poems published in *Tales of the Talisman, Strange Horizons, Apex, Space & Time Magazine, Mindflights, Shock Totem, Star*Line*, and others.

Nicolo Santilli is a philosopher, poet, and fiction writer residing in Berkeley, CA. He is currently engaged in writing a series of narrative fantasy poems which will serve as the prelude to a series of fantasy novels that have been living and growing in him for many years.

Mark Silcox is a Canadian citizen currently living in Edmond, OK, where he works as a philosophy professor. Mark is a co-author of *Philosophy through Video Games* (Routledge, 2008) and co-editor of *Dungeons & Dragons and Philosophy: Raiding The Temple of Wisdom* (Open Court, 2012). He also has had stories accepted for publication by *Perihelion SF, Dark Discoveries, Aoife's Kiss, All Hallows, Polluto,* and *Fear & Trembling* magazines. Mark belongs to the Codex Writer's Group and graduated from the 2011 Summer Short Story Workshop at the Center for the Study of Science Fiction at the University of Kansas.

Frances Silversmith grew up in Germany, where she lives with her husband, seven guinea pigs, and an Icelandic horse. She works as a software developer and splits her free time between writing, reading every book she can get her hands on, and riding and teaching circus tricks to her pony.

Jeffery Scott Sims, a degreed anthropologist and author of dozens of short stories published in magazines and anthologies, makes his home in Arizona, a region he has explored and photographed for several years, and which forms the backdrop for many of his sinister tales. As writer and reader he prefers the spooky and the fantastic, his favorite genre authors, and greatest influences, being H.P. Lovecraft, R.E. Howard, C.A. Smith, M.R. James, and E.R. Eddison. He is the creator of the serial characters Professor Vorchek, modern investigator of strange mysteries, and Jacob Bleek, cunning sorcerer of a dark, antique era. His recent publications include a volume of short stories, *Science and Sorcery: A Collection of Alarming Tales*; a novel, *The Journey of Jacob Bleek*; and the short stories "The Gorge of Pentono," "The Enemy From Nowhere," "The Journal of Reverend Winters," "Zirinsky's Swamp," "The Guardian of the

Treasure," and "From the Mud of Grasshopper Point."

Full information on his writings and publications, and a growing collection of essays devoted to the weird tale, may be found at the author's literary web site: http://jefferyscottsims.webs.com/index.html

Jason Sturner was born in Chicago, Illinois, and raised in small towns along the Fox River. His stories and poems have appeared in *Space and Time* Magazine, *Star*Line*, *Disturbed Digest*, and *Mythic Delirium*, among others. This is his fifth appearance in *Tales of the Talisman*. He currently lives in Knoxville, Tennessee, near the Great Smoky Mountains, where he is learning to play the bodhran. Website: www.jasonsturner.blogspot.com

David Lee Summers is the author of eight published novels and over sixty published short stories. His writing spans a wide range of the imaginative from science fiction to fantasy to horror. David's novels include the wild west/steampunk adventure *Owl Dance* and *Vampires of the Scarlet Order*, which tells the story of a band of vampire mercenaries who fight evil. His short stories and poems have appeared in such magazines and anthologies as *Realms of Fantasy*, *Human Tales*, *Cemetery Dance*, and *Taurin Tales*. In addition to writing and editing *Tales of the Talisman*, David has edited three science fiction anthologies, *Space Pirates*, *Space Horrors*, and *A Kepler's Dozen*. When not working with the written word, David operates telescopes at Kitt Peak National Observatory. Learn more about David at davidleesummers.com.

With over a million words in print **Patrick Thomas** keeps busy writing the fantasy humor series *Murphy's Lore* (*Tales From Bulfinche's Pub*, *Fools' Day*, *Through the Drinking Glass*, *Shadow of the Wolf*, *Redemption Road*, *Bartender of the Gods*, *Nightcaps* and *Empty Graves*) as well as the *After Hours* spin offs *Fairy With A Gun*, *Fairy Rides the Lightning*, *Dead To Rites*, *Rites of Passage*, and *Lore & Dysorder*. His Mystic Investigators paranormal mystery series has grown to include *Bullets & Brimstone* and *From The Shadows*—both with John L. French; and *Once More Upon A Time* and the upcoming *Partners In Crime*—both with Diane Raetz. He co-edited *New Blood* and *Hear Them Roar*. Patrick's syndicated humorous advice column Dear Cthulhu has been collected in *Have A Dark Day*, *Good Advice For Bad People*, and *Cthulhu Knows Best*. A number of his books are part of the set and props department at the CSI television show and have been

spotted on the show. His urban fantasy *Fairy With A Gun* has been optioned by Laurence Fishburne's Cinema Gypsy Productions for film and TV. Drop by www.patthomas.net to learn more or find out about The Patrick Thomas Show mockumentary.

Originating from the UK but now residing in the Canary Islands, **Teresa Tunaley** finds more time to devote to her love of art and writing. For more than 30 years she has been doodling traditionally with pencils and dabbling with watercolors.

Along with published stories and poetry, she can be credited with award winning cover art and illustrations for author stories. Her work can be seen online and in print across the UK, US, Canada and Europe.

"I like to think that I am very versatile in my choice of subject matter—my new surroundings provide the inspiration for me to paint on a daily basis and the fact that others may enjoy my work gives me the confidence to continue."

Louise Webster graduated with a degree in Communication Arts. She wrote the evening news for a small cable TV company.

While staying home to raise her children, she wrote for many of the small presses. She has also written an article for a psychology book, a horticulture magazine, and her poem on Lake Ronkonkoma won a prize.

Louise has written for June Cotner's anthologies *Dog Blessings* and *House Blessings*, *A book of Toasts* and was published in *Nurturing Paws* and *Miracles and Extraordinary Blessings* edited by Lynn C. Johnson.

She is proud that her work has appeared over the years in *Tales of the Talisman* edited by David Lee Summers.

Neal Wilgus has been writing and publishing SF/F/H poetry and prose for more than fifty years in the US, UK, and Canada. Some of his poems have been nominated for the Rhysling Award given by the SF Poetry Association and he has shared third place several times for the Data Dump Award for best SF poem published in England. His short stories have won the Fiction Contest at *Oasis Journal* several times. He also writes satirical *Leak News Service* stories and reviews book for *Small Press Review* and elsewhere. He publishes regularly in *Star*Line*, *Dreams and Nightmares*, *Tales of the Talisman*, *Monomyth*, *Poetry Cornwall* and elsewhere. His 1978 nonfiction book *The Illuminoids* is still in print.

William R. D. Wood lives with his wife and children in Virginia's Shenandoah Valley in an old farmhouse turned backwards to the road. His work has appeared in *Omni Reboot, Bastion Science Fiction Magazine* and *Animism: The Book of the Emissaries.* Other works and occasional ramblings can be found at www.williamRDwood.com.

Kathryn Yelinek lives in Pennsylvania, where she spends her days as a librarian. Her work has previously appeared in *Daily Science Fiction* and *Electric Spec.* She's a proud graduate of the Odyssey Writing Workshop.

Alessio Zanelli is an Italian poet who writes in English and whose work has appeared in about 150 journals from 13 countries. He has published 4 full collections to date, most recently *Over Misty Plains* (Indigo Dreams, UK, 2012).

Lee Clark Zumpe, a Florida native, lives in the Tampa Bay area and spends most of his time writing. By day, he is an award-winning entertainment columnist and reviewer with Tampa Bay Newspapers. At night, he writes Lovecraftian horror, dark fantasy and science fiction. He has penned dozens of short stories and hundreds of poems and his work has been published in a variety of magazines and anthologies. His most recent appearances include short stories in *Black Chaos: Tales of the Zombie* (Big Pulp), *Vignettes from the End of the World* (Apokrupha), *Steampunk Cthulhu* (Chaosium) and *World War Cthulhu* (Dark Regions Press).

Lee is also co-author, with David Lee Summers, of the book *Blood Sampler*, a collection of vampire flash fiction currently in its second printing from Alban Lake Publishing. For more information, visit www.leeclarkzumpe.com.

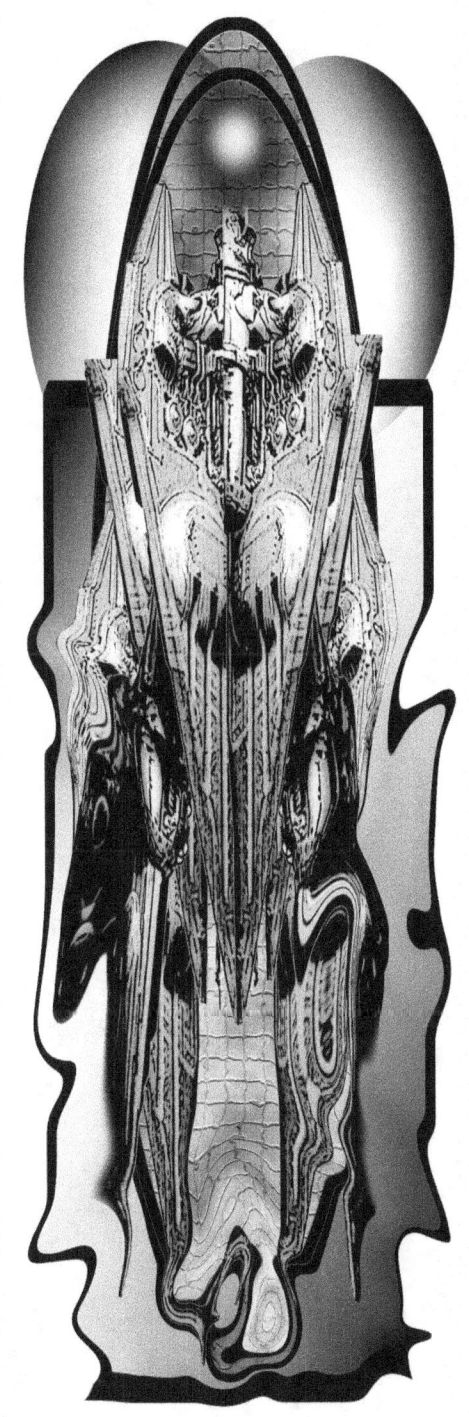

www.ingramcontent.com/pod-product-compliance
Lightning Source LLC
Chambersburg PA
CBHW080752120626
46557CB00005B/1233